Wild Sorceress Series, Prequel: Legacy of Magic

By Margaret L. Carter
and Leslie Roy Carter

Writers Exchange E-Publishing
http://www.writers-exchange.com

Wild Sorceress Series, Prequel: Legacy of Magic
Copyright 2017, 2023 Margaret L. Carter and Leslie Roy Carter
Writers Exchange E-Publishing
PO Box 372
ATHERTON QLD 4883

Cover Art by: Aprampar and Odile Stammane

Published by Writers Exchange E-Publishing
http://www.writers-exchange.com

The unauthorized reproduction or distribution of this copyrighted work is illegal. Criminal copyright infringement, including infringement without monetary gain, is investigated by the FBI and is punishable by up to 5 (five) years in federal prison and a fine of $250,000.

Names, characters and incidents depicted in this book are products of the author's imagination and are used fictitiously. Any resemblance to actual events, locales, organizations, or persons, living or dead, is entirely coincidental and beyond the intent of the author.

No part of this book may be reproduced or transmitted in any form or any means, electronic or mechanical, including photocopying, recording, or by any information storage and retrieval system, without permission from the publisher.

Legacy of Magic

..."If you would just listen to her--I know how you feel about magic use, but..."

Merina barely suppressed a scream, remembering where they were. "You know and you try to pull this trick on me. How could you?"

"I'm sorry, Mer. I should have told you why I wanted to talk with you tonight. I was afraid you would tell me you would not give me the chance to arrange a meeting between the Sorceress and us."

Tears flowed from Merina's eyes. She didn't want that to happen, but the frustration she felt with Trinames left her no other way to react. She realized he was only trying to make her accept his belief that becoming a Healer was the right choice for him. He just would not see that she could not accept his becoming a sorcerer without having to give up her distrust and loathing for magic.

Fighting the strong urge to lash out at him, to punish his wrong thinking, Merina swiped the stream of tears off her face with her right hand. "As you see, you would have been correct about how I would respond to such a meeting. What I don't understand is why you persist in thinking I cannot love you without loving magic. As long as your using Power does not lead to what happened to my mother, I could not care less if spell casting is what you want to do with your life. Just don't expect me to ignore any sign that magic is interfering with our lives."

Trinames nodded. That smile she loved so much found its way to his lips. Perhaps he had really accepted that he could not change her mind on magic. He stepped close to her and gently kissed a tear from her cheek...

With thanks again to our live-in editor, our son John.

Chapter 1

In a high-vaulted cave in the depths of the Non-Lands, a venerable female spoke. "Those whom we oppose, the Others, have accelerated their plan."

A younger, male voice replied, "I see no indication of that, Mother."

"There have been excursions off the settled land."

"They are a curious people, this is to be expected."

"No, son of mine, their memories should have prevented this. They are being encouraged to go where they cannot survive."

"I know that is what the Others want, Mother, but the will to survive is strong in the people."

"Just so, my son. If they cannot expand, they will turn on each other. Then the killing will begin again."

"So soon, after the last time?"

"They learn quickly, but they forget just as quickly. It is time, my son, to create the Chosen. We must use the Subject now. The Others are moving to interfere. They are making problems for her."

"Can we truly use her? She will resist."

The female voice reverberated through the vast caverns. "Trust me to shatter that resistance."

"Very well, I will send the Guardians for her as you have commanded, Mother."

"You're going away to become a Healer?" Merina asked in shock, pushing herself away from Trinames's embrace to look into his eyes, hoping to see a twinkle there that would tell her he was joking. All she saw in his face was anxiety. "When did you get tested? Why didn't you tell me you were going to do that?"

"I'm going after the fall ingathering, love. Byklandes only trains magic-users over the winter months. I'll be back in the spring." He cushioned his words with a tentative touch on her shoulder. "I would have told you earlier, but I knew you'd get mad--like you just have. I want to learn to use spells and--"

"You are a farmer's son, you work the land. That is what you know how to do. Why do you want to learn magic?" Sweeping her right arm in a wide arc, she pointed at the fields of corn growing next to them in the warm summer's sun. "What use do we have for it here? It doesn't take magic to make plants grow. What are you thinking?"

Merina knew she was quick-tempered and did not want to destroy the warm bond she always enjoyed with her lover. She let him go and turned her back to him, facing the barn so he would not see the tears in her eyes.

Trinames's anxious voice behind her continued to softly plead his case. "Farmers need healing magic as much as anyone. As a Healer I can help people, ease their suffering. And just as importantly, I could heal animals--"

"Magic-users are sworn to service; they forsake gathering wealth. More often than not they are paid off in dead chickens, eggs, cheese--not gold. I was born to manage a farm, growing produce for profit, not just being forced to live on what others give us. How can we afford such a life? We were supposed to become life-mates this midsummer. How could you change the plan without one word to me? Should I be grateful you told me now instead of the day before you leave?"

Trinames's refusal to match Merina's anger with his own exasperated her still more. She stiffened when he stepped behind her and put his hands on her shoulders, pulling her back against him so he could murmur against her hair. "We will be life-mates--after I become a Novice."

Twisting out of his grasp, Merina wiped the moisture away from her cheeks and spun to face Trinames. "That's just it. I don't know much about magic-users, but I do know this... They don't allow the students at their training lodges to have life-mates until they graduate and become..." she groped to find the words, "apprentices. You realize it takes four years to become a magic-user? Four years!"

"Graduated magic-users are called Novices, love. I know, believe me, I know. But the valley needs Healer support. I can provide that."

The earnestness in his voice told Merina her love was convinced of the right of his claims. It made her stop for a moment to think, remembering last summer, when she had spent half a night helping him spread wet towels over a colt with a high fever, only to have it die anyway. A messenger had been sent for the valley's Healer, Sorceress Helinu, who couldn't come in time because she had been tied up with a human patient. Merina recalled Trinames's bitter remark that if only their community had more than one Healer, the colt might have survived. So the harbingers of this decision were in front of me already, she thought bitterly. But she did not want to concede his point, saying "The valley needs a Healer? What happened to Helinu? She is not that old--only middle-aged. She has done the job alone now for twenty years."

Trinames tried to step forward to hold Merina, but she pulled back. She knew accepting his embrace would weaken her will to fight. She forced herself to ignore his familiar sun-warmed scent and the appeal in his soft, brown eyes. Soothingly, he said, "Sorceress Helinu has been accepted for the next level of sorcerer training after all these years of working alongside the people gaining the experience she needs to advance. She really deserves to be an Adept, but she can't leave until she is replaced."

"How nice of her to seek further training at the expense of supporting us." Merina shook her head. "This does not make sense, love. No sense at all. They are going to replace a Sorceress with a Novice. Your becoming a Novice is going to solve the valley's problem? I thought you said we needed more Healers, not one, and that one less qualified? Why don't her guild bosses accept their responsibility to replace her with a Sorceress or maybe even an Adept?"

Trinames shoved his rough farmer's hands into his pockets as if he didn't know what else to do with them besides reach for her. "Sorcerers don't have guilds, love--they have a Council of Magi. The Council has been short on magic-users for decades, especially Healers. They have been promising Sorceress Helinu for years that they would send a replacement when they could. But because the valley has grown so much over the last two decades, there is just too much work for one Healer at her level of skill. They finally agreed that if the valley found a candidate to go into training, they would send a substitute for her."

"You have lost me, Tri. This Council has known for years they needed to replace Helinu, but they can't train a replacement in all that time. Just how is that possible?"

"Merina, love," Trinames groaned with frustration, "there just are not enough candidates that take the Test and pass it--especially among those out in the provinces like ours. It takes a lot of Novices to be trained to be sent into service to develop the skills and experience to become Sorcerers. Not all Novices can become Sorcerer candidates, nor will all Sorcerers become Adept candidates. They want to support Helinu, but they are short of Neophytes--candidates for Novice. The problem, simply put, is the Council needs more Neophytes. Our valley has not sent anyone for training in decades, not since--"

Merina cut him off. "Not since my mother? Is that what you are going to say?"

Clearly Trinames did not want to bring up Merina's mother, a subject that always infuriated Merina. "It has nothing to do with your mother, love. The Council reminded Sorceress Helinu of the royal edict that all the youth in Saphradea between the ages of ten and fourteen are required to be tested--something all of the provinces have been ignoring. The towns and villages obey the law, but..."

Clenching her hands on her hips, Merina narrowed her eyes and glared at Trinames. "But dumb farmers and landowners need their children at home to help produce food so the rich craftsmen and merchants can idly enjoy their gold. So now, because Helinu hasn't been doing her job of testing farmers' sons and daughters all these years, she has been told to produce more Neophytes before they will find her a replacement. Isn't it rather strange to you that she, after all these years, has suddenly started finding candidates?"

"What are you asking?"

Throwing her arms up, Merina snapped at him, "You are the son of a son of a landowner. No one in your family has ever shown the least ability toward magic. Now all of a sudden you appear before Helinu and take the Test--and miraculously pass."

Trinames's tone sharpened. "Unlike you, the daughter of a woman who wielded the Power. Are you jealous that I passed and you did not?"

"Is that what you think?" Merina gaped at him in disbelief. "You know what I think about magic. I hate it! It weakens the mind and will and turns you away from what is good and right. It is unnatural, my misinformed love. You also know I have never been tested, nor would I allow myself to be."

"Why not at least try?"

"And prove what? Look, Tri, I think you have been lied to by our Healer. Everyone knows you come into magic when you come of age. We are both four years past that. Both of us are too old. If you passed, it is because Helinu is desperate to begin her Adept training. Tell me otherwise."

"Coming of age is when our bodies change to be able to have children--" he started, but Merina cut him off.

"Tell me about it. I thought you liked my woman's body," Merina said, emphasizing her words by passing her hands along her sides and down onto her legs.

Trinames's eyes followed her hands, and he sighed. "You know I do, but that has nothing to do with magic. Helinu says the mental discipline to learn to use Power works best just as our bodies began the change. The training lodges found that if they wait until boys and girls discover their sexuality they take much longer to learn the magic."

Merina cradled her breasts in her hands and smiled wickedly at Trinames's eyes locked on her fingers. "You are living proof of that wisdom, my love. You would leave me this winter knowing what we could be doing instead of your reciting age-old phrases and poring over musty scrolls! This is your choice?"

"No--yes. I do this for our future."

"Our future?" Merina retorted. "Your future, perhaps. My friends are having babies and starting homesteads. It is what I should be doing, what I have trained all my life for. Now you decide to take all that away from me. That is unfair of you. It's just not right!" Overcome by her indignation, Merina turned and ran from Trinames, wishing she could block out his cries of protest.

She fled up the hill to the lone, tall tree that stood at its crest. Under the huge canopy of the tree sat the chair she had made and placed there when she was ten years old. As she had proudly told her aunt and uncle, it was her sitting tree in her thinking place.

Merina dearly loved to contemplate the view from this spot, but not now. The hot tears flooding down her face obscured her vision. She blindly lowered herself onto the chair, burying her face in her skirt. She tried to choke off the unpleasant wailing she emitted so the noise would not bring her aunt from the house, but her heart would not listen to her mind. She succeeded only in causing herself to gasp for breath, which at least lowered the pitch. No one came out to check on her.

Damn it, why did he do that? Merina let the anger fill her mind. With each "why" she uttered aloud, further tears poured down her cheeks. She wiped them briskly away, only to feel them replaced by the next stream. Stop now! She ordered herself, Stop! The tears slowed, and she noticed with disgust that her nose was now draining in their place. Oh, now, how beautiful you must look.

She glanced down the hill to see if Trinames was watching her and with a surge of regret saw him riding away. Silly girl, you ran away from him. What did you expect him to do?

Merina sat back and watched her lover until he disappeared into the forest at the end of the road that led to her farm, leaving her with a dull ache in her breast. Why had she lashed at him so sharply? Was it because of being unable to fulfill her dreams of the past year to become his life-mate now, or was it waiting for four years, or was it his wanting to become a magic-user? It dawned on her that she had reacted most strongly when Trinames had brought up her mother.

Mother! Not that I ever knew you.

Merina had known no mother other than Alanu, the youngest sister of Delaphinu, Merina's birth mother. Auntie Alanu had become her foster mother almost immediately after her birth. Barely weaned, Merina was handed over the same night that Delaphinu left the valley for good.

At sixteen and unmated, Alanu raised the baby as her child, and until the birth of Alanu's first son, Merina had no idea she was not born of Alanu. Merina was old enough then to be aware of her aunt's pregnancy and had been fascinated with the development of the baby. When Merina asked Alanu if she had been as big as the coming baby, her aunt had told her the truth.

Alanu was the one who had insisted Merina recognize Alanu's oldest sister as the birth mother. Learning to call Alanu "Auntie" took many years--not that it changed how Merina thought of her foster mother. Feeling nothing for the woman who abandoned her, whenever Auntie had tried to tell Delaphinu's story to her, Merina had refused to listen, denying the truth.

Merina understood now the immaturity of that attitude. All she had focused on during those years was the fact that the woman who gave birth to her had deserted her. Anything that Delaphinu could be blamed for--being a drunk, sleeping around--was used to nourish the bitterness Merina had built up. The knowledge that Delaphinu was one of the few from the valley who became a magic-user was not a source of pride, but a reminder of why Merina had been left motherless.

Yet she hardly acknowledged what her mother had given her. Merina viewed whatever good her mother had provided as just due payment for the injustice she had suffered at her mother's hand. Now, in her present unhappiness, Merina saw that what she had previously thought of as unhappiness was the sulking of a child. Merina had not lived a hard life so far. What she was living was a life filled with what Merina wanted--very selfish of her.

Looking out across the fields, Merina took a fierce pride in the holding she considered hers--or one day would be, once the courts approved her grandfather's will. Romanus, Delaphinu's father, had left a major share of his land to his oldest daughter, hoping it would make the missing woman want to return to the valley. The farm her aunt and uncle held was part of Delaphinu's holdings, which would pass to Merina when the Prince of Princes' court finally acknowledged Delaphinu was dead.

Merina had fiercely wanted to believe that the lure of wealth would actually bring her mother back, but over the last five years the idea that Delaphinu was deliberately staying away to punish her family took root in Merina's mind. Why else would her mother not return? Merina had known of drunks in the valley who had one day sobered up, realized where they were and what they had missed, and changed their behaviors. Why not her mother? Merina, for all her anger, did not really want to believe her mother dead.

Merina stood and smoothed out her dress. She realized she needed help with her unhappiness, and she had a woman who had filled the role of mother within reach. It was time to reach out to her.

Alanu said as Merina entered, "I saw Trinames ride away. He looked pretty upset."

Slowly closing the door behind her, Merina nodded. "We had a fight."

"Something you did, or he did?" Alanu asked quietly.

Merina leaned against the kitchen door and thought for a moment. "It probably was as much my fault as his. He made a choice that I wished he hadn't. I told him so."

Alanu came closer to stand next to Merina. "We aren't talking about the color of curtains in your soon-to-be shared bedroom, are we?"

Merina shook her head. "No, far worse than that, Auntie. He has decided to become a Healer instead of the farmer he originally said he would become. You know how I feel about magic!" She started to weep.

Hugging her niece, Alanu let Merina cry quietly for a while. Merina pulled free, and Alanu wiped the tears off her niece's face with her apron. "Did he say why he changed his mind?" Alanu spoke in the same gentle voice she would use to calm a frantic calf or foal.

"He said he wanted to ease people's suffering. But what about the suffering he has caused me? All our plans--gone!"

Alanu guided Merina to the kitchen table and motioned her to one of the stools pushed underneath the large wooden work space. She then grabbed several cups off the counter by the ever-present teapot and poured them both a drink. Settling down next to her niece, Alanu waited till Merina took a sip before trying to talk. Alanu clearly wanted to give Merina a few moments to quiet down after the complaint about her future being ruined. "Until now, dear, the plan was for the two of you to be mated and start a life together. Has that changed?" Alanu asked.

"No, but..."

"Good, then we have something positive to start with," Alanu said cheerfully. "You will soon have the land to start your own holding and the means to pay for a nice home to be built on it. I have heard you tell him that it was your intent that he become more of a landowner like his father than one of the hired hands as he is now. You know you would be managing the farm anyhow--as you have told us many times, it is what you have trained your whole life to do. Whether Trinames works the land or not is not really the issue here, is it? Does it really matter what Trinames does for a living?"

Slamming her cup down, Merina said, "Yes, it does! Farming has value, magic use does not."

Shaking her head sadly, Alanu poured more tea for herself. "By value, do you mean gold? It would be very easy for magic-users to demand any amount of gold they wanted in return for their services. Long, long ago that was what they did. In their lust for power and wealth, they began to fight amongst themselves. This resulted in a terrible war. In killing each other off, they did not spare the innocent, the very people who needed their support. We, the people, harmed by their violence, suffered the greatest. We had to force the few remaining sorcerers to mend their ways. The sorcerers have taken a vow to serve the people and ask only enough gold in trade for the service they provide to meet their basic needs. This does not mean we do not value their services."

Merina poured herself another cup, refusing to look at her aunt, knowing Alanu was right. "I did not plan on an income separate from our farming. He would bring in more gold as a farmer working alongside me than in the time he would spend riding around the valley healing people." A new thought struck Merina. "And there is another thing--I would never see him. The Mayor would insist his Healer live in Dysandes. I would eventually have to sell my holdings, move there, and become a villager."

"Ah, I see. You would lose your standing in the valley farmers' eyes. Is that it, Merina?"

"No! Well, yes."

"There is no reason you would have to give up your holdings. One of my brothers--your uncles--would be happy to manage your land. Do you really think you will have the time to do so anyway when you intend to have children early and often? I've heard you tell Trinames that is your plan for a family."

Merina held her head up proudly. "I know I said that, and I think I can manage to do it as well as you have."

Alanu slowly smiled. "Then you are trying to prove something to the valley folk. Let me guess--that you are better than your mother, that you do not have her weaknesses, and you will do it without magic."

Merina simmered with renewed anger. "That's--"

Alanu quickly put her forefinger against her niece's lips. "Calm down and think about what I have just said. Whenever someone mentions your mother, you stiffen up and act offended. What did Trinames say that made you do that?"

Merina forced herself to relax, realizing her aunt was trying to help her through this problem. "He...he asked if I was jealous that he had passed the Test and I had not. Which is ridiculous, because I have never tried--and never will."

"I don't know how you will ever find peace in your heart, Merina, if you cannot resolve the pain of your mother's magic use and being deserted by her. Until you learned of it, you were the sweetest child I have ever known. It lies at the heart of this fight with Trinames, but I suspect there is another issue you have with his wanting to become a Healer. What is left if you rule out money, respect of your friends, or your hatred of magic?"

Merina closed her eyes against the tears that started down, wanting only to make this whole day go away. Then she remembered her words and said them aloud. "Four years, Auntie--it will be four years before I can begin the life I've dreamed of." Merina opened her eyes to see Alanu nodding, holding out a towel.

"Now that, my dear, will be the hardest problem you have to deal with here. You have to ask yourself if your love for Trinames can survive the wait. Only you can answer that. Take your time to think through this. You have plenty of time left before you must make a decision."

Trinames stood by one of the pair of huge trees that marked the entrance to Merina's holding and debated the wisdom of leaving his love in her upset condition. He should have stayed and waited for her to come down from her refuge, but he knew the day was already ruined because she would be so very careful to remain calm and reasonable. For her to return to the loving, caring girl she had been before their fight would take time-- it always did.

He stared at her sitting beneath her tree and ached to get back on his horse and gallop back down the long road to her side. She would see him coming and walk down the hill to meet him. They would kiss and hold each other, and he would apologize for being stupid. No, what do I have to apologize for? Granted, he should have given her more warning about changing what he wanted to do with his life, instead of waiting till midsummer, but he'd been avoiding the inevitable fight. Still, he had the right to determine what he was going to do with his life--a right she also claimed for herself.

That trait was what had drawn him to her. She was so determined, so clear in her vision of her life. All his friends told him she was the most desired woman in the valley. Heiress to one of the largest holdings, a skilled negotiator who always got the best price for her produce among a valley of strong male landholders, who found that they had to deal with a woman of quick wit when dealing with her. And beautiful! No woman in the valley drew men's eyes away from her when Merina was present.

He used to be almost afraid to look at her when she sat at her market stall in Dysandes on Settling Day. At thirteen, she had developed the body that made all the boys become aware of what men longed for in a woman. The crude remarks from his brothers concerning her breasts used to make him laugh because they all joked about becoming hard just looking at them. Now he felt angry at every man who looked at her, because they were thinking thoughts that threatened his possession of her.

Why did she want him? He knew she did--she had told him after the first time he had worked up the courage to visit her farm. He was not the catch that the valley mothers talked about. Markinis, the son of Calandis, the largest landholder, held that honor among the sons of the valley's farmers.

I am just the third son of a small farmer. I will never inherit my father's holding, and it is too small to be divided up. The farm that lay in front of him, Merina's current home, was just a piece of the land she would inherit. Mating with Merina would give him land of his own to farm, but that was not what he wanted in life. He had been given the opportunity to do something more with his life other than farming. To become a Healer, someone respected for a service provided. Again he savored the sense of completeness that arose from the idea of helping others, which he had tried so hard to impress on Merina.

After all, he was the one who tended his brothers and their hired hands when injured in the rough work in the fields. He helped in the calving and sewed the wounds on his father's livestock. With training, he would be able to use magic to assist the valley's lone Healer in treating injuries that threatened lives, human or otherwise. He could have prevented the death of his favorite colt.

But he had forgotten--no, not forgotten, not thought through--his love's hatred of magic. And it was the worst thing to bring up her mother. Was it worth the fight? He saw his love walk down the hill into her home. It was time for him to leave.

The road he was traveling on joined most of the farms in the north of the valley with Dysandes. Since it was well known to both Trinames and his horse, neither was paying much attention to their surroundings. Trinames was trying to figure out how he could get back into Merina's good graces and still reach his goal of becoming a Healer. A shout from ahead caught him by surprise, and he reined in his horse abruptly. The man who rode toward him was one of his father's hired hands, a good friend and companion Trinames had known most of his life. It was not like Jarkilis to be so excited by much of anything.

"Cow fourteen forty-three has disappeared, Tri. We need your help to find her."

It took a moment for Trinames to grasp what the man had shouted out. Cattle in Saphradea were taxed individually, and like most farmers in Saphradea, his family kept track of each animal using numbers branded into the inside of the cow's ear. Trinames did not like the practice of using their numbers as names, and he had to take a moment to translate the news. Bluebell! One of our best milkers. "Where did she disappear from, Jarkilis? I left her in the field by the barn."

"That's where I saw her last. Something must have spooked her bad, because she rushed the gate leading to the far pasture and knocked it open. Your mother and I searched for hours, but fourteen forty-three is not in that field."

Spurring his horse to a gallop, with Jarkilis right behind, Trinames called over his shoulder, "She's a pretty big cow and has never spooked like that before!"

"Well, her tracks headed out into the woods and they showed she was running hard." Jarkilis caught up with him.

"Any sign of dogs? I'm sure none of ours would chase her like that."

Jarkilis shook his head. "And the dogs we were using to track her did not want to follow her trail. Something big was after her."

"Where are my father and brothers?"

"Out on the north section. Your mother sent another hand after them, but I knew I could reach you faster."

Trinames nodded at the wisdom of that. They were an hour closer than his father could be. He glanced at Jarkilis and saw the same concern in the hand's eyes as he had in his--they might be too late to save Bluebell.

Reaching home, the two men grabbed bows from the weapons rack by the door, and Trinames stopped to take his medicine kit. He would need it if they were very lucky. His mother yelled to them as they mounted that she would send help as soon as someone showed. The ride to the barn pasture took only a minute. Trinames jumped down from his horse and scanned the tracks. Bluebell, a large heifer, had dug deep spoor into the dry earth. Whatever was chasing her had left no prints. He would have liked to know what the two of them would face when they caught up with the cow.

They followed the trail across the field to where it entered the wood. The trees here were far enough apart that the cow could dodge through them, but so could her attacker. Trinames spotted the start of a trail of blood soon after they entered the wood. *Why is she going in this direction?* The only thing out here was a small pasture used in the heat of summer to shade the stock. Trinames voiced his question to Jarkilis.

"She headed for the grotto, Tri. She'll be able to get inside and turn toward her attackers to make them face her horns."

"I believe you are right. She is the smartest of the lot that came out of Mavis years ago."

"Mavis? Oh, you mean twelve-forty. Yeah, now that was one great heifer."

As they suspected, the trail was heading for the grotto, and they quickly decided to stop tracking the animal and race as fast as they could through the woods to intercept her. Breaking out of the trees, they caught sight of the battle happening at the front of the cave.

"Look at the size of that wolf," gasped Jarkilis as he nocked an arrow to his bow.

Trinames was shocked by what he saw. There were at least three wolves weaving in and out in front of Bluebell--all of them bigger than any he had ever seen before. The leader stood a foot taller than the other two and was the most aggressive in charging the exhausted cow, who was barely able to thrust her horns forward to stop him. Screaming in anger, Trinames took off in a charge toward the leader. Trinames's action only incited the biggest wolf to spin around and face the onrushing threat. He realized he had no weapon prepared to strike with and clumsily pulled his sword from its scabbard.

He barely got it free when the horse he was riding reared up to lash out with her hooves. The wolf easily dodged the kicks, but an arrow slammed into one of its back legs with a thud, and the wolf yelped in pain. It spun around and bit at the arrow, snapping the shaft off with its powerful jaws. A second arrow whipped past its head, and the animal took off running away from Trinames. He reached for his bow to arm it while the other two wolves quickly ran after their leader. In seconds he had no targets to shoot at. "Thanks," Trinames said as Jarkilis rode up beside him.

"That wolf didn't look too scared of you, and I was afraid I would have to explain to your father why I let you take off on that foolish charge."

Trinames got off his horse and stepped over to Bluebell. As he examined the exhausted cow, he said over his shoulder. "Most wolves would have run from my approach, but not these. Look at her--they've torn her to pieces."

"She's bleeding out, Tri. Not much you can do. I'll cut her throat to put her out of pain."

"No," Trinames said stubbornly. "They did not get her jugular vein. I can clean up those wounds. The ones on her flanks and pasterns where they tried to bring her down are where she has lost a lot of blood. Oh no, look, they have cut the milk vein running along her lower torso. That's what is killing her!" Hearing a thrashing in the woods not far away, he looked up. "What was that?"

From his height advantage on his horse, Jarkilis peered into the distance and reported that he saw the wolves moving around just out of bowshot. "They're waiting to see what we're going to do. What are we going to do?"

"I'll stop the bleeding--just keep the wolves at bay until help arrives," Trinames said grimly.

Jarkilis turned his mount to face away from Trinames. "You're going to need someone to put pressure on those wounds to stop the bleeding while you tie off the bleeders. No way I can help you, Tri. The wolves look like they are waiting to rush us as soon as I turn my back."

Pulling off his outer shirt, Trinames ripped strips of cloth from it. He wadded the remains of the shirt into a ball that he shoved over the flowing hamstrung wound on the left leg and wrapped the strips tightly around the mound of material. "I'll do what I can by myself. Just keep them off us."

Jarkilis's bow snapped loudly behind Trinames, and from the lack of a scream of pain, Trinames guessed that his friend had missed. Trinames concentrated on the stomach wound. Applying a pressure bandage was not going to stop that bleeding. He reached into the wound and found the severed vein, holding it closed with his fingers until he could position a clamp to do the job. The vein would have to be sewn shut, but there was no time to do this now. Clamping the other part of the severed vein took only a moment, but it exhausted his supply of clamps. He turned back to packing the leg wounds with cloth, berating himself for not having the forethought to grab more supplies than he had.

Bluebell's legs were trembling under his touch, and Trinames knew the heifer was nearing the end of her strength to remain standing. His attempt to rally the cow with soothing words was interrupted by loud yelling from the entrance of the glade as his father and brothers rode onto the scene, driving the wolves away. He had barely finished dressing the forelegs when his father jumped from his horse and rushed up to see what had happened to his cow.

Glancing back and forth between the heifer and his youngest son, the old man clearly had a hard time figuring out who was hurt worse from all the blood covering both. "Trinames, son. Are you all right?"

"I will be, as soon as I get Bluebell stitched up."

Laughing in relief, his father said, "Oh, you mean fourteen forty-three. Go ahead and try, if you think you can save her. She'll die long before Sorceress Helinu could be summoned. I'll send for her anyway so she can witness your efforts."

And fix any mistakes I make in the process.

Chapter 2

Aweek later, Merina had not made much progress on her problem. Emotion and reason fought in her mind even as she did her daily chores, making it difficult to care much about the small things that made managing a farm so interesting for her.

As she pushed through the kitchen door and closed it quickly to keep the insects out, Auntie Alanu called out from the cupboard closet to her. "There's a scroll from Dame Brischelu on the table for you. It came this morning via a rider from Calandis's holding."

Merina walked to the table and picked up the letter, which was rather small and bound with a blue ribbon. Alanu came out of the closet wiping her hands on her apron, looking anxiously at her niece. It was not every day that one got a message from a noblewoman. Merina slipped the ribbon off and unrolled the scroll. It was written in the flowing script for which the Dame was so well known.

"She wants to meet with me the day after tomorrow afternoon at the Traveler's Rest. She doesn't say why. How odd!" Merina handed the scroll to Alanu.

"She rarely travels away from home unless specifically requested--like when we asked her here to tutor you and the neighbors' children in their teens in Saphradean social graces. That was such an uproarious gathering of young people, I'm glad we only had to do that once."

Merina smiled at the memory evoked by Auntie. Putting so many young girls and boys of mating age together in one house for an evening of instruction was bound to turn chaotic. "Maybe that's why she doesn't travel a lot. I remember you and Uncle Tomanis were wringing your hands the whole time, frantic that we would do something to upset the Dame. Ah well, it turned out all right."

Alanu finished reading the scroll and gave it back to Merina. "Dame Brischelu seemed to enjoy doing it. I wonder why she picked the Traveler's Rest, other than it's close to where she lives. Why not invite you to her home? That tavern is where the field hands like to gather after work. I see she's meeting you before they normally show up, but still..."

Merina shrugged. "I'll find out in two days. I doubt if we can provide her anything she doesn't already have, so I suspect this will not be a trade meeting." She left her aunt to go back to cleaning the cupboard and headed for her room.

Merina sat in front of her table mirror and brushed slowly through her short hair. She wore it that way because it was cooler in the summer and did not require much work to keep it tangle-free. Trinames wanted her to let it grow long, the way it had been when they first started noticing each other. He was fascinated by its color--a flaming red, as he described it. Aunt Alanu's hair was dark like that of her brothers, more brown than black. That used to puzzle Merina until she learned about her real mother. Auntie told her Delaphinu's hair had been red, slightly darker than Merina's, and worn very long.

Merina wondered what her real father looked like. The only image she had of a father was Tomanis, who had held that position in her heart for her entire life. The fact that he had not sired her did not change his love for her.

What was the color of her sire's hair? What else had he given her that she was unaware of? Merina leaned close to the glass surface so she could see her face in better detail. "Auntie said I looked so very much like my mother, sire. I have her green eyes, but my eyebrows are thinner and my nose longer. Is that from you? You must have had a name. No one has ever heard it, at least not anyone I've asked. And I have tried. Our Healer Helinu says she doesn't know. You were not from her lodge. She did not want to talk about you."

Putting down her brush, Merina asked the phantom in her mind, "Why would she not talk about you, sire? Was it because you were a sorcerer? Florinu's mother told her it was best not known you were a magic-user. Flo said her mother said that sorcerers should not mate and have children because their babies would go insane. She gave as proof that you all went insane centuries ago inbreeding like rabbits, brother and sister creating monsters. That was really stupid, sire. Everyone knows you don't breed together two get from the same dam."

Why would sorcerers think they can defy the experience of the ages and not suffer the consequences? Pure arrogance!

Merina began to wonder why she was talking to her absent sire about this subject. Her reason jumped into her mind. Mating! If nobody can mate with a sorcerer, then I can't mate with Trinames! Is that why his wanting to become a sorcerer angers me so?

"No, no, sire, that can't be true. I know I am not insane, and you mated my mother. But she was a sorcerer--at least one in training. Was she a sorcerer or not? Does it matter? I can't believe that it does. She is not related to you in any way, she couldn't be. You are from Delmathia. Oh, I just don't know. I need answers."

Fighting the rising panic, Merina forced her mind to rationality. "I know so little about magic-users, sire. I should pay more attention when the subject comes up. But it is just so hard. I get really angry when I hear about it. It made me so mad that I refused to listen during Brischelu's class on how the Domains were affected by magic use. I left the room when she started talking about it. Do you know why, sire? Because of what happened to my mother.

"Why did you mate with Delaphinu? If sorcerers should not mate with sorcerers, wouldn't it be wrong for you to do that? I thought you had some kind of law among yourselves that you swore to. Wouldn't it be dishonorable to bring a defective child into the world? Is that why Helinu won't speak of you, because you brought dishonor to sorcerers?

"Or is there another reason sorcerers won't talk about you? Just more questions. They just keep showing up." Merina shook her head. "Maybe, if I decide I will be Trinames's life-mate, maybe he could find out more about you, sire. Or is your reputation so bad now that your prestigious Training Lodge--Inhestia, wasn't it?--has hidden you away from prying eyes? Was what my mother did so heinous you could not even try to find out what happened to the child you sired? If you knew I existed, I think you would be proud of me."

She watched the tears pool at the corner of her eyes and, before her vision blurred, slowly trickle down her cheeks. The rejection she had felt since finding out she was not Auntie's child had always been centered on her mother, who abandoned her. Did her sire do so also, or did he not know she was alive?

"Did you love my mother? Auntie says Delaphinu was considered the most beautiful woman in the valley and could have had the pick of any man. Trinames says the same thing about me, but I think I have him rather smitten. Is that what my mother did to you?"

Merina sat back and turned away from her own face, wiping the tears away with her fingers. Her room's window looked out on her tree on top of the hill, and she stood to see it better. "First I need to know if I can be life-mate to a sorcerer. If I can, sire, I have to answer the question, do I wait four years until I can begin my family life with Trinames? If that answer is yes, then I could travel to where you are and ask you all the questions I can never get answered. I will have little else to do, so maybe that should be my plan. I'll have to think on it," Merina said to the empty room and to her thinking tree on the hill. She went in search of Alanu, finding her in the usual place, the kitchen.

"Tell me about the time my mother went to Dysandes for the Test, Auntie."

Alanu looked up from the bread dough she was kneading. "I didn't think you cared to know anything about your mother, Merina--but from the lack of disdain in your voice, I'm going to take it that you really want me to tell you."

"I'm interested in what made her want to go to the bother of making the effort. It isn't really required of anyone anymore, and from what my friends are fond of saying, Mother rarely did anything unless she was forced to."

Punching the dough harder than needed, Alanu set her mouth in a thin line. "That is not true."

"That my mother was lazy? Everyone says so, if only to politely avoid what they really want to say about her."

Slapping the dough into a wooden bowl, Alanu covered it with a cloth and set it aside on the kitchen counter. "It is not true that we are not required to send our children to the Test. It's just not enforced here among the farm people. If we lived anywhere near Byklandes, we would be hauled before the local Healer by the troops of Alexus and made to test."

"But we aren't, Auntie. The Prince of Princes hasn't cared what we do today, nor did his father's father before him. Neither he nor the--what are they called, Saphradean Council of Mages?"

"Council of Magi," Auntie corrected her niece.

"Yes, those people. None of them worry about rogue sorcerers practicing magic in the backwoods of Saphradea. If they did, they would have come after Mother when she sneaked back home after failing at Byklandes."

Crossing her arms across her chest, Alanu gave Merina a frown and said, "Your mother did not fail at Byklandes. She was dismissed from the Delmathian lodge's training school at Inhestia. Do you want to hear what I have to say about your original request, or are we going to dredge up my sister's failings all over again?"

Merina glanced downward, angry at herself for baiting her surrogate mother. "No, ma'am, I really do want to hear why."

"Good, then fetch us a cup of tea, and I'll tell you while the dough rises."

Sitting across from her aunt on a stool pulled up to the table in the middle of the huge kitchen where Alanu spent most of her day, Merina poured the tea and listened.

"Delaphinu was the oldest in our family, seven years separating us girls with six brothers in between and a sister that died at birth just before my birth. Your grandmother dutifully produced a baby a year after Delaphinu was born, including one set of twin brothers, until I was born, and then told her life-mate she was done--then died. Her death shocked your mother terribly, and I personally believe it was a major reason why Delaphinu turned out the way she did. My father loved my mother deeply, but being a son of the land, he had a family to raise and a rather large holding to tend. He made an arrangement with a widow named Jelisandu to move in and replace my mother. Delaphinu resented her deeply. She had already assumed the role of mother at nine years old and was distraught that Father thought it necessary to replace her."

Merina shook her head sadly, wondering aloud, "That doesn't sound like a ne'er-do-well person to me."

"She wasn't, but Jelisandu was strong-willed and determined to be mistress of the house. She taught your mother many things, and Delaphinu was quick to learn, but she learned too quickly to defy our foster mother, and it cost her. Father eventually took Jelisandu to his bed and made her his life-mate. Jelisandu's children by her first life-mate had been fostered out, and Father declined to adopt them. He had enough mouths to feed. Jelisandu resented his decision but did her duty to him, raising his children to become farmers, but with little love."

"What happened to Jelisandu?"

"After years of trying, she finally conceived. It was a very bad pregnancy, and the baby died stillborn. It nearly killed Jelisandu, and Delaphinu found herself back in the job of caregiver. Jelisandu foolishly kept trying to bear my father a child, and her next pregnancy killed her. Delaphinu was your age at that time. My father arranged with our neighbor to take his oldest daughter as a caregiver, with a promise to make her his life-mate. It proved too much for Delaphinu. She had spent her early womanhood caring for us and Jelisandu, ignoring the boys who saw her as a potential mate. When Father brought in a girl her own age to run his house, Delaphinu left."

"That must have been the Mistress Katreenu I've heard mentioned. Grandfather Romanus never life-mated her, if I remember correctly."

Alanu took a long drink, trying to hide the smile Merina saw on her lips. "Not for lack of trying on his part. I'm sure that was his intention when he brought her to the holding, but she had other plans for her life."

"If Delaphinu had no suitors who would take her as life-mate, why would she think running away from her home was going to work?" Merina asked, perplexed that a girl her age would do so willingly--and without thinking the action through.

Auntie finished the tea in her cup, tilting it around in a circle and watching the tea leaves swirl with the motion. Merina knew why her aunt was hesitating to answer. Auntie finally spoke. "It was not that Delaphinu did not have suitors--she had them by the score. It was more like she wanted to get away from her family, who she thought no longer valued her as a woman. Mating with a neighbor would not get her away from her source of disappointment."

Merina groped for the words for what perplexed her. "But creating and caring for a family was what she knew, what she had been born to do. What else could she do?"

Auntie gave Merina a wry smile. "Oh, there was more to my sister than we all knew. Sorceress Helinu was new to Dysandes and eager to send magic-user candidates to Byklandes. She had been very active in her visitations of the holdings, trying to convince the children who were becoming of age, or even past the time, to be tested. Delaphinu had rejected Helinu's offer when the Healer had first visited father's holding, insisting she was too busy to do anything else. When my sister decided to leave, she packed her few belongings and went to Sorceress Helinu's residence in Dysandes. She took the Test and passed."

Alanu stopped for a moment, her eyes on Merina and a hint of pride in her voice. "She passed with the highest score ever recorded in the valley, which wasn't saying much because so few test here, but it was also the highest recorded by Byklandes for all of Saphradea. Sorceress Helinu was beyond impressed and sent Delaphinu to Byklandes with a scroll of recommendation that urged the training lodge to admit her immediately. Delaphinu was gone before Father even knew she had left our home."

Merina refilled their cups. She had not known her mother had tested so high, only that she had passed. If Alanu thought so highly of magical talent, why didn't she take the Test instead of continuing the life of farming, unlike her sister? Auntie believed in the usefulness of magic--at least in its healing use.

While Auntie peeked under the towel to see how well the dough had risen, Merina pondered how to ask her next question. Auntie returned to her stool and looked expectantly at Merina.

"You said Mother was dismissed from Inhestia, but she had been sent to Byklandes. How did that happen?"

Auntie sipped her tea, then said sadly, "I wish she had never gone to that lodge. Magic-users throughout the Domains have such a high opinion of the Delmathians' skills, but they do not follow our Saphradean Order's rules as strictly as they could. If she had remained at Byklandes, she might not have been led astray down the path where her mentor took her. At least that is what I've been told by Sorceress Helinu."

"You mean my father, whoever he is?" Merina asked, tasting the bitterness in her voice.

Auntie nodded but did not attempt to answer the question. No one in Dysandes knew the name of the man who had sired a baby on Delaphinu, only that he was held at fault for not trying to provide any support for it. Alanu continued, "Delaphinu did exceedingly well for her first three years she was at Byklandes. We know this only because Sorceress Helinu insisted on keeping my father informed of her progress. She was very proud of the fact she had found my sister and sent her off to be a Neophyte. We would not have known otherwise, as Delaphinu did not come home during the spring for planting as was done by the rest of the Neophytes, making it clear she had quit the family. Father was heartbroken but too proud to show any interest in his daughter's progress. I think our Healer acted that way only to tweak his nose and let him know she also thought him wrong in his decision to bring such a woman-child into his home."

"Helinu is not from the valley. She was raised elsewhere," Merina said too quickly.

"Her title is Sorceress, Merina. Please show her some respect."

"I'll try, but there is something about her that makes me uneasy. Ever since I first started my monthly cycle I find her presence irritating. I can't stand to be around her. Grandfather Romanus had made the right decision to ignore our Sorceress Healer."

Auntie nodded. "Perhaps, but it was Sorceress Helinu who sponsored Delaphinu, and she was not going to let us forget that--at least as long as my sister was doing well. Which, as I said, she did. The Delmathian main training lodge was at Inhestia, where they send their best students. The Delmathians offer a limited number of students from Hermania and Saphradea the opportunity to train with theirs. Delaphinu was invited to study at Inhestia."

"Why would Mother go?"

"Your mother was studying to become a Provisioner sorcerer. They use Power to produce goods magically. It is something she loved to do, to make things with her hands. For example, she hated to bake bread because of the time it took," Auntie said, peeking under the towel again, "but loved to serve and eat it. With magic, it was a moment's task."

"This goes to prove what the villagers said about my mother's laziness."

"No," Auntie said with a weary sigh, "it shows my sister loved to nurture and care, to provide for the ones she loved, but, because of the demands on her time, was impatient to get the job done. At eleven years old she was providing for seven children, a father, and a bedridden stepmother. Four years later a new baby brother arrives and both he and his mother die. Delaphinu's strength in the Provisioner's magic was probably due to her will to succeed as a substitute mother for so many."

Merina bit her lip and cut off the words that almost escaped her. *If she cared so much, Auntie, why did she abandon me?* Merina drank the rest of her tea and checked to see if Alanu wanted anymore. Merina did not, but she had further questions she wanted to ask. Her aunt pushed her cup forward, and Merina filled it, hoping Alanu would not see the tears in her eyes from her unspoken question. Clearing her tightened throat, Merina asked, "What happened then, at this Inhestia training lodge?"

"Delaphinu was doing some kind of advanced studies with wines. Why wines? We weren't told. She apparently became addicted to whatever she was creating. Her drunkenness began to interfere with the completion of her study. Her mentor tried to help her by hiding her problem from the authorities. The rumors say she repaid him by seducing him to her bed."

"But," Merina cut in hesitantly, afraid to ask the question she had come to ask, "sorcerers can't mate other sorcerers. Why did she think it was going to solve her problems?"

Alanu dismissed that notion. "I thought so, too, but my sister laughed at me when I asked her why she had broken her oath and mated with her mentor. She said there was never any oath like that. What she did was commonplace among instructors and professors, although there were rules about students not sleeping with mentors. The onus was on the professors--they could lose their position."

"Then why was she forced out?"

"She said her research stopped because she was unable to control whatever spell she was developing. The wine was taking her mind off the spell. Then she found out she was pregnant. That sobered her up, and she realized what she had done. Her mentor offered to make her his life-mate, but she refused his offer of support. She quit and came back to Dysandes."

"What happened to this mentor person?"

Alanu looked into the teacup as if searching for an answer that would not upset Merina. "Your mother would not say. No one knows, or if they do, they are not willing to tell. That is the sad part of this story. Not having the answer as to why she did not take him as her life-mate leads one to believe that your mother had done something terrible or that she had to leave for some scandalous reason."

Why are the magic-users being so evasive? What are they hiding? Merina grabbed her cup and saucer off the table and slammed them into the sink almost hard enough to crack them. "You are so correct there, Auntie. I have heard from my friends many an explanation of why my mother came home. At least I learned who my real friends were and those who did not really care for me by what story they picked to tell me. I need to get back to our accounts. Tomorrow is Settling Day, and Uncle Tomanis will need our bills and charge records brought up to date. Thanks for telling me about Mother's decision to go into magic."

She hurried from the table. From the expression on her aunt's face, it was clear that Alanu wanted to stop her from leaving so abruptly, but Merina did not want to talk about her mother anymore. Anyhow, she really did need to get ready for the next day.

Settling Day was Merina's favorite day of the month. When she had been a little girl, it had been an excuse to leave her aunt's farm and travel to Dysandes, the one village of any size in the valley. The journey through the valley defined all she knew of the Domains. She only dreamed that one day she might travel beyond the mountains that confined her view of the world she lived in and held such wondrous lands named Delmathia, Saphradea, Hermania, the Seas, and the most mysterious of all, the Non-Lands. Until that day, her valley was big enough to hold her imagination quite well.

On Settling Day the valley's landholders would load their wagons with produce and goods they manufactured at home and would take to the roads early in the morning so as to reach Dysandes by high noon. There they would set up stalls where the field hands laid out what they brought for sale, and the women of the household would spread out through town, buying from both the local merchants and each other's wares. The farmers would gather in the center of the marketplace and settle the debts they had contracted with each other, while Dysandes's merchants gathered there eager to conduct trade and receive payment.

The children were mostly confined to the immediate vicinity of their family's wagon, if anyone could confine children to any place for very long. The family of her lifelong friend, Florinu, always set up their stall next to Merina's, and the girls would get to visit while they helped sell the fruits and vegetables stacked up around them. Merina took a much more intense interest in selling than Florinu, who would rather talk about her dolls and all the mischief she had gotten into. Flo was such a pretty and happy child she could charm the frown off the most crotchety farmer around. She would run off to visit their other neighbors and return with interesting bits of news, which she quickly shared, then rushed off to gather more gossip.

This pattern worked well with Merina. It kept her informed of what was going on around her, and, surprisingly, she found she could use the information to her advantage when she bargained with the folk who stopped at her stall. Tomanis noticed one Settling Day that she was selling more than those around her and remarked to his friends that his niece really had a heart for the business.

When her cousin Briamis became old enough to take Merina's place at their market table, Tomanis would invite her to go with him to see how the adults conducted trade. She found that listening to people and asking the right questions gave her useful information, sometimes the same information Florinu was getting. More often than not, it conflicted with what her friend heard and what she was told by adults. She came to realize that what little girls heard and talked about, adults frequently did not want anyone else to know. A father's complaints at the dinner table about a crop problem were not always repeated in the marketplace when his produce competed with others. She used such tidbits of information to her advantage when negotiating prices.

When she had finished conducting her business at today's Settling Day, Merina told her father she would not remain in town, as was her usual wont, because she had a call to make on Dame Brischelu.

Merina hesitated at the door of the tavern, anticipating that in there she would endure lustful eyes staring at her, followed by crude comments and suggestions no one in her right mind would respond to. That didn't really bother her since she was used to dealing with men and boys, like her farmhands, who did not have the means to support a family and could think only of their own needs. A chance for a roll in the hay was ever their dream. Nor did she think any man in there would try to force her to do anything she did not want to happen. After all, they were sons and brothers of people she had grown up with. And neighbors who had helped, or been helped, when times got hard. No, her apprehension was over what Dame Brischelu wanted to talk to her about.

The door opened directly into the great common-room of the tavern, where she found herself in the company of a half-dozen men standing along the bar that took up the entire wall on her left. On her right stood five round tables that served as both a dining area and a place for anyone who chose to sit with drinks. At a table in the far right corner sat the woman Merina had come to see. She closed the door and walked past the men, who gave her the measured stares she expected but said little, at most a stray hello as she went by.

"Good afternoon," Brischelu said pleasantly as Merina approached her table.

"It is indeed, Madam. I hope all is well for you and your family," Merina responded with what she hoped was the proper civility for addressing a noble. If Dame Brischelu had a title, no one in Dysandes had ever used it in Merina's hearing, but everyone held her in awe for whatever she was.

"We are losing animals to the wolves, which I am sure all of us are suffering from. They are becoming such a problem!" Brischelu sighed with a worried frown. "It has gotten bad enough that I am afraid to travel the roads. That is why I asked to see you here, Mistress Merina."

Sitting in the chair that Brischelu gestured to, Merina found she could not relax in the Dame's presence. Merina knew Brischelu was the life-mate of the richest landowner in Dysandes and a reclusive woman who stayed on her farmholding except for rare trips into town. She also knew the grand lady as the teacher who guided the older children in the valley. Although all the valley's children could read and write, having been taught by their parents or adult relatives, Brischelu had taken on the role of teaching what life was like in the rest of Saphradea and beyond that, in the Domains. There was little to do in the winter, and the children from the neighboring farms would be invited over to share in the learning. It was quite the honor to host the Dame.

Merina looked around the tavern, mildly surprised by how quiet the men at the bar were. Their presence this early in the day meant they were not local field hands, who would normally not get off work until sundown. She did not recognize any of the faces of the farmers her uncle and aunt traded with, and these men were more heavily armed than one would expect.

Dame Brischelu, noticing Merina looking at the men, answered the question that had jumped into Merina's mind. "This is my escort, Mistress Merina. Farmer Calandis hired them this spring. He usually has them patrol his lands, but when I said I wanted to go for a visit he offered their services to me."

Merina glanced away from the men and back to the Dame. She noticed Brischelu always used a title with her life-mate's name when she talked to anyone. A lesson in politeness Merina rarely observed. "I'm glad they are friends, Madam. With so few travelers on the road, being surrounded by armed men makes me think of them more as a threat than an aid."

"Well, you can relax, my dear."

Merina sat back in the chair with a little less stiffness, but she knew the wariness she was displaying was not a reaction to the men in the room. "I received your note, Dame Brischelu. It said--"

"Oh, what a terrible host I've been, Merina." The Dame waved to the bartender, who hurried over. "Please bring Mistress Merina whatever she desires, and I will have a glass of your famous Sweetwater Wine--chilled if you please." The bartender nodded eagerly and gave Merina a smile of greeting.

"I'll have the same, sir."

"Excellent choice, Madam and Mistress. It will take me a minute to fetch it from the cellar. Would you care for anything to eat with it?" he asked hopefully.

Merina was hungry, but she did not want to put anything into her stomach until she knew why she had been asked to come here. She suspected the wine was not going to settle her any more than food, but it would be rude to let the Dame drink alone. She shook her head in response to the bartender's question.

"Not right away, good sir--and please provide my escort another round of whatever they're drinking. But tell them to stay sober," Brischelu ordered lightly. She shot a glance at Merina and concluded, "I don't know how long I will be here."

The innkeeper hurried away. Merina said to his back, "This tavern has a reputation for ample rations of simple food and good beer, Dame Brischelu. I did not know they had fine wines also."

The Dame smiled. "What you really mean is the tavern has a reputation for cheap fare to draw a rowdy crowd that overindulges in its whiskeys and brews. I make them provide food fit for all, just in case a more sedate traveler should care to stay here."

"You make them..."

"Oh, yes. I own the tavern and several others in the valley. My family has large holdings in vineyards throughout Saphradea. I have expanded our wine business significantly since I came here thirty years ago."

Merina looked at the Dame in surprise. "Farmer Calandis has vineyards?"

Laughing merrily, Brischelu shook her head. "No, no. My father's estate--which is now mine. I dare say most of the wine Dysandes and its surrounds consume come from me!"

This surprised Merina, because she had always seen a wandering trader, a Tieri named Jalanos, making wine deliveries to the markets and taverns in Dysandes. She had assumed he was the source--or rather his people were. "I thought the Tieri--"

"He is one of my agents. You as a trades-woman should appreciate this--I supply the product, I also own where it is sold, and, except for one time in the past, I have had no competition to deal with."

Merina did see the advantage Brischelu spoke of and wondered how the Dame had managed to accomplish that feat of commerce. "But all of us who have farmholdings make wine for our own use, Madam, and brew our own beer."

The bartender hurried over from the cellar door, carrying a glass pitcher and two glasses on a wooden tray expertly in one hand, the other holding a towel to wipe the table clean. The two women watched him swipe the table surface, then, when he thought he was finished, silently waited for him to redo his effort. Several moments later, they had glasses in hand and took sips of what he had delivered.

"This is excellent, Dame Brischelu!" Merina said after putting her glass down carefully. She was used to pottery cups and wondered how glass survived in this environment.

"Isn't it! Can you truly say the wine you make is as good, my dear?"

Shaking her head, Merina admitted as much. "The berries we use can't produce such a light wine as this."

"And you don't grow them as a crop, which could be done at the expense of land you need for fodder or silage. The grapes I produce will not grow in this valley, though many have tried. The people of Dysandes have chosen to pay for my wines and beer because it is cheaper than the cost and work of doing it themselves, and they get what they can't make." Gesturing at the men by the bar with her glass, Dame Brischelu continued, "You would be spending all your time trying to keep your menfolk supplied with liquid refreshment. It is one reason we tolerate the Tieri people in our midst. They do most of their trade in food and wine."

What the Dame said made sense to Merina, but she had not known Brischelu owned the taverns scattered throughout the valley. She had always believed the Hospice Guild did. She mentioned her assumption to the Dame.

"They do," Brischelu said with a smile, lifting one eyebrow and looking into her glass as she took a long sip.

Merina realized what the Dame now implied. "So you really have no competition, Madam, since the purpose of the Guild is to control the trade in their market?"

Putting down her glass, the Dame filled it from the pitcher and offered more to Merina, who, looking at her glass, saw that she had unconsciously finished it. She pushed it forward quickly to get refilled.

"Mistress Merina, you seemed to have missed what I said about competition. My exact words were, 'except for one time in the past'."

Merina quashed her annoyance that the Dame was right, wondering instead why Brischelu had brought up the subject again. "If the grapes can't be grown here, how could anyone compete with you, Madam?"

The Dame swirled her glass in tiny circles, making the clear white wine rise up the side of the glass, and tilted the glass slightly side to side to see how the liquid flowed back down. "There was a very clever girl who grew up not far for here. She found out she had a gift and left the valley to learn how to develop that gift."

The anxiety Merina had been feeling rushed over her, as she suddenly realized she was hearing the reason Brischelu had summoned her. "You are speaking of my mother, Dame Brischelu?"

The older woman nodded.

"My mother never graduated from her training lodge. How could she become a threat to you?" Merina asked.

Brischelu looked at Merina in shock. "A threat? Did I say I was threatened by her?"

"No, ma'am, you did not. I'm sorry I used the wrong term."

"I respected Delaphinu very highly, my dear. It was in the result of her research that I saw the potential for her to become competition to me." The Dame took a tiny sip of her wine.

Respect? You would be the only one in the valley if you truly believe that. "My mother used the gift you spoke of to keep herself in alcohol. I suppose that kept her from buying your wine, if that is what you mean by competition."

Shaking her head sadly, Brischelu gazed at Merina with pity. "Your bitterness at your mother is unfounded, Merina. Delaphinu was a caring woman who thought to improve the lives of the valley farmers by finding better ways to increase their crop and livestock production. She came to me when she was offered a position at Inhestia with an idea to increase my wine production as part of her research there."

Chastened, Merina still could not hold back her cutting comment. "How, use Power to make more of your wine?"

"That is conceivable, but you obviously don't understand how magic works. You speak of Power as if it is limitless. I know I did not teach you such. Ah, now I remember. When I taught that subject you got up and left the room. Your friends said you hated magic and Power use."

The Dame's voice took on a motherly firmness when she said, "It is not good business sense not to know as much about what goes on in Saphradea and the Domains as you can. The origin of all magic, what we call Power, is very limited and is well guarded because it is so rare. There are only a few mines in Saphradea that supply the rock that contains the energy. The sorcerers call them sources. It would take quite a lot of these sources and even more Provisioner sorcerers than we currently have to even begin to compete with my vineyards in the south. That is not what she proposed."

"All I know about sources is that when she left that training lodge, she had one. I was told this, that she stole it," Merina said defensively.

"That was after she had studied in Inhestia--not when she first proposed her idea. Student sources are middling things at best--toys compared to working sources. And from what I heard from my friends at Byklandes, she did not steal a source. Do you want to know what she proposed or not, child?"

Merina finished her wine, putting her hand over the rim to show she didn't want any more. She took a moment to think, because the direction of this conversation filled her with an urge to get up and leave. It was not a reasonable response, and she knew that. "Yes, Ma'am. You have been very patient with me. I will not interrupt any further."

The Dame pushed her glass away from her and focused all her attention on Merina. "Your mother said she believed she could find a way to change the grapes I used in the south to grow here. Your mother wanted to know if she were to accomplish this, would I be willing to buy grapes from the valley farmers to produce my wine?"

Merina sat back, aware that her confusion showed on her face. "What good would that do for the valley landowners? We have only a certain amount of land that will produce crops, which we either use ourselves or sell. Adding a new crop would only increase the number of choices we have for rotation purposes. This would be a change of little value, Madam."

"Ah, the word that Dysandes residents resist so often--change. Do you know that since Valehanis first arrived in this valley three hundred years ago, the people have not lived much differently than he did? Nothing really changes--unless Power is used. Why is that, Mistress?"

"Because the way we do it works, and works efficiently and successfully. It takes hard work, but making it easier doesn't mean we can do more. That is the problem with magic, Dame Brischelu. People use it to do less work."

The older woman stiffened as if surprised at Merina's derision of magic. "Do you know the main requirement for advancement in the magic skills--to go from Novice to say, Sorcerer?" the Dame asked.

Merina shook her head. She really didn't care, but Brischelu seemed to think this point was important enough to bother her with the question. "I suppose to get more powerful spells."

"No. To advance in skill, you have to advance the knowledge of Power use. The higher the level, the more the spell has to affect magic knowledge. Back before the Sorcerer Wars, there were unbelievable spells that magic-users could control. There were legends of flying, walking through stone walls, and even slaying with a glance. All gone now, lost to us through time." The Dame leaned back, and wonder filled her voice as she said, "If we only had some of that back--we could change the Non-Lands into fertile land, stop people dying of disease, or stop death itself."

Merina crossed her arms in front of her chest and propped them on the table. It was a rude posture, but she wanted to show the Dame that this was all something she had heard before. "Making the Non-Lands fertile might, but stopping the population of the Domains from dying would only make it worse."

Smiling, Brischelu said, "So we argued when I was in court. The young don't always see the complexity in everyday life like farmers do. Excuse me for getting off the subject. Your mother's proposal was for a project she hoped to use to advance herself at Inhestia. She was trying to become a Sorcerer before she even graduated as Novice. She was very ambitious, your mother."

But failed. Merina asked the Dame, "How does her being ambitious make her proposal to you of any value?"

"Her ambitions supplied the drive to do something no one else thought could be done. She needed a supply of my grapevines to study. She believed the grapevines needed something from the ground of Dysandes that they could not get and the land in the south had. If she could discover what it was, then she hoped to be able to use a spell to make the earth correct for growing grapes. If she could do that, she reasoned that she might be able to go the next step in changing infertile soil, such as one finds in the Non-Lands, into fertile soil. The southern border of the Non-Lands is not that far away, at most several days' ride to the north of us. Close enough that she believed Dysandes' farmers could be persuaded to attempt planting the vines up there."

Merina sat up straight and folded her hands in her lap, staring down at them to focus the thoughts racing through her mind. A plan such as Delaphinu's could work, but only if magic delivered the secret of making the vines grow. She looked up at Brischelu. "Did you give her the vines?"

"Of course. Over the next two years I received reports of her progress. She excitedly wrote that she was very near to discovering the missing ingredient and was working with her mentor to conduct a test, and then I stopped hearing anything from her. For six months I received nothing, no news of her or her project. Then she showed up in Dysandes. I was saddened to learn of what had befallen her."

Merina did not want to hear anything more about her mother than she already knew. "Why are you telling me all this, Madam? If you think my mother left anything of what she had been doing in Inhestia with her family, I can assure you the only thing she left was me."

Brischelu smiled at Merina's sarcasm. "I see a lot of your mother in you, dear. You have a drive for trade that is well known in the valley, and I know you have the courage to risk doing things no one else would try. I am looking for someone to help me--manage, I think is a good word--a problem I have."

Merina wondered how she could help the richest noblewoman in Dysandes.

"Magic use has been shown to run through the bloodline. It is very strong in yours. I believe you have the same gift your mother did. I can arrange to have you tested and admitted to Byklandes--I have very influential friends in the Saphradean Mage Council. You will succeed there, I'm sure. I need you to then go to Inhestia and find what your mother discovered..." Brischelu stopped, for Merina's face must have mirrored her horror at the Dame's scheme.

"Merina, my dear, you look distressed. Do you hate magic so much that you cannot bring yourself to use the gift your mother left you?"

"You, you..." Merina could manage to force only those few words out past the turmoil raging in her mind. She put her hands around her ears and closed her mind, shutting down every sense she could to cut herself off from the world. What is she asking me to do? she screamed in her mind, over and over again. Taking several deep breaths, she willed herself to be calm. After a few minutes, she realized she had succeeded.

Lowering her hands, Merina opened her eyes and found Dame Brischelu watching her, a slight smile on her face. The Dame held out Merina's glass filled from the pitcher and Merina took it, swallowing half in one gulp. Setting the glass down carefully, Merina spoke calmly. "No, Madam, I can't hate something I don't want or need. I don't accept this gift you say my mother gave me. I do appreciate and accept the gift of the body she gave me. What you are asking me to do is to become my mother, and that I will never do. I will use my body and mind to raise the family I intend to have, and I will not abandon my family to chase foolish dreams. My life is here in Dysandes--not in far-off foreign lands."

Sitting back in her chair, almost lounging, if a noble lady could do such a thing, Brischelu drained her glass and put it on the table. "Then let me ask for what I really want from you."

Merina reached for the pitcher, and, leaning forward, filled first the Dame's glass, then her own. Either the drink of wine she had just taken was washing through her body and making her slightly light-headed, or she did not understand what had just happened. "Pardon, Madam, but..."

Taking up her glass, Brischelu sipped from it. She turned and frowned at the bartender, who immediately rushed over. Both he and the men at the bar had been studiously trying to ignore the two women but obviously had not succeeded. The Dame pointed at the pitcher and told him to bring another because this one was warm, and to give the old one to her escort. He scurried off to obey her command.

"Everything I have said is true," Brischelu said to Merina, "so don't think I am trying to convince you with lies. You are at an age when you need to make decisions about the choices you have before you. I would truly love for you to do what I asked first, but I knew it would force you to think of what you really want in life. I need a strong-willed woman who can simultaneously manage an estate, raise a family, increase the fortune of that family, and think beyond the troubles of today and see ahead to the future. The problem I am asking you to take on is my son."

"Markinis?" Merina said with disbelief. She took a long sip of her wine and waved the half-empty glass at Brischelu. "It would take a half-dozen more pitchers of this wine to convince me to even linger in his presence. Your son has chased after every girl over the age of eleven in the valley, and notice I did not say anything about an upper age limit."

"I don't deny that, Merina. He is young, and, like a bumblebee, is attracted to every flower his path crosses."

"Your son is long past the age where the sight of a woman's body disconnects his mind from all reason. His mind is focused on exactly what he wants it on."

"That is true also, Mistress, but as a mother I can tell you it is because he, unlike you, does not have a goal in life. He can afford most anything he wants, but having it does not fill the void in his life. He needs direction, purpose, and a firm hand to guide him. I cannot give him what he is seeking."

Merina pushed away the ugly thought that jumped into her mind and asked instead, "Which is?"

"A family of his own. Someone to love him and for him to love," the Dame answered with conviction.

Were that only true. I am sure he wants someone to love him, but he has not acted that way with any woman I know. Does she not know what he did to Florinu or what I had to do to him to stop it?

Merina finished her glass and pushed it away. She knew if she drank any more, it would probably work the same magic that had ruined her mother. Merina glanced at the Dame, who seemed to be waiting for an answer to a question not asked. "Madam, I appreciate your interest in my life and thank you for what you told me about my mother. Whether or not your son becomes a part of my life depends on your son. It is getting late, and I must take my leave."

Brischelu nodded, that same faint smile playing at the corner of her lips. Merina wondered if she had just unwittingly agreed to whatever the Dame had been trying to accomplish. Merina stood and said her goodbye with a slight bow.

The Dame watched the young woman walk away from her and knew Merina was the one for her son. Having spent her early years in court, Brischelu knew what caught a Saphradean nobleman's eyes and what men of power wanted in a woman. She knew that like all males, they lusted after the body first, but unlike the simple people, a nobleman considered three other things he wanted more in a life-mate. First was the influence a woman brought to his bed, second the obligation it placed her family under to her life-mate, and third the creation of heirs.

Scanning her guards by the bar, Brischelu smiled to herself. These simple men had a whole different priority in what they wanted from women, but they were not men of power. Like most of the men in this valley, they were trained to do the work they had been bred to do. Few if any thought beyond anything besides what was handed down to them. Not that she objected to that situation, since she needed them to do what they were told and not get any ideas counter to her will.

Finishing her glass, she poured another. The guards glanced at her, and she saw them relax. Her staying for another drink would give them the chance to consume more on their own. It was so easy to please men when you know what they wanted. Her life-mate, Calandis, was not unlike these men. The fact that he was the richest landowner in the valley made him also the most powerful in a society based on trade. His wealth had given him the means to purchase her, a bastard daughter of Saphradean nobility, with the hope of influencing the Prince of Princes. She had given him that and an heir. He had not gotten her gold, though. She had worked to earn that, on her own, by managing him.

Yes, influence worked many ways, sometimes to another's advantage, but always to hers. Young Merina would find that out soon enough.

Chapter 3

Merina arrived home just in time to help her aunt finish the preparations for dinner. Having little time to tell of her visit with Dame Brischelu, Merina decided to save the news for after-dinner talk. Alanu's boys, the nine-year-old twins and their eleven-year-old brother, were full of nervous energy and, once fed, did not want to be tethered to the table to listen to anyone. They had talked excitedly about finding wolf tracks near their secret place, which, of course, alarmed Alanu, but Uncle Tomanis assured her the tracks probably came from a fox. This idea worried Merina's aunt even more and led to a discussion of chicken predators and losses to them. The boys kept insisting the tracks signified wolves, and Merina got volunteered by Alanu to go check, since adults were not allowed to see the secret place. The boys did not consider Merina an adult. The four of them left the table before Merina could deliver her story.

The secret place, which everyone knew was located in an old shed behind the chicken coop, was too small for Merina to crawl into--which was fine for her because it was unlikely to have any tracks left intact with the boys crawling in and out of it that day. They wiggled inside and emerged with crudely manufactured spears. Briamis, the oldest and leader of this gang, insisted the weapons were needed to protect Merina. She pulled her knife from her belt sheath and examined it, then the sharpened sticks, and nodded that she was glad for their protection. The boys raced away to the site of the tracks.

"See, there in the dirt. That's no fox track, Mer." Briamis pointed out the spoor with grave authority.

Merina looked at the impression--made quite a while ago when the ground, which was now dried, had been soaked and muddy. She knelt and measured across the print with her knife blade. "It is big enough, Briamis. Too big for any of our dogs."

She surveyed the yard to see if any other tracks remained. There were none that she could see. The boys, with weapons poised, stalked around the area to help. From the number of people that usually used this path by the chicken house, she thought it interesting that even this one trace had survived. Neither she nor the boys found any further prints. Her cousins stored their spears in the secret place and marched Merina back to the dinner table to proclaim their skill at animal tracking.

Uncle Tomanis was finishing a piece of pie when the scouting expedition returned with their report. By the time the boys had poured out their findings, a listener would have thought an entire pack of wolves had invaded the farm but had escaped the boys hunting them down. Aunt Alanu managed to shift their interest off the wolves and onto the pie waiting for them, giving Merina a chance to tell what she had seen. "A single pawprint in the dried-up mud along the chicken house path was all I found, must be several weeks old. It was very large and deep. I'm sure it was a wolf. I wonder why our dogs had not picked up on the scent?"

Tomanis looked worried. "That rain we had a while ago could have washed away most of the trail and scent. I'll take a couple of the men and scout around the barns and the main pasture. It is not like wolves to come this close to any holding."

"I'm riding to see Florinu tomorrow morning. I'll ask if they have been visited as well," Merina said, sitting at her place and savoring the sight of the plate in front of her. The boys had already finished their pie and raced away to catch the last rays of the sun to play.

"What did Dame Brischelu want?" Alanu asked.

Having just put a piece of pie in her mouth, Merina took the time while chewing and swallowing to frame her reply. "She asked me to consider becoming Markinis's life-mate."

Tomanis barked out a laugh, then stopped himself, saying, "I guess nobility doesn't follow Saphradean customs. Does Calandis, or even Markinis, know of her request?"

Forking in another piece of the excellent berry pie, Merina waited for Auntie's shocked expression to change into a quizzical one. Next came the question she knew Alanu would ask. "Does the Dame know you're spoken for?"

"If she did, she didn't mention it. It would not have mattered to her if she knew, because as a woman of trade herself, she viewed her offer as better than the one I had. I suspect the Dame knows more about what is going on in the valley than we think a woman so reclusive would know."

Alanu pushed her uneaten dessert away, her annoyance evident in the frown on her face. "She must not have any respect for you, thinking you can be bought like a side of beef."

"Perhaps, Auntie, that is true. We all think Farmer Calandis paid the highest bid to make her his life-mate, but I am willing to bet she was more involved in that negotiating than we think. She wants what is best for her son, and she thinks that is me. I take that as a compliment, which shows respect from her." Merina finished her dessert and took a sip of her hot tea.

As Alanu started clearing the plates, Tomanis posed the question that his life-mate wanted to ask. "Did you accept the offer?"

"I did not stop the negotiation, is a better answer. If her son Markinis wants me as a life-mate, it is up to him to pursue me--not I him," Merina said flatly. She stacked her knife and fork on the empty plate before her, carefully not looking at Tomanis, because when the memory of the last meeting she had with Markinis flashed before her eyes, she could not keep her revulsion at him from her face.

Alanu smiled as she picked up Merina's plate and carried it to the kitchen. Merina reminded her uncle, "Tomorrow I'm riding over to Florinu's holding to check on her and talk woman talk."

"And ask your friend for advice." Tomanis smiled. He seemed to know Merina would not think that highly of a man's opinion.

Merina knew all of the families in the valley, but could count only a dozen of the women her age as friends. They had grown up together, meeting at Settling Days, festivals, and funerals, attracted to each other because they were of the same age and interests and banding together for protection from the older children who would order them around. Her closest friend was Florinu, because Florinu had lived within walking distance of Merina's homestead and they could meet more often, provided they could take the hour's one-way walk between their homes. Florinu no longer lived close. Like many of the valley women, she had mated after reaching her sixteenth year. Her life-mate, Denathis, the oldest son of a landholder, had been given a share of land near his parents. Florinu was now a two-hour ride away and a mother-to-be. Merina did not usually mind the length of the trip, but today, with the threat of wolves around, she was pushing Marigold to a faster pace than the old horse wanted to go.

Florinu was hanging out the wash when Merina rode up. Her friend was beginning to show, which meant she would bear her child in the winter's months. It seemed to be the way of farmers' wives to begin their children in spring like the rest of the livestock. Merina had made her decision to take a life-mate in late summer and have her baby in the spring.

Not this year, she mused.

"Hello, Merina! Just in time for a cool drink under the shade--I really need one today."

"How are you feeling?" Merina asked, a natural question to a mother-to-be, but not the one she had ridden this long way for.

"Just fine. Denathis's mother has been very helpful and has explained everything I need to know to be prepared for birth. I haven't even bothered to talk to Healer Helinu yet."

Merina poured them cups of water from the pitcher on the table under the tree that supported Florinu's wash line. She handed her friend a cup. They sat on the long bench underneath the cool shade of the tree. "I would rather have the advice of a woman who has borne many children and assisted in the birth of hundreds, than help from a childless sorcerer. Magic may be useful for treating injuries, but having a baby is a natural process, not a wound to be healed. Your life-mate's mother is a highly respected midwife."

"Oh, I agree with you about that, but it is still required that a Healer be notified of a pending birth. I haven't made the trip into town because I don't want to pull Denathis from his work to escort me. With these wolf attacks getting worse, I am afraid to go alone. I am not as brave as you."

Waving away Florinu's deprecating remark about herself, Merina said, "Nonsense, you are being prudent with the safety of yourself and the babe. Trying to outrun a pack of wolves would not be good in your condition. Speaking of wolves, Briamis found a pawprint near our home. Has Denathis seen any around your place?"

Her friend shook her head, losing some of the joy that usually filled her eyes, after Merina mentioned the predator track. Florinu had something to say on the topic, by the way she was glancing around nervously.

"Have you heard of any attacks on travelers?" Merina probed. "The only ones I know of have been on stray cattle and sheep."

Lowering her voice, her friend said, "My father told me he was followed last week while riding into Dysandes. The wolves trailed him for at least an hour, which is rather strange behavior. He was armed with his bow and had it ready for them. I don't know if they recognize weapons like our hunting dogs can, being wild and not used to men, but since our hounds have learned, I don't know why not. They stayed out of range the whole time."

"That is not natural, all right," Merina said, sipping thoughtfully from her cup. "They surely know death awaits them with the presence of men. The Guard has hunted them in the past and taken many a hide. It has been a while since hunters last thinned out the population. Maybe their numbers have increased too much, and they are coming out of the deep wood because their natural prey is getting scarce?"

Florinu nodded, renewed excitement sparkling in her eyes. "Which is what Father said, but he has talked to the other landholders and they say it is only happening in our valley, which is very strange. And even stranger, he said the wolves were a lot bigger than he had ever seen around here. He believes they are coming out of the northern mountains--in fact, he thinks from the Non-Lands."

"The Non-Lands? Really?" Merina laughed. Her friend was a little naïve about anything other than valley history. "The Non-Lands will not support any life as we know it, Flo. If they came from there, they would be ghosts."

Florinu pouted. "So my momma said, Mer. Maybe they are ghosts."

Merina scoffed. "As have all our mothers, my friend, because mothers use the legends of the Non-Lands to scare their children into obedience. If we were to believe them, nothing good lives in the Non-Lands, only evil. I'm willing to wager that you will tell your children as well, but no one has ever proven the existence of ghosts, walking dead, or, for that matter, dragons."

"Not true, I saw one last year at the fair," Florinu countered.

"You saw a magic-user--what are they called, an Illusionist, that's it-- an Illusionist's creation. They make those things up in their minds and use magic to bring them to life. That is what they get paid to do, to entertain us backwoods types."

"You said, Merina, that dragons do not exist. I just proved they did."

Sighing, Merina poured the two of them more water and muttered aloud something about the heat and Florinu's mind. "I will concede the existence of legends. But back to my point, do you remember when we were little girls, about ten summers ago? We were at Settling Day and we saw the Prince of Princes Alexus's soldiers arrive on that huge ship that sailed up the river into Dysandes. There seemed to be so many of them that they filled the village to bursting, and the horses--"

Florinu burst out with, "Oh, yes. The mighty horses, so sleek and powerful, some wearing armor. And the knights riding them! Do you remember that officer--"

"The lieutenant! She was the first woman knight I had ever seen," Merina added.

Pushing Merina's shoulder playfully, Florinu laughed. "Like you had seen any knights before. She looked so formidable, yelling orders--all dressed in armor. All those men jumping to her commands, except for the lead foreman--"

"Commander. He was called that--the army doesn't have lead foremen," Merina corrected.

"Yes, of course, but that is what he did. What else do you call a man who runs things? I suppose I could have called him the mayor--that's who met him when he walked off the ship." Florinu gave Merina a smug smile and continued, "I remember we stood there gawking at all the soldiers and horses milling around. There we were, our mouths hanging open, when the lieutenant walked over to us. We must have looked so stupid."

"But she didn't think so. She was nice, and called us Mistress like we were somebody." Merina smiled at the memory, then sighed, returned to her original purpose, saying, "She told us they were going to the Non-Lands and asked if we knew anyone who could guide us."

"And we did, we did. We told her of our Guard Captain, Garlantis. You ran off to get him, but he was already coming to see what the fuss was about at the pier. I remember it all so clearly. They formed up in a big long line--"

Merina broke in, "A column, that's what Uncle Tomanis called it. They filled the street. Then off they trotted, flags flying at the front of the line, people cheering at them."

"Oh, but do you also remember how after they had ridden out of the village, the farmers in the market made jokes about the soldiers chasing ghosts in the Non-Lands?" Florinu said, laughing.

Merina gazed at her friend and said slowly, "And do you remember what happened after they left?"

"Of course. That's your whole point, isn't it? I wasn't there when they rode back into Dysandes a month later, but on the next Settling Day we got to visit their camp outside the village where they waited for the ship to pick them up. It was so sad, the horses..."

Nodding, Merina finished Flo's sentence. "...were starved. You could see all the bones under their skin. And the soldiers were so worn and thin."

"You ran off and grabbed a basket of apples off your selling table," Florinu reminded Merina, "and we found the lieutenant and gave them to her. She smiled so prettily and thanked us."

"And remember, she told us what happened. They had spent weeks searching the Non-Lands and found nothing but rock and sand. The soldiers did not explore very far because they nearly ran out of food and water, not finding any. Nothing can survive there," Merina said, finally reaching her point.

Florinu took a quick sip of water and poked her index finger into the air. "See, my point exactly. The wolves could not survive there, so they are leaving it."

They both broke down into giggling. After a few pleasant minutes, Merina stood and grabbed a shirt from the wash basket to hang it on the line. She waved Florinu back her seat and began hanging the rest of the clothes while relating to her friend the tale of the meeting at Traveler's

Rest. She glanced at Florinu to see how her friend would take the news of the Dame's proposal. Florinu had fallen in love with Markinis when girls reach the age of fascination with boys, but the older man had been too busy with his latest conquests to notice her--not that he had not tried later.

"Oh my, Mer. What I would have given to be asked that four years ago." Florinu sighed.

"Think about it, Flo. Where is Denathis right now?"

Florinu looked to the west and pointed across the field to the far tree line. "He's fixing the water sluice."

"And where is Markinis right now?" Merina asked, the scorn plain in her voice.

Puzzled, Flo stared at Merina as if to say, how would she know, then she smirked. "Either mating with some man's life-mate, or drunk--"

"Or both," Merina finished for her. "We both know you made the right choice when you picked Denathis over the son of Calandis. Markinis is not a catch, he is a trial."

Agreeing with her, Florinu nodded in thought.

"Do you remember..." Merina began.

"No, not really, at least most of it. I know I was the talk of the valley afterward," Florinu said, her face reddened by the memory.

Merina shook out an underskirt and made soothing noises at Flo. "It was the Harvest Gathering, Flo. Everyone was celebrating too much. That was the first year we were allowed to take spirits beyond a child's taste."

With a dry laugh, Florinu shook her head. "What a polite way of saying I drank myself into silliness."

Merina made her point. "You had help from Markinis. He brought you drinks that night and made sure your glass was never empty. I saw what he was doing and tried my best to distract you."

Sighing, Florinu said, "I remember that part. He was so charming and attentive. And he, forgive me, Mer--he convinced me that you were trying to steal him away."

"As I thought. That's why you suggested I spend more time with Trinames and leave you alone."

"I'm sorry."

"No reason to apologize. I saw he was not drinking as heavily as he did with the other men, so I knew he was planning on taking you off into the bushes. I found Trinames and told him what I feared. He agreed to watch the two of you with me and be ready to intercede. Unfortunately, when that moment came, he had gone over to the drink table and was getting a beer. I was returning from the outhouse and saw Markinis maneuvering you toward the barn."

"That part I don't remember," Florinu groaned out.

"I didn't think so. Your eyes were not focusing, and you swayed a lot. By the time I got to the barn, he had your blouse untied and was pawing your breasts."

Flo turned her eyes downward. "Do I want to hear the rest of this?"

Merina lied, telling her friend, "Nothing else happened. I showed up, you had passed out, and he left."

The memory of what actually happened jumped into her mind. She had found Markinis straddling Florinu, her underpants in one hand and the other pulling his rigid manhood out. She ran up behind him as he knelt to enter Flo and laid the blade of her long knife across his throat. The cut was slight, but it served the purpose she had intended--making the big man freeze in place.

"She wanted it."

"No, I don't think so, sir. She is passed out. It looks like rape to me."

Markinis pulled his pants up and spread his hands out away from his sides. "It is your word against mine. She was begging me for it."

"The only begging I want to hear about is yours. I'll cut your throat faster than you can move if you try to turn on me."

Markinis spoke with a calmness that Merina could not believe he was feeling. "Look, no harm done. Let me walk away and I'll forget this whole incident if you will."

Merina gasped out with acid rising in her throat, "You must be joking. You will apologize to Florinu and her parents for your crude behavior."

"If I do that, then I will have to explain what really happened here, and the story will be all over the valley by morning. Everyone saw her throwing herself at me earlier. You are just jealous because I would not pay attention to you. Is that want you want?"

Stepping back, keeping her knife ready to slash the man, Merina knew Markinis would do just what he said, ruin Flo's reputation. "You're disgusting, Markinis. One word of this gets out and I will finish what I started. Now leave."

The man stood and leered at her. His eyes locked on her chest and the erect nipples under her blouse. "I love a woman with fight in her. You apparently like what you saw. Let's go into the barn and satisfy both of our needs."

Merina knew the surge of energy flowing in her body was not sexual, but due to the need to defend herself. Gesturing with the knife, she said, "If I see that thing again today it will be lying on the ground for all the ladies to appreciate."

Markinis had then excused himself and left.

Florinu coughed politely, drawing Merina back to the present. "What about Trinames? Does he know about the Dame's attempted arrangement for her son?"

Returning to the bench, Merina sat beside her friend and accepted a filled cup of water. Merina did not have an answer for Flo. She had not seen Trinames since the day of their argument. She was not sure how he would react after she ran away from him. Would he think I am even considering it? Merina sipped her water and turned her attention back to Florinu. "He doesn't know."

"I'd love to be there when you tell him. He really does not like Markinis," Florinu said, apparently relishing the scene in her mind.

The thought of what Florinu was alluding to made Merina gasp, and she blurted out, "Oh, Flo, we had a fight the last time I saw him. He'll probably think I've broken our promise to each other and am chasing after Markinis! He won't understand and he'll leave me!" Merina started to weep.

Florinu moved to Merina and hugged her, then gave her friend a good shake. "No, he won't! He loves you too much to be that stupid. Now, what was the fight about?"

Merina got control of herself, ashamed that she let the sudden emotion take her over like that. "You're right, I am being stupid. He just made me so mad, telling me he was going to become a Healer instead of a farmer without even talking to me about it. I know it is his life--but it's mine, too!"

Flustered, Florinu said, "Wait, wait! A Healer? He's talked about that before!"

With a shocked look on her face, Merina said, "When? Not to me!"

"Umm, probably not. He knows how you feel about magic use. He told me he had thought about it at a Settling Day years ago, before he got serious about you. He has always been interested in doing things for animals and helping people. You do know that, right?"

Annoyed that her lover had told her best friend things he wouldn't tell her, Merina said a little sharply, "Of course. That is what I like so much about him, he's kind and considerate."

"Then you should not be surprised he would want to be a Healer. Now I grant you, it is surprising that he is trying to do so now. Isn't he too old for the Test?" Florinu let go of Merina and sat back to take the pressure off her baby.

"Yes--for all I know about it. Helinu somehow convinced him that he should try despite his age. That is really what makes me mad about this, not that he wants to be a Healer. He will be in training for four years, and our mating will have to wait till then. Does that seem fair to you, Flo?"

Florinu patted Merina's knee. "No. I can see why you're upset. But think of it this way, your inheritance could come in during that time and you'll be busy setting up your own home. The time will fly by!"

"Or it could not. In the meantime, Markinis will be haunting my homestead trying to get me to give him what both of us separately want-- a home and a family to raise. Dame Brischelu is a sly and scheming woman. She knows I will not accept Markinis as he is, but she believes I can change him." Merina leaned forward, staring into her friend's eyes. "Here is my dilemma, Flo. I resent anything that alters my life--look how I reacted to the change Trinames presented me. Realizing that, I would expect the same resentment from anyone else if I set about to change their lives. People can change their lives if they want to do it--but not if forced."

Florinu smiled and nodded. "That is so true."

"The problem is, I am trying to change Trinames to fit my way of life, and here is a man who fits my life exactly as I want it. If I change Trinames, he will be unhappy as a landowner because he wants to be a Healer. He will come to resent me--magic will have come between us. I don't know how I can get him to remain a farmer willingly unless I force him to choose between magic and myself."

"I don't see a way either, Mer. To solve that problem, you are going to have to make changes in your life--particularly about magic--if you are to be the life-mate of a sorcerer."

"I don't think I can do that. I have dreamed of what I feel I was born to do--run a farm and raise a family. If I accept Brischelu's proposition and take her son as a mate, I will have what I dreamed of--but I will have to change Markinis. I am sure I can make it very unpleasant for him if he continues his ways, but that will not make him change his behavior. I could love and care for him with all my heart, but I don't think that will stop him unless he willingly loves me in return. That is not his nature--he is not the caring person Trinames is. If I fail to change Markinis, one of us will suffer, and I guarantee it will not be me!"

Florinu shook her head sadly. "Which means once again you are the one who will have to change--abandon the love of your life-mate to keep what you have. It seems the only question is which way are you willing to change?"

A flash of jealousy made Merina realize her friend already had what Merina wanted so desperately, without having to change herself. Standing abruptly, Merina stalked away from the bench to stand beside the shade tree. In the distance she could see Denathis riding away from the spot where the sluice was located. Apparently he had finished his repair. He headed out along the waterway, probably to ensure it was clear and flowing properly. A man who knew what he wanted, whose goals were set and within reach. Not a man who was either chasing after a dream or living only for the moment. Flo was the lucky one, and she had offered the correct answer.

Returning to the bench, Merina slowly formed the answer to Florinu's question in her mind. Which way am I willing to change? But why do I have to change? Is there another way for me to be happy? "Flo, I guess I need to know more about magic than I do now. There is something frightening about it that keeps me from thinking clearly about it. You know I love farming. It seems natural to me. There are seasons and cycles to it--like nature itself. If you carefully and wisely make the right plans, at the right time, and use the right material, your crops will grow, or your herd will prosper. If you try to do things differently to avoid the work, more often than not you fail. Dame Brischelu made a strange comment to me during our meeting. She said that since Valehanis first arrived in this valley three hundred years ago, the people have been living much the same as he did. If anything had really changed, it was because of magic."

Florinu thought about that for a moment. "I can't say I have noticed any change even with magic--maybe it has in Byklandes? I don't know. Why should we care? Everything is fine--except for the wolves."

"That may be my point, Flo. I see magic as forcing a change in our lives, and it certainly is doing something to my life again. It has already caused me so much trouble by what it did to my mother. Your mother and mine were best friends--just like us. What did she tell you about Delaphinu?" Merina finally asked the question she had come for.

Florinu's smile faded to neutral, her eyes saddened. Merina knew her friend must have been told many stories about Delaphinu because Florinu's mother was the one everyone quoted when passing on bad rumors about Merina's mother. Florinu had never spoken to Merina about Delaphinu. It was a subject never raised between them for fear of hurting their friendship. The dismay that shadowed Florinu's face told Merina she had violated the rule.

"Don't ask me, Mer. Please!"

"I have to. I need to know more about her because she represents magic use, which is coming between Trinames and me."

"Ask your aunt," Florinu begged.

"I did, and I got the type of answer you would expect from a sister. My mother was a hardworking daughter of the land, a dedicated servant to her father, and a mother to her siblings. She was a strong-willed woman who took her future into her own hands and decided to become a sorcerer--a user of Power. To hear Auntie talk, my mother was a person who should be revered instead of ridiculed."

Florinu reached out to touch Merina's wrist and flashed a smile. "Then leave it at that. It is the truth. My mother said those same words to me. She said she felt so sorry for Delaphinu because they could not visit and play often, since your mother had so many responsibilities."

"What about her responsibilities to me, Florinu?"

Her friend sagged back, releasing Merina's hand. "That...that was later, she--"

"A drunk who got pregnant without a man to support her. Damn it, what did she need a man for when she could supply herself with unlimited wine and beer? The only need she had of a man was to rut endlessly with him for her own pleasure. Where was her vaunted motherliness when she abandoned me and ran off alone?"

Florinu would not meet Merina's eyes. The tears that ran down from the corners of Merina's were soon matched by Florinu's. The two friends wept together, one out of anger and the other out of sadness.

Merina brought her tears under control first, since anger can evoke strong responses for only so long, taking much more energy to sustain than sadness. She pulled a cloth from her belt pouch and wiped her eyes. Pants were easier to ride in but were warmer in the summer, and you could not wipe off sweat or tears on them. Florinu used her skirt hem for that purpose while Merina stuffed the cloth back into her pouch. Merina was just about to ask another question when an older woman stepped onto the side porch from the kitchen door and hurried over to them. It was Serafinu, Denathis's mother, looking worried.

"Is something wrong, girls?"

"No, ma'am," Merina said quickly.

"Please, Merina, tell me the truth. I saw two happy young women laughing and giggling one moment, and the next, tears. Rapid swings in emotions in a pregnant woman are not uncommon, but..."

Merina glanced at Florinu, then said, "It was my fault. I asked Florinu about my mother. I wanted to know why she left me like she did."

Serafinu sat next to Merina on the bench and took her right hand, clasping it between both of hers. "I understand the tears now, Merina. There is probably no one else who knows that answer better than me. I attended your birth because Delaphinu would allow no Healers near her. She was living in a hunter's hut on the northern edge of our homestead for the last few months of her pregnancy. She was very depressed, and her health was getting worse because she was not keeping herself fed and exercising like I begged her to."

"Too drunk all the time?" Merina asked, choking back a sob.

"No, your mother was sober the whole time I tended her. She was in a lot of pain, with really bad headaches. I was so worried about her. You know twins run in your family. Your grandmother, your aunt, and from what I was told your grandmother's mother had two sets of twins. In her weakened state, if she was growing two babies it could have resulted in both her death and that of the baby or babies."

Merina nodded. The fertility of the women in her line was well known.

Serafinu continued, "I found her one time talking to herself, and she seemed to be listening for a reply to her own words. She asked me if I knew of any herbs that could take the pain away, but I could not give them to her because they would affect the baby."

"Why did she not go home? She could have asked forgiveness of Grandfather Romanus--he would have taken her in!"

Nodding, Serafinu patted Merina's hands gently. "And he would have, but your mother was afraid that the mages at Byklandes would send their guards to her old home to take her back. She was frantic that they would find her. The Delmathians had held her prisoner for several months before she escaped and notified our mages she was missing. I had to swear I would not expose her presence to anyone."

Merina began to feel entrapped as her mother must have felt. She pulled her hands out of Serafinu's. "Then Byklandes must have told Helinu to look for her!"

In a calming tone, Serafinu replied softly, "She was told. Sorceress Helinu came to me because she knew Delaphinu was pregnant. Helinu was very worried about your mother, because she said something about grid burnout and the danger to both of you. I am sure she knew I was caring for Delaphinu."

"Grid burnout..." Merina started to ask.

"I don't know what that is--it is nothing I have ever heard associated with birthing. She tried very hard to convince me to get your mother to put herself under a Healer's care, but I knew Delaphinu would not do such a thing. Helinu was wise enough to let the matter be."

Florinu asked anxiously, probably herself feeling the tension in the story and projecting her own fears into it, "Who provided for Delaphinu?"

"Your mother did, Daughter, with the help of Alanu."

"And after the birth?" Merina whispered.

Serafinu obviously realized she had two emotional girls hanging on her every word and tried to make her answer as light and encouraging as she could. "It was an easy birth for your mother, Merina. Fortunately it was just one baby--and such a healthy baby girl. She had very little pain with her delivery, and the headaches even ceased for a time afterward. Her health picked up, and she was able to nurse you with no problems. For the next three months she did just fine, then the headaches came back. She begged me to allow her to drink again. She said the pain was too much. I told her that was bad for you."

Florinu asked fearfully, "Bad for Merina?"

"Alcohol passes through breast milk, Daughter. It affects the baby as much as it does the mother. Delaphinu knew this and made the decision to wean Merina as soon as she could. She bore the pain for several more months. She would not allow me to find a nursing mother--she insisted on providing for Merina herself. Finally her health deteriorated to the point her milk dried and she had to give you up."

"Why? Why did she have to give me up?" Merina asked, the agony in her voice raising the pitch of her last words.

Serafinu's own speech took on a roughness that showed she also was having trouble talking. "The voices. She said voices were telling her to flee, to go north. I begged her to seek help from Sorceress Helinu. She tried to explain why. She knew of this grid burnout disease, or whatever it is. She said no Healer could help her, Merina. She had to get away."

"What did you do, Mother Serafinu?" Florinu choked out.

"I gave her a powder I used for numbing pain, which she took gratefully. She didn't suspect I had given her too much, and she fell asleep very quickly. I sent your mother to get Sorceress Helinu. Alanu and I watched over Delaphinu for hours until the baby became too restless and I was afraid she would wake her mother. Alanu took the baby to my home. I locked Delaphinu in the hut, afraid she might overpower me in anger at my betrayal."

"What did Helinu do when she got there?" Merina asked quietly.

Serafinu folded her hands in her lap and looked down at them. The girls could barely hear her response. "I was listening at the window for any sound of Delaphinu stirring when I heard a noise behind me. Thinking it might be Helinu, I turned to greet her and..." Serafinu wrung her hands in distress, then continued, "I...fainted. Blacked out--I'm not sure. I wasn't hit. I awoke with Sorceress Helinu bending over me, several village guards standing around looking puzzled. They said there was no one in the hut. They had broken into it because the lock was still on. The window was closed and locked from the inside. Delaphinu had escaped."

The sad ending to Serafinu's story brought the tears the women had avoided until then. When she could, Merina thanked Florinu and her mother-in-law for listening to her and for answering her difficult question. She left shortly thereafter.

Florinu sat on the bench as Serafinu took the wash basket into the house, her eyes following Merina trotting away on her horse, riding with such confidence and poise. Florinu was Merina's oldest and dearest friend, knew the red-haired beauty better than anyone in the valley, and still felt a pang of jealously whenever she looked at Merina. Her friend had never put on airs with anyone, although that was what all their friends expected Merina to do.

Heiress to a huge landholding, self-assured, a trained fighter who could defend a friend when she needed it, a beauty who took men's breath away. Merina could bear twins while plowing a field and never break a sweat--not like Florinu herself, who was exhausted after hanging a wash out on the line. And deal with men! Denathis told her the farmers at market would rather deal with Merina's uncle than her. They always came out short in a trade.

Florinu grimaced, telling herself it was not because they couldn't think straight while looking at that body. Merina had been good at making deals long before their bodies developed. She certainly could be charming, or quick-tempered when she had to be. Florinu saw Denathis in the distance making his way back to their home. Reddening, she looked down at her lap and struggled with the surge of shame the memory gave her every time it came into mind. She had not been passed out that night.

Markinis's hands had been stimulating her breasts long before their walk to the barn, and his baring them was what she had desperately been seeking. After he had pulled her underpants off, she remembered saying no over and over in her mind, realizing he was not going to stop with kissing her breasts. If Merina had not shown up--but she had.

Her friend had saved her honor. Maybe Denathis would still have life-mated her, maybe not. Markinis never would have, for he had fixed his eyes on Merina. And now Merina had a decision to make. Florinu knew what she would answer the Dame and felt weak, knowing what Merina would think of her answer.

Chapter 4

Merina trotted around the bend in the road and caught sight of the last person she wanted to meet. It was too late to turn her horse around and avoid the robed woman, and to ride by without speaking to her was not an option--especially as Helinu was waving and calling her name. Merina slowed her horse to a stop and sat watching the magic-user's approach. That odd feeling Merina always got when the Healer came around grew stronger the nearer the middle-aged woman came. It felt like ants crawling around the back of her head underneath the scalp. The feeling made her uneasy. Helinu was smiling and looking expectantly at her.

"I was just riding to visit Florinu, who I'm told is four months pregnant. Oh, Merina, that silly girl should have come to me as soon as she knew."

Merina replied in the least confrontational tone she could muster after hearing her best friend called silly. "She has sought care from the best midwife in the valley, Sorceress--one who has had multiple children of her own."

Still smiling, Helinu said, "That's good, very good. Expecting mothers always receive advice much better from those who have been through a pregnancy. Unfortunately, a midwife cannot monitor the new mother and her child for serious problems that can occur before symptoms start to show and alert a caregiver something is wrong."

"So I am told, Sorceress. I know the law."

"Anyway," Helinu said, not reacting to Merina's cold statement of fact, "I was thinking of riding to your farm after I visit Florinu. It's so fortunate for us to meet like this. Trinames asked me to talk to you."

"About what, Sorceress? We have nothing to discuss, as I am feeling perfectly well and do not need your assistance in any way."

Helinu stopped her horse next to Merina's and rested her hands on the saddle horn. If Merina's coldness discouraged her, the healer was not letting her reaction show.

"He wants me to test you for magic use. I think that is a wonderful idea! You have such potential and--"

Merina cut her off. "He wants? He is not of my family, nor does he have any authority over me to ask that of you. I am not a child, that I can be forced to take the Test."

"That is not what either of us wants, Merina. He is hoping that you will test as highly as Delaphinu did and the two of you could study together at Byklandes in the fall. I said I would be happy to administer the Test if you were willing. Just give me the chance, dear."

Merina raised her right hand, palm facing the magic-user, and retorted, "There is no chance of that happening, Sorceress. You know how I feel about Power use, since my aunt has told you so to your face."

Helinu's face turned somber. "You were a foolish little girl when you would not let me heal your broken ankle. Even Alanu agreed with me that I should have done so despite your refusal. There are times when Power use is necessary. I felt the pain you were suffering."

"My ankle healed fine, and it no longer gives me any pain. Besides, it was little compared to the pain I have lived with all my life from what magic use did to my mother. A loving, caring woman reduced to drunkenness and debauchery."

The sorceress reached out toward Merina, who recoiled from the touch. Helinu said sadly, "Drunkenness is not caused by magic. I admit in your mother's case it made it easier for her to find the alcohol she craved, but she didn't need to create whiskey from Power. She was well trained as a farm girl in the arts of brewing and distillery. No, she had lost the discipline needed to control her use of Power. She was weak-willed."

"Weak-willed? This about a woman who left her family and refused to be supported by them because her father betrayed her trust. What does will have to do with controlling magic?"

Helinu eyes tightened at the corners, and a touch of anger shadowed her face. "Why would you question me about something you have no belief in?" The Healer visibly forced herself under control and continued, "Wait, don't answer that. Your question is fair. I will answer it so that you can make a better decision based on knowledge instead of emotion."

"I do not want your answer, Sorceress. I know the answer. Being able to have what you want without working for it is what leads to excess use. The value of working for something becomes so little that you lose sight of why you work to get it in the first place."

Helinu stiffened in dismay. Shaking her head, she said, "Your growing reputation as an expert bargainer and woman of business is based on both being fair and having a willingness to see both sides in a negotiation. I fully agree that the value of a service is dependent on its cost, but that principle does not apply to how magic is controlled. Will you at least let me give you the reason?"

She is right. I shouldn't have lashed out at her. I'll never learn the answer to my questions if I stay close-minded. She nodded at Helinu to proceed.

"Power exists in an energy form that magic-users can gather in and hold within their body." The Healer took a box from her belt pouch. "This is my source, which provides me the Power when I expose myself to it. No sorcerers can cast spells using Power from a source directly. I have to meditate in its presence to build up enough Power to cast a spell. The spell drains the energy from my body. Does that make sense, dear?"

"No," Merina said warily, "that is why it is called magic. Why is it you can do this and the rest of the valley people can't? Do you have some organ inside you that we don't?"

"Definitely not, Merina. As a Healer, I can tell there is no organ in my body that is different from yours. Control of Power is done by the mind."

Merina had heard this explanation before, and asked the same question she had asked at that time. "So those of us who don't use magic must be dumber than you. Is that right, Sorceress?"

Shaking her head, Helinu gave Merina a wry smile, as if she had heard that accusation many times in her life. "You have witnessed the slaughter of animals--you know that brain size differs from one type of animal to another, and I am sure you have seen differences among specimens of the same kind of animal. It is not the size of the organ that explains the ability to control Power. If that were so, women would not have the capacity to use magic, compared to men. But I bet we can agree that many women are smarter than men. Whether one is dumber than the other is debatable, but yes, magic-users seem to be smarter. That is what the Test shows us."

"Let me guess who came up with the Test--Sorcerers. And who determined pass or fail--Sorcerers," Merina said, her voice edged with sarcasm.

Helinu just nodded, as there was no use in denying the obvious. "The Training Lodges have many years of experience teaching the control of magic to our people. They have found that those students who succeed at magic have certain mental abilities that can be measured and have demonstrated the ability to discipline their thinking to use those abilities. I will not be revealing any secrets of my training to say that how our minds control Power is a mystery. But we do know the kind of person I am determines what kind of magic I can do."

Frowning, Merina said, "I don't understand how a person's temperament should affect magic."

Helinu seemed to perk up when Merina asked the question. She thinks I am showing interest.

"Oh, dear, it is a hard idea to follow. Let me give you some examples. As a group, Aggressor magic-users are sullen, easily angered, hot-tempered, brooders, and meticulous planners. They are quite capable of killing and, unfortunately for their area of discipline, willing to do so. Illusionists, on the other hand, have a whole different personality. They are schemers, dreamers, humorists, fanciers, far-seeing, and playful tricksters. They have the most vivid imaginations and tell the most wonderful stories. They love to entertain--"

Merina cut in, "And spread lies or falsehoods to trap the unwary. I have seen them in the market place on Settling Day. I see no value in what they do."

"Those are Tieri witches, Merina--not real magic-users--but if people find amusement in their images, then that is not a bad thing. I am not trying to justify the use of magic to you, Merina. Let me tell you about my discipline. Healers are people who have a strong desire to stop pain, care for the helpless. They're listeners, strongly observant of how people act and think, gentle, persuasive, acting with reason, not out of rashness. They have intense feeling for the needs of others."

A memory flashed into Merina's mind. When she was ten she had visited Trinames's family one summer day. Trinames, all excited, had wanted to show her a rabbit he had rescued from one of the family dogs in his father's barnyard. He had bandaged the lacerated leg and sheltered the animal in a box in his room, feeding it leafy greens from the kitchen garden. He was going to release it that day. Merina had told him that the rabbit would probably get eaten in a week or two by a fox or some other farmer's dog. He'd said with a sheepish grin, "I know, but I couldn't watch it get torn apart before my eyes." Helinu had just given her a fair description of Trinames.

Is that what the Test measures? Could this be the truth she is telling me?

"And Provisioners," the Healer continued, "you know what they are like, for your mother was one."

"I never knew my mother, Sorceress. From what the valley people say about

her--"

Helinu stopped her, a flash of anger in her eyes. "Do not pay attention to what they say about how she seemed when she returned. She was not that way growing up. I knew her then. She was indeed loving and providing, and she always tried to be supportive."

"But weak-willed--those were your words, Sorceress. Are all Provisioners weak-willed?" Merina cut in.

Sighing, Helinu said, "Let me finish answering your question. For anyone to control Power, they need to have discipline. They must be able to focus on what they are trying to spell and not be distracted by stray thoughts or emotions. We are taught precision in everything we do. Without control, our magic can go astray and become something we did not want it to be."

"You passed her, Sorceress. You thought she had the ability to work magic. She was invited to leave Byklandes to attend Inhestia because she had such great success. Alanu told me you were very pleased that she had. She must have had control to do that."

"And she did!" Helinu said with a passion that surprised Merina.

You're afraid blame for my mother's failure will fall on you!

The Sorceress continued, "Whether a Neophyte can create a spell is known within months of her start of training. It takes years to know if she can control the complex spells that a Novice must demonstrate."

"My mother was beyond Novice training in her first two years, Healer. Did her instructors fail to teach her correctly and pass her to hide their failure?"

"No, you are misunderstanding what I'm saying," Helinu said, frustration roughening her voice. "She was well taught. Your mother chose to study wine production. She probably sampled too much of her work. The alcohol caused her to be distracted. She was weak-willed and became addicted. From then on, she lost her discipline and her control. She avoided being expelled from Inhestia by sleeping with her mentor and--"

"But we are told non-sorcerers cannot mate with sorcerers. Is this another lie that your kind perpetuate to keep from bringing impure blood into your lines--like bull breeders do?"

Shocked, the older woman just stared at Merina for a moment. "You believe that old tale. I spend most of my time trying to stop the spreading of that nonsense--generated mostly from old women who can't understand why I have not mated and borne children of my own. Is that why you are objecting to Trinames becoming a Healer? Oh, child, you have been misled."

So now I have heard it from a sorcerer myself. Cutting Helinu off before she could say more, Merina said, "I am not a child, Sorceress. Then the tale of sorcerers breeding with sorcerers and creating monsters that caused those sorcerer wars is also not true?"

Grimacing, Helinu stuttered, "No, I mean, yes--that happened, but you know it was not because they were sorcerers. You are a farm girl, you know about not inbreeding. Saphradean law forbids its people to mate parent and child or brothers and sisters. Mating is not an issue with sorcerers."

Folding her arms across her chest, Merina gave the Healer a wry smile. "Mating is not an issue? Why are, what do you call them, Neophytes--why can't your Neophytes mate while training? You take them when they are just learning about their bodies and begin training them before their first kiss."

Sighing again in obvious exasperation, Helinu said flatly, "The reasons are so numerous, and they are clearly stated in the law that the Prince of

Princes decreed centuries ago about testing children. I am sure you know them, and I will not repeat them. But it does come back to what I was trying to tell you about control. Sexual activity distracts the Neophyte's mind and prevents them from learning control."

"Trinames is not a child. He is a man, but your rules prevent our mating while he is at your training lodge. That is a good reason for me to be against his going. You are stopping us from starting our life. And now you suggest that I should be tested and enter training, to be beside my lover day after day, and not be allowed to mate? Is that a reasonable idea, Healer?"

"It is not such a long time, Merina. Your mother was as old as you when she went. She obeyed the rules."

She is hiding the truth from me. The horse shifted restlessly as if sensing Merina's agitation. "You seem to forget that she was mating with her instructor. Which got her expelled. Was she weak-willed because of lovemaking, or debauchery? What story is the one you believe about the root of this lack of control? Could it have been something else?"

"What makes you ask such a question, Merina?"

"Midwife Serafinu told me Delaphinu suffered something called--ah, grid burnout. You magic-users tried to hide that fact." Merina spat out, "Power made her ill."

The older woman's body swayed away from Merina in shock. "You take the word of a midwife over mine?"

"My mother told Serafinu the same thing. Inhestia could not cure her, so they locked her away."

Groaning, Helinu raised her arms to plead with Merina, then dropped them back to her side. "No one knows the real cause of grid burnout, except we know the few who have experienced it and lived had tried to do more with Power than they could control. It damages their minds, and they need to be protected from themselves. I am not lying when I said lack of control caused your mother to fail."

Merina's anger did not abate. She pointed her right forefinger at the Healer. "Hiding the victims of this grid burnout damage is wrong. Are you afraid it will drive away people who want to be sorcerers? Don't you warn candidates of the danger? Did you warn Trinames?"

Helinu snapped back, "No, there is no need. It is so rare, so very rare. How many people die in farming accidents every year? I tell you since I treat them--far, far more than from grid burnout! You prevent accidents by being careful. We teach Neophytes control, control, and more control."

Merina lowered her hand and relaxed, forcing herself to not display so much anger. "And you want me to Test to use magic? Aren't you afraid I will follow down her path? Wouldn't I be as weak-willed?"

The Healer so quickly regained her composure, Merina wondered if she had done it by magic. Helinu gently laughed. "Everyone in Dysandes knows you are strong-willed, dear."

Merina's horse settled into calm with the fading of Merina's own indignation, but her voice still held an edge when she said, "So by your description that makes me an Aggressor, strong-willed and quick to pick a fight. But you think I ought to be a Provisioner because my mother tested so high. Does temperament really have anything to do with it, or is it what the person administering the Test wants it to be? Did you recommend Trinames for Healer because you--I'll repeat that, you-- wanted him to be?"

"The Test does not tell us what you will be, child. It tells us if you are even capable of controlling Power. From the results of the Test we then make our own judgment of what discipline we recommend for you. The Training Lodge reviews the result of the Test and has the final say. I am not allowed to discuss Trinames's results with anyone else."

Merina wanted to tell the Healer she had not answered the question and was hiding behind the convenient rules of the Council of Magi, but she had no desire to continue this conversation. She said instead, "You need not visit my home after Florinu's. I have nothing further to talk about."

The Healer pleaded, "Will you let me Test you?"

Gathering her reins tight, Merina spurred her horse forward, throwing Helinu a firm "No" as she rode by.

In the darkness, the watcher stirred out of his trance. "She resists as vehemently as ever, perhaps more."

"As I foresaw. We must have patience."

"But as long as her hostility remains so deeply rooted, how can her potential awaken?"

"Only through a sharper threat to what she cherishes. You will see, my son."

"Perhaps we should use the wolves as well as the Guardians."

"A good notion. At the proper moment, make it so."

Arriving home, Merina was still angry over her confrontation with the Sorceress. She stormed through the house greeting no one, grabbed a towel from the storage chest, and marched out of her room. Alanu watched her as Merina pushed open the kitchen door and said something about going swimming. Alanu shrugged but did not ask what had upset her niece so much.

The Silveron River formed the eastern boundary of Romanus's Pride, the parcel of land from Merina's grandfather's original holding that made up Aunt Alanu's homestead. Cascading down from the mountains above Dysandes, it slowed to a sedate flow past the port town and through the valley. Fortunately, the prevailing winds blew from the south, providing the wind to drive the barges that sailed upstream, bringing goods for trade, and returned south with cattle and grain. By the time the Silveron reached Merina's home, it was a gently flowing body of clear water that ran deep in the center and became shallow to about waist high along its banks. Merina had spent many an hour swimming in a pool formed by the river as it coursed around a rocky island in the middle of the streaming water. She planned to spend the next hour on that island, mulling over what she had just learned that afternoon and trying to decide what she was to do with her life. She was unbuttoning her blouse to shed her clothing when she heard a polite cough behind her. Whirling around, she had her knife in her right hand and pointing at the man standing ten feet away in an instant.

"Pardon, Mistress, I mean no harm."

He looked to be the same age as her Uncle Tomanis. His face was weathered, his black hair long, almost to his shoulders. His eyes, as dark as his hair, were deep set. With his long nose, those features marked him as Tieri. A wanderer, someone to be wary of. His people were only tolerated in the valley because they brought useful trinkets and commodities from the far Domains to trade, including the Dame's wine.

What was not tolerated was their reputation as thieves, a people not to be trusted, especially with their men around vulnerable women. She kept the knife at the ready, her left hand pulling the opened shirt closed across her breasts. "This is my land, Tieri. You are not welcome here."

The man pointed downstream about a fifty feet to where a small boat with furled sail was pulled up on the river bank. That was why Merina had not seen the craft when she walked to the river down the path from her home. Inside the boat lay a large pack stuffed full of lumpy objects, which at this distance looked like pots from the shapes visible through the leather sides. "The river is like a road, Mistress, its use is allowed to all. I am traveling south on my trade route. I stopped to eat."

"You are not the Tieri who trades in Dysandes," Merina said flatly. "I know Jalanos well, and he is at least twice your age."

"He is my uncle. He is ill and asked me to carry a load of promised goods to a customer who lives two farms down. I did not want to arrive there during the evening meal hour, so I came ashore here early to eat."

Merina relaxed ever so little, lowering her blade to point at the feet of the man. "You obviously have finished eating so you are welcome to leave now. I have no interest in looking at your wares."

"Perhaps your aunt?" the man asked hopefully.

"I told you it is my land, sir."

"My uncle was kind enough to tell me about his trade customers in the event that I should chance to meet them. He said this homestead was owned by Alanu, youngest daughter of Romanus. She had three sons and a niece, Merina--who I am guessing is you. You are among the most eligible of woman"--the Tieri glanced away from her left hand with a sly smile--"and a good prospect for us to approach, as you will be setting up your own homestead soon. It is our business to know our customers, Mistress. Has anything I said not been true?"

"You know too much of my business, Tieri. And yes, you have spoken untruth. This land belongs to Delaphinu, the eldest of Romanus's children. I am her only daughter." Sheathing her blade, Merina shifted her weight to one leg and buttoned up her blouse, crossing her arms across her chest when she was done. As pleasant as the man was trying to be, she still felt uneasy with him. Something about him made her think of Helinu, perhaps the soothing way of talking to people they both had. "It is disquieting that a complete stranger knows so much about me."

"Then let me give you a name to make me less of a threat to you. I am Tieri Delnos Pathla m'Lothur. Saphradea is not the land of my birth, as you can tell from my accent."

"You speak my language very well."

"I speak all of the Domains' tongues. One has to if one trades across the land. Tieri are a people of clans, Mistress Merina. My clan name is Pathla. My sire's name was Lothur. We are born in wagon trains that roam our trade territories. These territories do not recognize the boundaries set up by governors who rule the Domains. My clan is more at home in Delmathia than it is here, but we do trade across Saphradea, all the way to the mountains surrounding Dysandes. Your name is Delmathian--did you know this?"

"Yes. They end their women's names with an 'a'," Merina responded with a little less coldness than before.

Delnos nodded. "It is a custom handed down for as many years as anyone can remember. The Saphradeans use a 'u', the Tieri an 'ee', the Hermanians a single 'e'. Your mother Delaphinu--a Saphradean, but she named you in the Delmathian fashion. Curious."

"My father was Delmathian. She did it to please him."

"You had another ancestor who had a Delmathian name--she was called Lenora."

Merina said with no humor in her voice, "Obviously my family's daughters should avoid visiting Delmathia if we want to keep our line pure. How do you know of my lineage, Delnos Pathla m'Lothur?"

"Tieri do not keep our histories in scrolls. We rarely write anything on paper. Histories are information, and perhaps you did not know, we deal in information--as well as pots and pans. We have learned it is best to pass stories from clan member to clan member, sometimes in song, most often tales told around our campfires. Since we trade among all the people of the Domains, our stories are often interwoven with those of our customers. Lenora was a very powerful Mage who became the first sorcerer to lead the Delmathian Council of Magi after it was created following the Sorcerer Wars. Do you know about the wars?"

Waving her hand in dismissal, Merina spat out bitterly, "Only that the magic-users went insane and tried to take over the Domains from the common people. They killed themselves off. The few remaining ones begged forgiveness from the people and set up the lodges where they control themselves or face extinction. I have no use for sorcerers, past or present."

"They are a great help to the people, Mistress. Their Healers alone make up for the wrong they did two centuries ago. Your Saphradean order has taken a vow never to use magic to harm. People can change for the better."

"So you say, Tieri, but they can also change for the worse. If you know of my family, look to my mother for an example of that. I am tired of this conversation. I wish to bathe, so it is time you leave." Merina pointed at his boat and waited for him to respond.

Delnos nodded and strolled back along the shore. He pushed the craft into the water, jumping in as it cleared the shore. He sat facing the stern, unshipped the oars, and pulled away with powerful strokes. In moments he was gone. She wondered how far she would have gotten undressed before noticing the Tieri if he had not made a noise. The men of the wandering tribes had a reputation for taking advantage of helpless women, but perhaps that was not true.

Merina unbuttoned and removed her blouse, draping it over a bush that she had planted as a young girl for just that purpose. This was her spot, and she felt slightly violated that the Tieri had been here. Removing her shoes, she placed them on a flat rock next to the bush, then looked downstream once more to ensure Delnos was still out of sight. She slipped her leather pants off her hips and folded them on top of the shoes. Her cotton shorts completed the pile of clothes, and she put the smaller rock beside the flat one on top to keep the occasional breeze from blowing her things away--as had happened once before. She smiled at the remembered image of chasing her dress across the field, naked to the world. It almost got away, and she had been in a panic that she would be seen sneaking back into the house with only her underpants on. Not that anyone would have noticed an eight-year-old girl that much.

She looked down at her large, well-rounded breasts and thought, They certainly would love to do that now. She took no special pride in what nature had given her, although Trinames was not the only male whose eyes constantly swept over her body and lingered on her chest. She relished his appreciation but found the stares of the others something of a nuisance. She patted her flat stomach and splayed her hands on the curves of her hips. Wide for their purpose, but not so that it made her bell-shaped like some of her friends. She did not like to hide her legs beneath a skirt and, when walking around the homestead, sensed the farmhands following the sway of her hips. If her mother had left her anything, it was a woman's body made for what only women could do. She had never had the problems other girls had complained about with their monthly cycles, and although untried by a male, she was sure childbirth would not be a problem for her. Stepping into the water, she waded in 'til it reached her nipples and watched them grow taut in the chill. Taking a quick breath, she dived underwater.

Delnos watched from behind the tree that had shielded him from Merina's searching eyes. He wondered why he had been sent by the Rhuhani to determine if the young woman was really the one who had been chosen. The Tieri Jalanos had watched the women of her line for several generations and knew more about Merina's family than any man alive. It had not bothered Delnos in the least that he had lied to the young woman about Jalanos being ill. The old man was secluded in Dysandes to remain out of sight.

Jalanos was not his uncle either. Delnos was not sure what the ancient Tieri's relation to him was, if there was one at all. Jalanos had been a watcher over this valley for nearly a century. For all that time his Saphradean language skills were still poor, having an accent that made the valley folk think of him as simple. The old man was not. Maybe that was why he did so well with his trading business.

It was Jalanos who had sent word to the Rhuhani that the Chosen One had been found. Whether Merina was or was not the Chosen One, she was definitely a fully mature woman. Maybe that was why he, Delnos, had been sent. Perhaps the Rhuhani worried that the old man might not remember what a beauty like her did to a man, but Delnos did. A man of vigor, he felt the hardening at his groin and wondered if her physical appeal was to be the basis of his evaluation of her.

He knew from his short time working Jalanos's trade route that every man in the valley was aware of Merina. The mention of her name in a conversation evoked enthusiastic responses. Somewhere in their answers always lurked the desire to possess her. The reason might be given as her

pending wealth, trade wisdom, quick wit, or just being a strong woman--
the fact the true motive was the desire she stimulated in them.

With all the valley to choose from, it was ironic she had picked a man
who wanted to become a sorcerer. For her to say she had no use for
sorcerers, that hatred of things magical was going to cause her problems.
And as for the other men of the valley, they hoped it would drive her
from Trinames and give them all another chance.

Delnos watched as she emerged on the shore of the island and lay
back in the grass to dry herself. He turned away out of his guilt from
having spied on her. Yes, he would tell the Rhuhani that she was ready.

Merina had not intended to fall asleep after her bath, but the summer sun
shone warm on her skin, and the river burbling by at her feet was too
hard to resist. As her mind drifted through her encounter with the strange
Tieri, she wondered if she should risk lying outside as she was. Normally,
she was not afraid of being seen on this side of her island--not that it was
really hers. Very little boat traffic traveled between the island and her side
of the shore because, unless the river was swollen by spring rains or
melting snows, the water more often than not was too shallow to allow
passage of any sizable craft. But then the memory of the last time she had
watched a boat pass by here stirred a passion in her that she would not
allow herself to think about awake.

It had been last summer, just about this same time, when Trinames
had delivered a wagon of lumber her uncle had ordered to build a new
storage shed. While the field hands had emptied his wagon, Merina,
wanting to be alone with the young man who had frequently visited her
stall on Settling Day, suggested a sail on the river to cool him down from
his hot ride over. Happy to have something to do besides help unload the
wood, Trinames readily agreed. The slight breeze was refreshing, but not
enough to keep the boat from drifting south. The two of them were so
busy talking about who was doing what with whom that when they ended
up by the island, Merina steered the boat onto her beach to avoid going
too far south. It would take long enough to sail the boat back to the
house as it was, which might force them to man the oars and really work
up a sweat.

Merina helped pull the boat up on the beach and took Trinames's hand to show him the rest of the island, which really wasn't that big. As they started away from the beach, Merina looked back and saw the boat's bow floating off the sand and heading downstream. She squealed a warning and ran to grab the boat. They both ended up hanging onto the side of the boat, up to their waists in water, and laughing so hard that they managed to fall over more than once dragging the boat back to the beach. Trinames secured it there with a bowline to a tree and joined Merina sitting on the grass above the shoreline.

They spent the next few minutes blaming themselves for being careless, then insisting the other was not at fault. Trinames stripped off his shirt, wrung the excess water out, and laid it across the bow to dry. Merina had seen shirtless men before, but stared at the muscles of his arms and chest as if seeing that sight for the first time. Trinames was truly a man, not the skinny boy she had known for all these years.

As he removed his boots to pour out the water in them, Merina did the same with hers, handing them to him to place on the middle seat along with his. When he turned back to sit beside her, his eyes fixed on her shirt. The soft material clung to her breasts, and she was pulling the shirt away to keep him from seeing them. The memory made Merina's nipples stiffen even now.

Trinames gallantly looked away and sat with his back toward her. Merina thought for a moment of boldly exposing herself, but accepted his offer of privacy to remove her blouse and squeeze out as much water she could before putting it back on. She abandoned the idea of wringing her pants out, as he was not making any effort to do so with his. Leaning forward at the waist, she hugged her knees up to her chest and told him he could turn around again. When he did, his eyes darted immediately to her breasts. As she intercepted his glance, he blushed red and turned back away once more.

His awareness of her as a woman excited Merina. She tugged at his shoulder to get him to turn around again, but he refused. He said he was sorry for getting her wet, then staring at her. She laughed, saying, no, he wasn't. They sat for a while that way until she convinced him she didn't mind being looked at. His thoughtfulness touched her heart, but that was not where she wanted to be touched, then or now. When he turned around, she bent her arms behind her back to support herself and leaned on her elbows, facing up at the sun with her eyes closed. She lowered her knees till they were level and thought about just lying back. Trinames actually groaned.

She opened her eyes to look at him. His eyes met hers, and he leaned forward to kiss her. It was their first kiss, and she remembered it did not last long enough. Trinames broke off because he started to fall over onto her, since he had not taken her in his arms as she hoped. Instead he flipped over her, did a somersault, and jumped to his feet. He grabbed his shirt off the boat and put it on, telling her they had to leave now. They had sailed back in a silence filled with warm looks and smiles.

Merina awoke with a start and looked around in confusion. The memory had merged into a dream so real her heart was beating quickly and her breath was near panting. She stood and waded into the water, the coolness shocking her back to awareness of where she was and what she had been thinking of. She swam to the shore where her clothes lay waiting and dressed hurriedly, content to let the sun dry her off as she walked home.

Chapter 5

Sitting in her chair under the thinking tree, Merina stared out to the north over the valley where the many farms' cultivated fields took up most of the open land. The dense forest that surrounded the farms cut off the open pastures from the rest of the homesteads that dotted the valley. She thought of the painting she often looked at in the Dysandes meeting hall. It depicted a coastal village far to the south, the ancestral home of Dysandes's founder, Valehanis. The village sat on the edge of a huge body of water, with many hilly islands scattered along the shore. She often wondered if anyone lived on those islands.

Here, the cleared patches of land among the trees reminded her of the islands upon the water. But she knew each patch of land in this picture before her had people living on it, and each farm housed people she knew almost as well as her aunt and uncle. The islands were a mystery to her; this valley was not. Merina surveyed the distant farm to her right and asked herself if that was to be her new home in a very old place, or would she choose the faraway Dysandes--that dot at the edge of the mountains to the north with pillars of smoke rising from the smithies. Or even, if Dame Brischelu's proposition to her were to come about, the large holding on the left where Markinis would have her live.

It was a decision she did not want to make now, but one she could not escape. Movement on the road below drew her attention, and she saw Trinames emerge from the forest on the northern edge of her aunt's farm, riding down the road from Dysandes. It was time for his weekly courting call, and, as ever, he was very prompt. She usually looked forward eagerly to this end-of-the-week visit, but today she knew it would probably break off with an argument. Helinu's chance meeting a few days ago would fuel the fire of their disagreement, as he would first try to apologize for acting on Merina's behalf, then justify himself for doing so. Merina was not ready to forgive him yet, no matter how much he professed his love for her.

He was riding toward her house at a leisurely pace, not in a hurry because he had made this trip numerous times and knew how long it took to travel from his homestead to hers. As was the custom, he timed his arrival to coincide with the evening meal. It was an arrangement as old as time itself for their community of farmers. They would eat Auntie's feast and then sit on the porch watching the sun go down. When it finally disappeared below the horizon, her aunt and uncle would excuse themselves to get their younger sons ready for bed, and Merina would take Trinames for a stroll to the river. It would be there that they would argue.

She wondered if he was rehearsing his arguments as he rode along. She could see him making hand gestures and laughed when he waved his right hand back and forth in front of his chest as if he was wiping away what he had just said and started over again. Yes, he was practicing--as she had already done. He looked up as he passed through the gate and saw her. He waved, and she waved back.

"Time to begin this dance, my love," she said aloud as she stood.

Merina helped Alanu clear the dishes from the table and dried as her aunt washed the plates. Both women were listening to the men talking at the dinner table over cups of wine. Alanu's three sons, although under the age of maturity, had been granted the privilege of remaining and participating in the ritual passing of the latest doings in the farm community. If it had been women talking, it would have been called gossiping. Merina stopped smiling when she heard Trinames answer her uncle Tomanis's question about planting. She turned to peek into the dining area, where she could see her uncle facing her love.

He had just said, "Father has released me for the summer. He doesn't need me to tend our herd because he has hired a new worker. I am to leave for Byklandes in a month."

Tomanis glanced in the direction of the kitchen and nodded at Merina. She heard him ask, "Does my niece know?"

Merina didn't hear a reply, and since she could not see her love, she guessed Trinames had shaken his head in reply. She put down the plate she was drying and started to go through the door when Alanu stopped her with a touch to her arm and shook her head. Merina reluctantly picked up the plate and continued drying it.

"Have you decided what discipline you will study for, Trinames?" her uncle asked.

Her love answered, "I tested highest in Healing, which is what Sorceress Helinu was hoping I would, but I am rather shy of dealing with people."

"Why would Helinu hope you would become a Healer?"

He explained what he had already told Merina about Helinu's plans to begin her study for the Adept rank. "The Council of Magi told her there is a shortage of Healers, so she is trying to find a replacement herself. I told her how I felt about people, and she told me what I learned about healing men applied just as well to animals. I could even concentrate my studies on animal healing. It's a new branch of healing that is becoming in demand. I really like that idea."

Tomanis said, "There is indeed a call for Healers to take care of our stock with the high demand for meat from the Domains. Although the other countries in the Domains are beginning to produce their own cattle, Saphradea has been the main supplier of meat because we have the land and resources to do so better than they. The problem is that the Domains' population is increasing in numbers so fast the land available is hard-pressed to supply the food they demand. There's talk of opening roads into the mountains to farm the high valleys. Some fools prattle about venturing into the Non-Lands--as if they think they could make a life where none exists now."

"As little as I know about magic," Trinames said, "I don't think Provisioners have enough Power available to transform rocks into anything useful. If they had unlimited Power, it would be an easy task to create more land to turn into farms for grains and feed, or for that matter, grasslands for pasture."

"Aye," Tomanis said, "the need for the rock that supplies Power is almost as strong a driver of greed as the lust of gold is to the nobility. My job in the army was to protect one of the few source mines Saphradea owns. Delmathia and Hermania have far more mines since their lands are mostly mountains, and even simple farmers know mines are in mountains. They have almost all the metal production under their control. Our smithies in Dysandes produce a mere fraction of what Delmathia can. Both Hermania and Delmathia have control of most of the source mines. I don't know how magic-users get Power from staring at rocks, but maybe one day you can tell me how it is done."

Merina scoffed aloud, "I doubt that, Auntie, you have to be special to use Power. I bet Trinames will be warned not to share their secrets." Alanu put a finger to her lips and shook her head at Merina.

Trinames spoke in the other room, "Sorceress Helinu said the control of the source mines was a major reason there were Sorcerer Wars, which nearly destroyed all the Domains. I'm sure I'll learn the details of that in my Novice training, but magic use has also got to be controlled because it upsets what the Council of Magi call 'the balance in nature'. We should only be using from the land what we can replace. We farmers know this because we don't plant the same crop in a field every time, year after year, because that crop will not yield as much as it had. Letting land go back to the way it started refreshes it."

"And taking forest for farmland means no wood for building and burning," Tomanis said, adding with a harsh laugh. "Those bastard Hermanians would really like that, since they have most of the coal."

Trinames's voice continued, "So if we can't take more forest, we have to find a way to produce more livestock on the land we possess. We are already letting the herds get too big. In these crowded conditions, an outbreak of disease can quickly ravage a herd. And in the 'balance of nature' idea that I mentioned earlier, more prey seems to encourage predators to breed as well. We are losing more stock to predators than my father remembers in the past. He says it is time for a great hunt."

Merina peeked through the door and saw her uncle shake his head. "Normally I would agree with your reasoning, but predation has increased only around this valley. I don't think the Prince of Princes would be bothered enough by our problem that he would send troops. As much as Alexus loves to gallop all over Saphradea hunting and slaying wild beasts--which he claims is protecting his people from threats--he has decided that our greatest threat is from Delmathia. He tells us they are preparing themselves to make a land grab." Tomanis laughed harshly at his own statement. "What he really means is that he is the one thinking of taking land. He must be insane if he believes a war to grab land will solve our problems."

Trinames said, "It's not Delmathia he is worried about. I know you dislike them, but I have heard also the Hermanians are making trouble in the southeast. They hold the worst lands of the Domains and--"

"Aye," Tomanis cut in, "they are a hard, cruel folk who would not hesitate to move into Saphradea or Delmathia if they thought they could get away with it."

"If they did," Trinames said, "then many of us farmers will be called into the army. Our Sorcerers are not allowed to use Power against another human, but I've heard Delmathia and Hermania do not force their sorcerers to make that vow. Even so, the Prince of Princes would take many of our Healers from the villages and towns to support the war. That would include animal Healers being pressed into service to support the cavalry. I hope that doesn't come about before I finish my training, Tomanis. Until trained, I am at risk to be called into service as a soldier, along with all the other young men in our valley. I am not against fighting to protect Saphradea, but I would hope a peaceful way can be found to feed our people."

Tomanis stood and stretched. Merina heard Trinames push his chair back and stand in dismissal. Tomanis glanced into the kitchen and nodded toward Merina. "Your time with Merina may be shorter than you think. My niece told us that Johanis, Florinu's father, was nearly attacked by a wolf pack. If the Prince of Princes doesn't respond to our plea for a hunt, you may find yourself busy with the town militia on a hunt of their own. Have a pleasant evening, Trinames, and watch that you don't become a meal yourself on the way home."

The full moon lit the path to the river so well Merina and Trinames did not need a lantern to guide their feet. She strolled along slowly, not wanting to rush the moment when they would begin the argument she knew they would have. Trinames, holding her hand, swung it forward and back in a rhythm that matched their pace. His eyes were locked on her face, when not looking down her blouse. She had deliberately not laced the front of her dark blue shirt up very high and left the leather thongs tucked in the space between her breasts. The white light of the moon reflected off the tops of her breasts and drew her lover's eyes. He would have wandered off the path if she hadn't been tugging him back to her side.

He said hopefully, "A ride in the boat would be nice."

"No, not tonight. Let's just sit on the dock and enjoy the view," she said, pointing at the beam of moonlight running across the river toward them like a white road.

Trinames was only a head taller than she, so he did not have to shift his gaze much upward from where he was looking to see her smiling face. "That would be just as good, but you are much more fun to look at than the water."

"And less effort. Rowing the boat would distract you from me," Merina said coyly, but did not add that it would put her in a position of being trapped on a boat, unable to leave if their conversation went the way she feared.

They reached the dock that jutted out a dozen feet into the water and sat on the bench at its end. He took the side nearest the water, lest a wind-blown wave splash her. It was a good place to fish from, and she had spent many an afternoon in her childhood doing so with her aunt and uncle. Trinames licked his lips and turned to speak to her, but Merina stopped him with a kiss. She pulled herself against him with her right hand behind his neck to stop him from talking, teasing his lips with her tongue. He responded the same way, and they kissed for a long moment. Warmth radiated through her.

Merina released his lips and moved back a little to take a breath through her mouth, still clasping his neck and staring into his eyes to see if he had enjoyed it as much as she had. His smile gave proof of that. She felt his left hand move along her arm and drop down to cup her right breast. His right hand wandered to the center of her back and held her in place. His eyes flickered downward, and she waited till he gazed back at her face before she arched her neck backward and exposed her throat to him.

She knew he loved to kiss the hollow of her neck, but what he really wanted was farther down. His lips brushed her neck as they sought the space between her breasts and his warm breath puffed across her skin. He pushed the breast upward, and his tongue licked across her nipple. She shivered with pleasure.

Her hand caressed his neck as he kissed her exposed skin, and she let her passion rise. His right hand moved to her hip and stroked down to her bottom. Suppressing a moan, she pushed him away with her left hand to make him sit up. She pulled the blouse back around her breast and tugged the thongs together.

She was breathing as deeply as he was, but she shoved both hands against his chest to stop him from pulling her against him. The want in his eyes was hard to look at, but she gave him the most loving smile she could, followed by a light kiss meant as a promise of more to come.

"Let me bed you now, love. We can post the announcement tomorrow and begin our lives as life-mates then," Trinames begged.

Merina sighed. She had hoped he would be stronger. The reason for allowing him to kiss her breasts was to remind him of the promise of her body, but not to tempt him to think only of mating and make promises she knew he would regret in fulfilling his lust. "So you have given up on the idea of becoming a Healer, my enamored love? One kiss and your mind goes from discussing Domain affairs to visiting the barn for a roll in the hay?" Merina asked, pouting her lips at him.

"I...I..."

Moving a few inches away from him, Merina put her hands in her lap, smoothing out the apron that had been slightly bunched up. "Gather your thoughts, love. I saw you rehearsing a speech, so I know you have the words to say. When were you going to tell me that you'll be gone in a month? I tried to show you what you will be missing when you're gone. You are going?"

Groaning, Trinames rubbed his face with both hands before taking a deep breath and saying, "Yes. I leave in a month. Sorceress Helinu says my starting earlier will give me a chance at getting more attention from the instructors, which will give me an advantage over my classmates. I will be the oldest Neophyte there and can expect to win a leadership role."

Merina turned to stare at the reflection of the moon in the water. She was afraid Trinames might see the flash of anger that Helinu's name ignited in her eyes. "So it is more important to you to achieve a position of authority than to spend time with me--what little time we had left." Merina let a trace of bitterness creep into her voice. "Is there something else Helinu has suggested to you that you wish to tell me?"

Sighing, he said, "I know about your meeting her on the road to Florinu's. Sorceress Helinu really thinks you are the ideal candidate. I hate the idea of not seeing you, and I asked her to talk to you. She told me she would try, but she cautioned me that even if you passed the Test, Byklandes would not allow us to be mated until after our training. I can see now why that is so. Your seduction just proved I can't think clearly I am around you."

Merina almost regretted making the decision to entice him. She just might have given him reason to know their separation would have to be and forced him away. She had not thought of that, but then she had not thought she would be so affected by him. Sitting under her tree and planning this night had been easy, but Merina had not considered that she, too, would be aroused by his passion.

She remembered the evening eight years ago when she had seen Alanu and Tomanis strolling hand in hand toward the barn. Her aunt was acting very flirtatious, and the two of them laughed more than usual. Curiosity got the better of her, and she followed them. Sneaking into the hay loft, she looked down into the back of the barn and saw them doing what she had just let Trinames do. But they had not stopped there.

The memory of their lovemaking inflamed her passion anew. She had seen animals mating many times before and wondered how something that seemed so violent would bring any kind of pleasure to anyone. Watching her foster parents had taught her the part love played in the act. It also taught her the results, for her twin cousins had resulted from that night's pleasure.

Even though Trinames knew he would not be allowed to train with a life-mate, apparently he wanted her so badly he would take her. And she wanted him now.

Merina toyed with the laces at her throat. Trinames's eyes were fixed on her hands, as if he knew what was going through her mind. She lowered them to her lap. "I received a note from Dame Brischelu last week. She wanted to see me."

Trinames's eyes flicked away from Merina's face, and a flash of disappointment crossed his face. Moments later, when his gaze shifted back to hers, she saw wariness that was not there before. "She mentioned that to me," he said cautiously. "I had noon repast with Dame Brischelu yesterday. She stopped me as I rode into town and passed her at the Wolf's Head. She was most eager to see me."

"About what?" Merina tried to make her voice light, but a twinge of dread crept in. The Dame had gotten to him before she could tell him.

Trinames noticed it and hesitated before answering. It was now obvious he knew Brischelu's son was trying to court Merina.

Was that why he wanted to make love tonight?

"She had heard I was being put forward as a Neophyte candidate to be a Healer and wanted to congratulate me. She sounded genuinely pleased by the news."

Hoping that you'll soon be out of my sight and mind. "She must be aware that you and I are going to post our mating. That makes you a rival to her son. Doesn't it strike you odd that she would be happy for you?"

Shaking his head, Trinames tried to keep the conversation off his having a rival. "Not at all. I didn't know it before--I don't think any of us valley children were aware of it either--that Dame Brischelu is the main source of recommendations to Sorceress Helinu for children to be tested."

"What?" Merina gasped out.

"It makes perfect sense. As the highest educated person in Dysandes, and the most knowledgeable of the world outside our valley, she is in the ideal position as instructor to young adults to evaluate them for magic use."

Merina turned sharply toward Trinames, crossing her arms across her chest, and glared at him. "You mean to say she is the Prince of Princes' spy, to report our compliance with his stupid law?"

Leaning away from her angry posture, Trinames stuttered, "No, no, love, not at all. That can't be it. If she was, we would have troops in here all the time forcing families to get their children tested. Think about it!"

Merina lowered her arms and faced the river, doing what Trinames suggested. "Yes, that does make sense, but it also forces you to believe that the children of farmers and herders are not smart enough to use magic. Otherwise, why has she not recommended any for all the decades she's been here?" Did my mother's failure cast doubt on Helinu's reputation as a tester?

Before Trinames could respond, Merina turned slowly back to look at him, letting suspicion show in her eyes. "And why of all the valley people does she recommend you, and long after the time--years even--when children are asked to take the Test?"

Her lover fidgeted under her half-closed eyes. He said softly, almost pleadingly, "I told you, Sorceress Helinu wants to leave here to study to be an Adept. I am willing to wager she went to Dame Brischelu for a recommendation."

Merina stood and walked to the piling nearest the end of the pier to them, leaning back against it. When she was little she would climb up to sit on it, staring at the river flowing by. Now she could just barely sit up on it if she tried, but since she was broader than back then, sitting there was uncomfortable. She did not mean to make her lover nervous or upset, but something really bothered her about Trinames's gaining a recommendation now. *Brischelu told me I had the gift of my mother. Why didn't she recommend me for the Test?* She pulled gently on her lower lip with the fingers of her left hand, trying to pin down the thought that was dodging away from her. A question popped into her mind, and she looked over at Trinames, seeing the tenseness in his body, as if he anticipated her next words.

Calmly she asked, "Assuming Sorceress Helinu did go to Dame Brischelu for a recommendation, when did the Healer ask you to come in for the Test?"

Trinames closed his eyes, tapping out a number on his right thigh with the fingers of his right hand. "Three months ago."

Shoving away from the post, Merina paced over to sit beside her nervous lover. She realized in the space of the last hour she had shown him passion, love, and anger. It was time for her to be understanding, which was going to be hard because she did not understand. Dame Brischelu was making problems for Trinames and her, but for what reason?

"Love, consider this. Four months ago we announced to your parents and my aunt our intention to be mated this summer. Almost the moment the valley learned of our engagement, the Healer begins to talk to you about becoming a Healer, then asks you to be tested--and you pass. Does it make sense to you that Helinu has been trying to get out of Dysandes for years and years and is just now seeking a replacement? And the one she picks is the one recommended by Dame Brischelu, who has decided on her son's life-mate?"

Trinames reached for Merina's hands, which she reluctantly put in his. "When you say it like that, it does sound suspicious, love. But what does the Dame accomplish with this, this plot you think she has?"

His hands were warm, and Merina realized the chill off the lake had made her cold. The comfort waiting in his arms presented an almost overwhelming temptation. She resisted, saying, "She removes you from the valley to give her son time to woo me, is the first thing that comes to my mind--and should also enter yours. The next is she is using my known, intense dislike of things magical to force a barrier between us. She tested that on me by asking me to take up my mother's work--and got the reaction she expected, my total rejection of magic. And finally, the thing I fear as much as any, is that you have been tempted to become something you may not be qualified to be. What if you were to go to Byklandes and fail? I won't care, I would still love you, but we will have wasted all those years."

When Merina spoke of failure, Trinames gripped her hands tightly, blurting out, "I won't fail."

Merina winced in pain, and Trinames let go of her hands, telling her he was sorry. She wiggled her fingers and said she was all right, then put her hands on his cheeks, turning his face to give him a gentle kiss. "Love, I don't want you to fail, but I think you have been lied to. If you have, and you can't do magic, we will know very quickly. Healer Helinu told me instructors know within months whether a student can do simple spells. If the plan was to get you away from the valley to make me choose between Markinis and you, my love, this lie will be exposed by winter's end. We can be mated in the spring."

Trinames sighed, "And if I have succeeded in casting spells, Mer, what then?"

Merina lowered her hands and broke her gaze from her love's. "Then I will have to make the decision I can't make now."

Tomanis entered the kitchen and gave Alanu a kiss on the cheek, whispering something into her ear. She glanced at Merina and nodded. Her aunt wiped her hands on her apron and brushed past her life-mate to exit the room. Tomanis turned toward Merina.

"You know our visitor?" he asked.

"Farmer Calandis, who owns the farm nearest to Dysandes. He is the valley's richest farmer. Everyone knows him."

"He is looking for a life-mate."

Shocked, Merina almost knocked over her glass of tea, catching it just before it would have fallen to the stone countertop. "What? I saw his life-mate last week--she was very hale and hearty."

"Not for him." Tomanis smiled. "For Markinis--his only son."

Merina frowned her displeasure at hearing the name for two reasons. First from the realization that Dame Brischelu was going ahead with her plan. She is making her life-mate ask for permission to allow his son to come call on me. And secondly for the reason she was about to give to Tomanis. "That lout! He has chased every woman in the valley and some he should not have been chasing."

Nodding, her uncle agreed with her, but said, "I know, I know. He has seen the error of his ways and is ready to settle down. He wants to begin a family and has asked his father for a section of land to call his own. His father won't give it to him unless he proves his intent by taking a life-mate. He knows his son well enough. To his surprise, Markinis agreed."

"And Markinis chose me? How honored I should be," Merina said with as much sarcasm as she could muster. She wondered if Dame Brischelu had used her motherly wiles to suggest Merina would make a good life-mate or had simply told him whom she wanted him to mate with.

"You could do worse."

Shaking her head angrily, Merina did not spit out the words as she wanted to, but still said sharply, "I have chosen a life-mate."

"As is your right, being the inheritor of your mother's claim to her share of her father's land."

"Which includes this farm and several others," Merina said matter-of-factly, not wishing to offend her uncle but determined to assert her right to decisions about her life.

Tomanis just nodded. She knew he had never held any grudge against her independence, although the talk in town was that she seemed ungrateful for the fact that his life-mate, her aunt, was the only family member who would take in the bastard child of the first born. As the third son of his father, he would probably never inherit the land his oldest brother held now. His life-mating her aunt was a lucky circumstance that had given him the status of landowner instead of just a hired hand.

"I will not back out of my mother's agreement with Auntie. I am beholden to her and truly feel she is more mother to me than an aunt. She will get this farm when I am recognized by the Prince of Princes as the rightful owner of the holdings Grandfather Romanus's will stated were Delaphinu's. I just wish these proceedings took less time than the decade they have."

"Delaphinu has to be given the chance to claim her land," Tomanis said. "Romanus's will was very specific that every chance must be given her to return to the valley and reclaim her land."

"Posting notices on trees throughout Saphradea and scribing them into Dysandes's meeting diaries has not brought her back, Uncle. It is more likely she is dead."

Tomanis shrugged his big shoulders. "She is missing, not dead, Merina. Your other uncles are in no hurry to give up the portions of your holdings that they control, so time is not in your favor."

"My status was not in any way brought up with Calandis, was it? Is that the real reason he came to see you?" Merina asked, watching her uncle's face to see if his expression would reveal anything. It did not.

"Calandis has twice the holdings of anyone in the valley. He doesn't need to provide for his son from another man's land. I told him I have no authority over you and thanked him for the courtesy of asking. I did tell him I would accept a visit from Markinis with the same courtesy, but whether you would meet with him also was entirely up to you."

Merina bit back the words that almost escaped her lips. Tomanis was only being respectful to a neighbor, but he should not have allowed Markinis the privilege of asking for her hand. She thought a moment, aware that Tomanis expected a sharp response. "I will see him," she said, smiling at the shocked look on her uncle's face.

Chapter 6

Standing with her back to her tree, Merina followed the progress of Markinis as he galloped down the entrance road to the farm. He was late, as she had expected he would be. When she had agreed to a visit from him ten days earlier, Merina had assumed he would appear within a few days, so eagerly had his father presented Markinis's suit for her hand. A week went by before a field hand delivered the expected formal visit request, written in--as she had remarked to her aunt that it would be--Dame Brischelu's script. That Markinis had not penned it himself confirmed what she knew of him, a farm boy who placed so little value on education that he had rarely been seen in school.

She looked down at the note in her hand and marveled at the beauty of the script. Dame Brischelu could have taught her son the skills she had learned if he had shown any interest. As a lady-in-waiting at Alexus's court, she'd had the benefit of the finest education. Odd that she did not pass some of it on to her son. Perhaps the likelihood of her ever presenting him to the Prince of Princes' court was not in her plans for Markinis.

Valley men tended to have large families, for the obvious reason of needing more hands to help. Yet the most powerful landowner in the valley had only the one son. That could not have been his choice. Merina chided herself for showing a sudden interest in the family of the man riding to woo her, especially since she had no intention of becoming his life-mate. But since Dame Brischelu was taking more than a small interest in her family, perhaps she should find out more about the Dame. Who better to ask than her son?

As for his being late, she knew the Traveler's Rest stood between their farms. Merina suspected her suitor needed courage before facing her.

Markinis slowed to a trot as he approached the front porch, where Tomanis was waiting. Her uncle pointed up the hill toward Merina, and Markinis turned in her direction. It was too much to expect that he would dismount and spend a few moments greeting her foster parents before walking up to present himself to her. Merina deliberately moved her chair to put the approaching rider off to her left side and sat. She put her wide-brimmed hat on, looking away from Markinis and feigning interest in the setting sun.

The tall, burly young man was half again as old as Merina. He dismounted and removed his hat before saying, "Good afternoon, Mistress Merina."

With his voice deep and strong, he was not the least tentative in his greeting. Still staring at the sun, Merina answered with a lighter tone than she wanted to use, "Closer to evening than afternoon, sir." Waving the note in her left hand, she continued, "Your request was for the fourth hour past noon." Adding a playful lilt to her voice, she turned and peeked from under the hat's brim. "Lose your way?"

The large man did not expect that question, and his huge hands turned his hat around as if to buy time for his reply. "No, ma'am, I stopped for a few beers to calm my nerves."

"I see. Is my reputation so frightful? I bet the boys in the tavern think I am a harridan."

Markinis stammered, "No, no, Mistress. That is not true. They think you're..."

"I'm what?" Merina asked. She stood, removed her hat, and turned to face Markinis, her hands on her hips, her shoulders back. She knew this pose would show her full figure to the man in front of her.

"Beautiful, the most desired woman in Saphradea!" His eyes were seeing what she wanted him to.

"And you needed a drink to tell me that?"

"No, speaking the truth is never hard for me. I--"

"Tell lies better when your tongue is lubricated. I still have a strong memory of your seduction of Florinu. I see I did not leave a scar to remind you of that night."

Markinis touched the spot where she had cut him, and the slight scowl on his face testified that his memory of the incident remained clear. She remembered he had left her by the barn and spent the remainder of the evening drinking heavily and picking fights. She had thought it likely that he would not have remembered anything, considering his being driven home in the back of a wagon, along with the rest of his gang of friends.

Markinis spread his hands out away from his body in an appeal for forgiveness. "Merina, I know I have a reputation of chasing the girls. That is all behind me now! I am ready to settle down. I'm seeking a life-mate, not a roll in the hay."

"And what are you expecting from this woman you would make your life-mate?" Merina crossed her arms in front of her chest. Her eyes stayed fixed on his face, watching for the expression that would tell more about his motives than his words. She was not disappointed.

"A mother to my children. To run my household staff and manage my affairs. To feed and care for me and give me the pleasures of my bed." The want in his eyes told Merina his last demand was all he really cared about.

"And she would get what for her effort? Let me guess. Well-fed and sheltered for the rest of her life as long as it would last while having to produce a child every year. Since you will use her body to give you pleasure, she could look forward to the times when she is pregnant and you will be turning to another source to get those pleasures you value so highly."

Markinis's face looked as if she had slapped him. "I will care for you and never look elsewhere. You are everything I want in a woman--strong, beautiful, farm-trained."

"Did you hear your words, sir? My children, my household, my affairs, and my bed! What of our? Everything is about you. Is there to be no love in that relationship? If you think me strong, don't you realize that I could make the household staff mine, run your life as I want, give you children when and if I wanted to, and take my pleasure from you when it suits me? Is that what you want in a life-mate?"

"This is not going the way I had hoped. Can I start over, Merina?"

"Certainly." Moving her chair to face the flustered young man, Merina sat and put the hat back on, although she no longer needed it with the sun rapidly setting on the horizon. She pulled out the lamp she had stored under the chair and lit it, setting it off to her left side so that it cast light on both of them.

Markinis looked at the hat in his hand and turned to put it on the saddle horn. He walked over to Merina and sat in front of her. "My father is rich, and someday I'll inherit his land. I like working the land, and I want to make something of myself instead of just being the heir. I want the responsibility of being my own man and making my own decisions. So yes, I have a plan for the things I want. As you know from my father telling your uncle, he will let me have some of his land early. It will be of value to me only if I work it since I will not be able to sell it and use the money to continue the life I have had. I don't want that life anymore."

"I can believe all you have just said is true, except the last part," Merina said softly. "Every man I have ever known wants the life you have." Except Trinames, she silently corrected herself.

"That is fair, but they wouldn't want it after living it for as many years as I have. What they want is to have the lives they've currently built and be free of owing anyone."

"So you want what they have. Families, people who need them and care for them."

Markinis nodded. "Our lives out here follow the cycles of the land. We have children so that we will have help in our later years. To get them to the place where they can do it means we have to care for, feed, teach them the skills to work the land. We need women to bear those children and raise them while the men work the land. The women share our lives, and the men protect and care for their life-mates."

"So you do recognize that women are not just cows to be serviced by a bull to bear calves and produce milk."

"I see your point, Merina. The boys in the tavern really do think you are beautiful, but their praise tends to compare you to the prize heifer of the herd, the giver of the most milk."

"Ah, the perfect woman. And to win her, the perfect man has to be found."

Markinis glanced away and gave a little shrug. Merina smiled. He is a stud, I have to admit. And the rumors are that he's built like a bull, which

I can verify from having seen him erect. Being serviced by him would not be a bad thing, but in the end it is still being used.

"It might surprise you, Markinis, that women feel the same need you have expressed. We are built to have babies and are equipped to care for them. Perhaps that is why we seek the attention of men who we think will give us the things we want. I have a body that I know men want. I see it in their eyes. I don't need to be in heat like an animal to get them to want to mate with me. But like an animal, if I do so, I will become pregnant. Then I have no choice but to be dependent on a life-mate to provide for me, or do like my birth mother did and abandon the baby to be adopted by the herd or die."

Markinis glanced quickly back at her when she spoke of her mother. "I said I would never leave you."

"Yes, you did, but at that point I would have no options left in my life. If we are together only to meet each other's needs, then we are living the lives of animals instead of men and women. You are offering that life to me."

"But you said you have the same needs!" Markinis said urgently. "We share so much in common."

Merina shook her head. "What makes you think we have anything in common? What do you know about me other than what your friends in the tavern have told you?"

"My mother has told me a lot about you."

A smile crept up from the corners of her lips as Merina said, "Ah, your mother! I'm sure she did her research on me because it was her idea for me to be your life-mate."

Markinis recoiled in shock. "That is not so, I..."

"You would begin lying to me before we are even engaged, sir."

"No, it was my idea. She--"

"Markinis, your mother met with me a month ago to discuss my becoming your life-mate. She wanted a strong-willed woman to take over the job of running your life. What she didn't tell me was why. Is your mother ill?"

Flustered, Markinis shook his head. Before he could speak again, Merina asked him another question. "Is there a reason why you have never had brothers or sisters? You seem to share with all the rest of the valley men a willingness to support a large family. Yet your mother only had you. Isn't that odd?"

Markinis looked at his shoes and shrugged. Merina asked another question that she was now sure he did not have an answer for. "Your mother is of noble blood. She served as a lady-in-waiting in Alexus's court. What was her title? Who was her father?"

"I don't know," Markinis mumbled.

"Don't you talk with your mother? Didn't your parents ever talk at the dinner table? Did you ever ask your father about his courtship of your mother?"

"What does this have to do with my proposal, Mistress?" Markinis asked, his lips tightening and his voice turning harsh.

"It has everything to do with it. You said we have things in common, but my idea of what a family is bears no resemblance to yours. You grew up alone with a domineering mother and a father who pays little attention to the other members of his family. I know your mother has her own separate gold, and I suspect she is wealthier than your father. I suspect she is tired of living in the backwoods of Saphradea and wants to return to the court. If she can ensure you are in competent hands, she will have fulfilled whatever bargain she made or was made for her. Either that, or she is dying--you say she is not. Why else would she seek me out to take over the reins?"

Markinis just stared at Merina. His mouth hung slightly open, but no words came out.

She continued, "I look at your life and don't see sharing in it. Therefore, I see no sharing in your offer. I do see there is something we have in common, sir. We both want to take control of our own lives and become our own man or woman. But your mother would want me to take control of yours, as well as mine. That is not sharing either. Now tell me the truth. Did your mother tell you to come here and ask to be my life-mate?"

Probably for fear of saying something wrong, Markinis just nodded.

Merina smiled, glad that he did not try to lie to her again. She said, "There is no love in your heart for me, only lust. If I give you what you want, and believe me I can do so better than anything you've had to date, you will be happy because you will have your prize heifer, and your friends at the tavern will envy you. After I create a herd of your children, you will have everything you need from me and will began looking for another challenge or another woman."

"That...that is not true," he said with a tinge of anger and hurt.

"Perhaps," Merina sighed, "but here is a truth I know. I would work very hard at making our--note I said our--farm productive. I would bear our children and raise them to respect the land and the animals we own. I would expect you to honor my values and remain loyal to me and our family. If you strayed from that, I would leave you and return to my own holdings with our children, who would then become mine. You would have your farm, and you would have an heir when our first born is old enough to leave me."

"You would do that?"

"You expect less from a headstrong woman who has trained herself to manage an estate? Your mother and I have a lot in common, but I am not gracious and noble. It is said your father paid a great price for her, but I am not willing to sell myself for your offer. I have chosen a life-mate who I believe will love me and with whom I can share my life."

Markinis's voice shook with anger. "Sharing a life of poverty? You know sorcerers have forsworn wealth and power. That craving for control is what drove them centuries ago to try to conquer all of the Domains during the Sorcerer Wars."

"Trinames seeks fulfillment in his life by way of service. I'm not happy with his choice of magic use because of what it did to my mother, but I know his heart is still with the land and not for personal gain. I would rather he not leave farming, but--"

"You'll try to change him anyway. You could use your threat of taking his children and running home," Markinis cut in sarcastically.

This remark only succeeded in igniting Merina's anger. She lashed back, "I am not trying to change him, any more than I am you. If you behave with me like a rutting bull, I will treat you like one. You have already experienced that. If you try to force me to become something I'm not, I will fight back." As if to drive home that fact, Merina stood over Markinis, who jumped to his feet as well. He was a foot taller than she and easily a hundred pounds heavier.

Markinis grabbed her by the arms to prevent her raising them up. "You're a fighter, missy--everyone knows that. It is that fire in you that excites me."

Merina could not move her upper body. It had not been her intention to attack Markinis, but now she found herself unable to pull away from him. She fought back the urge to kick him in the crotch or hurt him in any of a half dozen ways her uncle had taught her. She slowed her breathing and let herself relax, gazing up into his eyes and waiting for a sign that he was going to do something they'd both regret.

"I'm sorry, Merina," he said, letting go of her. "Since that night I have tried very hard not to take things I want. I will fight for them, win the right to have them, but not force myself. I have changed, Mistress."

Merina did not step away. She continued to stare at him, curving her lips in a wry smile as she released the tension from her muscles. "I was surprised when you did not run around the valley bragging of your deeds of that night. Perhaps you have changed in some ways. Maybe time will show it is really true and not a fancy of the moment."

"I have changed, Merina. Please believe me!"

Shaking her head, Merina gave her answer to his proposal. "I know you hate to lose, but there really is no fight here. I have already accepted Trinames's proposal. So think of my answer as not rejecting you, Markinis. I met with you because most of the valley folk have heard about your proposal and are expecting us to become life-mates. Having your offer turned down by me sets you free to find a woman who is willing to live under the conditions you set. If there is to be a loser here, I will be viewed as that one. I will be topic of discussion for all the valley folk who will laugh about my loving a sorcerer and hating the very thing he stands for. It will amaze them that I would give up the wealth and power they all assume I should want, not seeing that it is only what they want for themselves."

He stepped back and looked as if he was going to try again to persuade her otherwise. After a moment, he turned and took his hat from the saddle horn. "Forgive me for grabbing you, Merina. I should not have touched you without your permission. You are right, Mistress. I hate to lose. But you are wrong to say there is no fight here. There are things happening in Saphradea which may change all our lives and undo decisions made. I have not given up. My offer still stands." He mounted his horse and urged it to a trot as he rode down the hill.

Merina strolled down the hill, following the path she had worn between her house and the tree. She had extinguished her lantern, preferring the light of the moon, which allowed her to see more of the land around her instead of just the small circle of light cast by the lantern. Restless and uneasy, she worried over how her meeting with Markinis had ended. She needed more time to think of what she was going to say to her foster parents.

Ahead, she saw her aunt and uncle's silhouettes on the porch, backlit by the living room's lamps. Telling them she had turned Markinis down was not her worry, for they knew of her vow to Trinames. Telling them he had not accepted her answer would make them anxious about their relationship with one of their closest neighbors and a powerful leader in the valley. They might even try to convince her to change her mind, which would then lead to a family argument, and everyone would go to bed upset.

Hearing her slow approach, Tomanis lit the porch light, and her aunt moved to put her arm around his waist. Merina emerged from the darkness and hung her lantern on a peg in the post near the foot of the steps. She climbed up the stairs to one of the chairs at the right of the main bench. Her foster parents sat on the bench as she hung her hat on a coat hook.

"I take it from the lack of joy in your face that you did not accept Farmer Markinis's life-mate offer," Tomanis said lightly.

With a faint smile, Merina told them what Markinis had proposed. "Even if I had, Uncle, I would not be filled with joy. The man is so focused on himself that being his life-mate would be considered hard labor by anyone's standards."

Alanu sighed. "That was a very generous proposal, Merina. The rewards for that labor--"

"Did you and Tomanis stop at three sons because you could not have any more, or because it was as many as you both desired? Markinis has the same drive to prove himself that Grandfather Romanus had. I would be producing kin for Markinis until I became barren just so all of Dysandes would see what a great man he was."

Alanu smiled, trying to cut across the sarcasm in Merina's voice. "I wasn't talking about that kind of labor."

"I know, Auntie. Thank you for your gentle humor. And the sad thing about saying no is that I know in my heart if I really wanted to have that way of life, I would have tried my best to be the mother all of Dysandes would be talking about forever. I just don't see myself as the

Great and Grand Mother of Saphradea who saves the Domains from extinction."

Tomanis glanced at Alanu, then said hesitantly, "You would have the land you wanted to develop into your own farm long before your inheritance comes in. You could start with an advantage that few women have in this life."

"Which I'm sure is why all of Dysandes thinks I should take his offer. In truth, Uncle, Markinis did not mention anything about my inheritance in his proposal, nor do I think he had even given it much thought. If he had, I might have received a different offer."

"Why do you say that, Merina?" her aunt asked, glancing at her life-mate.

"My having a source of wealth would counter his offering to provide for me, making me independent of him. You noticed he promised me free rein to run his farm, because I am known to be a shrewd manager of gold. He realized that if he didn't, he would be asking me to give up something I really wanted to do. So he did not consider that I had something to bargain with. He offered a generous price for me, not expecting I had conditions of acceptance. When I confronted him with his bullish behavior, I made it clear to him that I had my own means of support and would leave him to chase all the females he desired. I could not be bought--it is he who has a price to pay."

Sighing, Tomanis rubbed his face with his hands. "You don't throw such a thing in a man's face, Merina."

"Why not? Am I supposed to accept his reputation as a rake and ignore it? I gave him an excuse to tell his drinking companions I was not worth the price."

"No," Tomanis said with another sigh, "you threw down a challenge that he has told you he will fight for. Pride and humiliation are the causes of more conflict than greed has ever been."

Merina was returning from her morning security patrol around the farm, one she had imposed on herself after her nephews found the wolf print weeks before, when she saw a rider departing the front of the house. It was no one she recognized, and callers did not normally appear before noon. Unstringing her hunting bow, she stowed it and her quiver of arrows in their rack by the door and called out her presence to Auntie. Alanu answered from the kitchen that the Dame had sent a message.

I wonder what she wants now. The scroll was not very big, about the size of the one Merina had received before. Pulling off the ribbon securing it, she took just a moment to read what was written. Alanu appeared from the dining room door as Merina finished the note.

"She wants to see me again," Merina said, handing the scroll to her aunt, who wiped her wet hands before taking it carefully by the corner and unrolling it.

Alanu cooed, "At her home in Dysandes this time! Oh my, Merina, she never entertains guests there. She always has her parties at Calandis's home, the more to impress the other landholders."

"She probably doesn't want me to refuse the visit because going to Calandis's puts me at the mercy of running into her son--or for that matter, her husband. Surely she is not going to try to talk me into changing my mind, would she?" Merina asked her aunt.

"Look, tomorrow is Settling Day. She knows you would be in town anyway and that you would certainly not want to lose the day to travel to Calandis's when you have business to take care of." Alanu handed the scroll back, shrugging. "You said she was a shrewd businesswoman. Perhaps she feels there is room to negotiate a better deal for her son. He did tell you he was not giving up his courtship, and you did make it clear to him that you believe his mother was behind this. You can be sure he had to report to his mother what happened last night. She will try to make amends."

"That she wants to support him in his courtship is all the more reason why I don't want to take up his offer. When I told Markinis I thought his mother was looking for someone to take over the responsibility of running his life, I did it deliberately for two reasons. The first was to make him see he was being manipulated and make him angry. The second was that I could not see why she would be giving up control unless she wanted out. If she does not leave the valley, I now see I would be fighting for control of Markinis until one of us dies. I'd best end this as soon as I can."

Chapter 7

Merina rode into town accompanied by her uncle and a single wagon carrying baskets of berry products that the forests around the farm provided them. Since she was meeting with the Dame in the early afternoon, she hoped to get most of her business conducted that morning. They had left before sunup to arrive several hours after first light. The crowd gathered in the marketplace confirmed that the majority of the valley's farms shared the wish to get business done early.

This summer season Settling Day was held more to arrange for the selling of the fall harvest than to display produce grown in the past month. Farmers were guessing what their fields would yield in the next month and looking ahead to what they would need for the spring planting. The summer had not been too hot, and the rains were adequate, although more would have been better. Expectations ran high for an abundance of crops, but that would drive prices down. The wolf problem was growing worse. Sheep and cattle were taking losses, which could only get more severe when winter set in. Much of the talk in the market square focused on solving the problem. The official response to the Dysandes appeal for help from the Prince of Princes' court was that no troops could be spared.

Merina asked Tomanis how that could be. He said, "The rest of Saphradea is not having our problem. There are rumors floating around the Merchants Guild that we are inventing a reason to charge higher prices for our goods. Business is brisk throughout the Domains. The bad news for farmers is Alexus has increased tariffs on all the guilds and is seeing an increase in his coffers. The good news for the smithies is he wants more weapons and armor produced. The saber rattling with Delmathia and Hermania is getting louder. All three are starting to impose fees on trade across their borders. This does not bode well."

"It certainly does not, Uncle. Raising tariffs on us will make any negotiations we do today almost meaningless. I suggest we hold back on making any commitments and plan on watching the mood develop."

Tomanis nodded.

The wagon goods sold briskly, as there was always a demand for sweet produce this time of the year. Merina was closing her stall when Trinames found her. He looked troubled, and more so when she told him of her pending visit to the Dame.

"I need to talk to you, love. Can you stay in town after your meeting?"

The worry in his voice bothered her. "Of course!" she said, trying to cheer him with her light tone. "Go the Wolf's Head and arrange a room for me. I will meet you there at five hours past noon. My meeting with Dame Brischelu is less than an hour from now. We could eat at the inn and spend the evening together. That will be so nice."

He gave her a quick kiss, thanked her, and rushed away before she could ask why he wanted to talk. She finished closing up and told Tomanis of her change in plans.

Dame Brischelu's village home was one of the few that sat within a walled enclave, in the far west of town away from docks to the east and their surrounding smithies. The mayor's house stood next door, but it had no walls and almost gave the impression it was a servant quarters for the large home behind the walls. Two other walled houses completed the street opposite the Dame's and mayor's. Merina knew they belonged to the head of the Smiths Guild and the Dockmaster. She had never been in any of these homes as the landholders and villagers rarely associated with one another, meeting only for business.

She approached the iron gate blocking the walkway that led through the thick stone wall. Through the gap she saw a lush green garden with a waist-high hedge leading up to the entrance of the house. The building itself was made of stone, quarried from the same rock as the majority of the village houses. Dysandes had a lot of stone. It was a major export for the town, sent down river with farm produce and cattle. Merina's home was wooden, made from the trees cleared for the fields and pastures surrounding it. She wondered how cold a stone house would feel in the winter. Her dislike of cold made her leery of living in town, which she might have to do when mated with Trinames.

The latched gate opened smoothly when she pushed on it. A bell tinkled from behind her as she closed the gate, announcing to the servants that someone had entered the grounds. A maid came through the front door and greeted her cheerfully. Merina had expected a male servant, one who might serve as a guard. Surely the Dame wouldn't rely solely on the walls for protection. Merina followed the maid into the house, noting in passage the solidity of the door.

The maid led her through a wood-paneled hall and past a dining room, easily as big as the downstairs of the Traveler's Rest, but small for what Merina had expected. For such a big house on the outside, the interior gave her an impression of snugness. The sitting room she was led to was definitely intimate. A large fireplace occupied the center of the wall facing the door, and it was surrounded by portraits of exquisitely dressed women that looked down at any visitor who sat before the fire. The maid bade Merina sit while she notified her mistress of Merina's presence.

The chairs were overstuffed, made of the finest leather. As she sank into one, a thought came to Merina that she might have trouble getting out of it. She decided to move to one of the two straight-backed chairs before the fire. The sudden appearance of Dame Brischelu found Merina struggling to get free of the chair. The Dame smiled and offered a hand to pull Merina out. The older woman was stronger than Merina had expected. The women took seats in the wooden chairs opposite each other.

"Thank you for coming so promptly, Mistress Merina. After hearing of my son's visit, I was afraid you would not. I warned him not to visit the tavern beforehand."

Merina shifted toward the rear of the chair, pressing her back against the hard lattice. "As nervous as he was, I don't think the drink did him any harm. He was very much the gentleman you raised him to be."

Wishing she could take that back, Merina realized that her sarcastic tone implied an insult to Brischelu's mothering.

The Dame folded her hands in her lap, sitting as rigidly as Merina. She said, "Gentlemen do not restrain women by the shoulders, for whatever reason, good or bad."

Even when provoked, is that what you mean?

"He told me he lost his temper and apologized. I sincerely hope he did," the Dame finished.

"He did, Madam. But in the passion of the moment I, too, have a share in the blame. I had just refused his offer, and he brought up my relationship with Trinames. That led to an argument, and I stood up to leave. I should have kept my peace and let him depart first."

Dame Brischelu nodded, reached for the silver bell on the table beside her, and gave it a quick ring, summoning the maid. Merina hoped it meant she was being dismissed herself. That was not to be, since the Dame instructed the maid to bring wine.

As the maid left the room, Brischelu locked her eyes on Merina and said in a firm voice, "I am the bastard daughter of the Duke Frohtonis, Alexus's Right Hand Sword. Saphradean nobility do not get their titles from land grants, to be handed down from one generation to the next. They get them from deeds accomplished or from loyalty purchased. My father was made the young Prince of Princes' bodyguard when Alexus was five years of age and was by his side through every battle and fight until ten years ago. He was by then too old to protect the Prince, so he stepped down, replaced by a younger man." Merina listened raptly, not understanding why the Dame was telling her this.

"My mother was Alexus's mother's handmaiden. As frequently happens in court, the Duke, being in close proximity to the heir and his family, became familiar with those who serve the Prince of Princes' needs. My mother took the Duke as a lover, but she was not interested in life-mating a soldier, particularly one who was gone from court a lot doing his Prince's biding. Alexus's mother allowed the offspring of her ladies-in-waiting to be kept in court, and I was raised like a baby sister to Alexus. I later became one of his mother's ladies. When I was thirteen, my mother sold herself off to a very rich merchant--who got a Barony out of the deal."

Brischelu stopped as the maid returned with a tray with chilled bottle and two glasses. Within moments the wine was served and tasted, Merina recognizing it was the same as she had had at the Traveler's Rest. The maid slipped out and left the two women alone.

The Dame continued, "You looked shocked, my dear. Have I said something you don't understand?"

Merina nodded, finding it hard to voice her question. "Your mother sold herself off?"

Sipping her wine slowly, Brischelu savored it, then put her glass gently on the table. She smiled. "The court is like a nursery, Merina. My mother's mother was born a bastard. Her father was Alexus's father. Girls and boys born of such relationships are a trading commodity. They are used to exact influence, to make trade deals, and carry on the business of power. Remember I said titles are earned or bought. The land is taken by your landholders, who regard it an asset to be kept in your family. Not so for nobility, we trade in power and influence."

"But your father was a Duke? Doesn't that make you a Duchess?" Merina asked, now completely puzzled.

Laughing, the Dame was clearly enjoying Merina's confusion. "No, because that was his title. I would not want to have him acknowledge me just to have a title. He died relatively poor. His pension kept him in the style of life he had lived all those years, and he still had a major influence with Alexus--which gave him power. As his daughter I had little influence on the Prince."

"As daughter of the daughter of the Prince of Princes you would be Alexus's cousin?" Merina asked.

"And if his father had not had a male descendent I could be Princess of Princes--which in the history of Saphradean noble males was very unlikely. They produce children until the male succession is assured."

"That's..." Merina gasped out.

The Dame cut in, "Wrong? No, it is the way of our Princes. It works exceeding well for the women of the court. They have their influence on the succession, and they trade their bodies as they want. My mother did exceeding well with her deal and even has a title of Baroness, which to her means nothing. As for me, I got what I wanted. I mated the most prosperous landholder in the northern valleys, and I have my own source of wealth, plus now what my father left me--small as it was."

Merina downed her glass and did not object when the Dame refilled it. "This influence idea... It seems so odd. Not wrong," she quickly added, "just..."

"I know," Brischelu said, refilling her own glass. Merina saw the Dame relax, as if talking with her was like talking with a friend. This was not what Merina had expected. The Dame swirled her glass to sniff the aroma of the wine. "It all made sense to me while in the court, but when I mated and moved out here, I found the questions from you, the young of valley, making me question why--where I had never done before. The answer lies"--Brischelu leaned forward, head cocked to one side--"in the role nobility plays. We govern, but for no reason other than we have throughout the centuries. Why is that? Because we have the power to do so. We have the weapons, the armor, the horses--all the things that allow us to make war on our enemies. And I suppose, on our own people. Yet the people let us rule and support us."

Merina found she, too, was relaxing, perhaps more from the wine than the conversation, which she had so many questions about. "You took on the job of protecting us, so we can do what we are trained to do--produce food."

"Exactly my point. You have your job to do, and we--I should say the court--has theirs. Now I am one of you--a merchant in her own right, a producer of goods. It is what I wanted to be, until you rejected my son."

Alarmed, Merina stiffened. This is why she asked me to come!

"Calm yourself, Merina. This is a good thing you have done. It has awakened me to why I have lived here in the valley all these years."

Not knowing what else to say, Merina asked, "Why?"

"I had been living the life of court intrigue for so many years, I did not know anything else. You asked Markinis why I had only the one child."

Merina nodded, afraid of what was to come. Had she stepped too far into the Dame's life, and now was she going to be taken to task?

The Dame continued, "It is not the way of the valley people. It is the way of the nobility. I sealed my bargain with Calandis by bearing him a son. I could have had more--but we of the court know of ways to stop bearing children. I enjoyed my life-mate, and he, me, but I did not want to have the responsibilities of more babies. My plans did not have multiple children in them. So I didn't. Do I regret it now? No."

What Merina heard made her feel as if she had intruded on the pain of another person. She almost wanted to cry.

"See, you are sad, Merina. Sad because your way of life includes many children. Understand me, child! I did not want them! If Markinis had died growing up, I would have produced another--that was my duty. That is not your way of thinking, and I understand that now. I should have realized that when Markinis voiced his desire for a life-mate. He is, after all, a man of the valley."

Nodding, Merina lowered her eyes, a tear falling--not for Brischelu, but because Merina felt sad that she had not thought of anything but how Merina would feel. She would want those children.

Seeing the tear, the Dame produced a cloth from her sleeve and handed it to Merina. "You see, dear, you are moved by a sadness I don't feel. But I do now, because my eyes have been opened. You spoke to him of a coldness in my family."

Merina jerked her head up to protest.

"Stop, whether you said that or not, I don't care. It is true to me. Calandis got what he paid for, and no more. Not because he didn't want more, but because I let him know nothing more was needed of him. It is not his fault his son was not a major part of his life, but mine. Relationships are power, Merina. You know that, as well as I, who used that power to keep my influence on Markinis."

"Madam, Dame--I only--"

"You made your point, Merina. And Markinis understands it all too well. He wants to be his own man, as he said. He made it very clear to me that he did not want my meddling in his life. But at the same time, he wanted my help to solve his problem with you. I can't do that, dear Merina. But I will warn you..."

Here it comes. Merina reeled back in shock.

"Do not close your eyes to your future like I did, knowing only what I wanted to know. You might make the wrong decision!"

Merina walked slowly back through town, mulling over what Dame Brischelu had told her. The street was unusually empty of people for Settling Day, and she did not meet anyone she knew. She really missed Florinu at a time like this because her friend would bring a fresh insight into what Merina had experienced. As she finished repeating the conversation in her mind for the fifth time, she gave up trying to figure out why she felt something was wrong.

Entering the Wolf's Head, she strode to the front desk and asked where her room was. The landlord told her it was the next to the last on the left of the long hall. He ordered the maid washing cups at the bar to fetch hot water and gave Merina her room key. Her uncle had carried her things in an hour before--not that she had very much in the way of evening wear. She always had a change of clothes in her traveling box, having learned in the past that trips to Dysandes often lasted longer than she expected.

Her room was reasonably clean and, for the price, spacious. The large bed would sleep two, but she did not intend to take advantage of it this night. There were two chairs before the fireplace with a round table between them. At the foot of the bed stood a wash stand and a rack for towels. Her box was sitting on the bed. As she walked over to open it, a knock on the door interrupted. The maid from the bar carried in a large pitcher of steaming water and quickly deposited it on the stand. There was already a pitcher of water on it, but that would be room temperature now. Merina thanked the maid and asked her to tell the landlord that she did not want to see any visitors for at least half an hour. She knew it was close to the time Trinames had said he would call, so she rushed through her wash.

Merina was running a comb through her short hair when a knock came almost to the minute the half hour was up. She put a smile on her face and opened the door to her lover. Expecting to see his usual warm smile, she was taken aback by the stress in his eyes and the tightness of his lips.

"What is wrong?" she asked.

"I don't have very much time to explain. Sorceress Helinu has me making calls with her. She thinks by working alongside of her I will pick up the non-magic techniques I'll need to know. She is waiting for us at her home. We need to go now!"

Shocked, Merina stepped back from the hug he offered and held out a hand, palm facing him. "No, that is not what you asked to do this evening. I have no desire to speak to that woman. I told you of my meeting her on the road to Florinu's farm, and I made it quite clear I had no further reason to talk. I do not trust sorcerers, especially Healers. They have lied to me about what happened to my mother. They are deliberately keeping the truth from all non-magic-users."

"Sorceress Helinu would not lie--"

Merina cut him off. "She did, right to my face. Midwife Serafinu told me Delaphinu suffered a grid burnout. Helinu tried to cover that up."

Trinames shrugged. "I don't know what that is, but perhaps her answer sounded evasive because we non-magic-users don't have enough knowledge of magic to understand such things."

Trinames stretched his arms out, imploring her to go with him. "I am the one asking you to talk to her. I wanted her to explain why I am leaving early and..."

"And what? Give the two of you the opportunity to pressure me into being tested. Why are you doing this, Trinames? This is not like you at all."

"If you would just listen to her--I know how you feel about magic use, but..."

Merina barely suppressed a scream, remembering where they were. "You know and you try to pull this trick on me. How could you?"

"I'm sorry, Mer. I should have told you why I wanted to talk with you tonight. I was afraid you would tell me you would not give me the chance to arrange a meeting between the Sorceress and us."

Tears flowed from Merina's eyes. She didn't want that to happen, but the frustration she felt with Trinames left her no other way to react. She realized he was only trying to make her accept his belief that becoming a Healer was the right choice for him. He just would not see that she could not accept his becoming a sorcerer without having to give up her distrust and loathing for magic.

Fighting the strong urge to lash out at him, to punish his wrong thinking, Merina swiped the stream of tears off her face with her right hand. "As you see, you would have been correct about how I would respond to such a meeting. What I don't understand is why you persist in thinking I cannot love you without loving magic. As long as your using Power does not lead to what happened to my mother, I could not care less if spell casting is what you want to do with your life. Just don't expect me to ignore any sign that magic is interfering with our lives."

Trinames nodded. That smile she loved so much found its way to his lips. Perhaps he had really accepted that he could not change her mind on magic. He stepped close to her and gently kissed a tear from her cheek.

Merina hugged him tightly, burying her forehead in the hollow made by his collarbone and neck. He responded with a hand pressing on the back of her head and another patting her gently on the back. She felt more tears leaking from her eyes and wetting his robe but stifled the urge to say anything. The relief she felt in the comfort of his arms should not have made her cry, but nothing about herself lately made sense to her. She lifted her face to welcome the kiss she hoped was waiting for her and watched in shock as Trinames was hauled backward out of her arms.

The hand clasped over his mouth bore a tattoo of a fierce animal, and the eyes that stared at her from behind Trinames's head were deep set. The hooked nose completed the identification of her lover's assailant as Tieri. Merina started to lunge forward to help Trinames, but a sword flashed from her left, and the point cut through her shirt and pierced her chest between her breasts.

"Don't try it."

The command, in Saphradean with a very heavy accent, came in a female voice. It stopped Merina as effectively as the steel cutting through her skin. Merina looked at the wielder of the sword and realized the woman's face was as hard as her voice. Middle-aged, heavily tanned--the woman could easily be mistaken for a man. Her stare betrayed nothing feminine. The woman raised a hand to her face, where Merina saw the same tattoo on the back as on the one holding her lover's mouth shut. The woman's fingers opened, and she blew a white powder out of her palm. Merina instinctively closed her eyes but gasped in surprise. A numbness began spreading across her chest, and she collapsed, blackness enveloping her mind.

She stabbed me! Am I dead? But I don't feel any pain. I can't move! Merina tried to cry out, but all she heard was a low moan.

"Be still," a voice said from the blackness beyond her mind. "The poison is wearing off."

Calmness spread through Merina's body. I felt that, I must be alive! She drew a breath and heard the sound of air flowing into her lungs. She exhaled it slowly, but a coughing spasm cut off the question she tried to ask.

"Relax!" the voice ordered more sternly. Another surge of calmness, and Merina realized a spell was being used on her. Her cry of protest came out as a whimper to her ears, and she lost consciousness again.

"You can open your eyes now, Merina."

Merina awoke in a whirl of confusion. Had she been knocked out or spelled into a trance? She willed her eyelids to open and fought back a moment of panic when all she saw was a blurry flicker of light. As she concentrated on the light, the shape of an oil lamp on a table above came into focus.

She sensed the softness of a bed underneath her and the warmth of a blanket over her. She reached with her right hand across her chest and found the hole in her blouse. Her fingers pushed through the cloth and touched where the sword had cut. The skin was whole.

"It was just a nick, dear. Getting the blood out of that pretty blouse will take you more work than I had to perform in healing you."

Merina recognized Helinu's voice now. "You used magic on me?"

"I know, I know. To tell the truth I didn't need to heal that wound, but since I had to stop the poison anyhow, I went ahead and did it. It did not cost me much Power."

"Poison? The blade was poisoned?" Merina croaked out.

"Don't think so, don't know for sure. The wound was very clean. No, the poison I had to stop was from a powder. You had it in your eyes, nose, all over your face. I couldn't tell from your life signs whether you were near death or in a deep trance. I have never seen anything like that before. I didn't want to take the time to analyze for what kind of poison, so I used the strongest spell I had. Now that, my dear, took a lot out of me."

Merina realized she owed Helinu her life. Anger at the Healer for violating her with magic was no way to show her gratitude. "Thank you for saving me," Merina said grudgingly.

Helinu looked pleased. "You're welcome. Now, do you know where you are?"

Groggily, Merina looked around. "Yes, this is my room in the Wolf's Head."

Nodding, the Healer asked, "And what day is this?"

The room had no windows. Merina had no way to tell how much time had passed since she fell unconscious. "It was Settling Day."

"It is now the morning after. Do you know where Trinames is?"

"They took him--I think. Two men and a woman were pulling him from the room. I tried to stop them. You haven't seen him at all?" Merina asked with mounting panic.

Shaking her head, Helinu stretched a hand out to calm Merina. Perhaps she did not use a spell because she was drained of Power and, besides, knew it would only make Merina's distress greater. "The town guard is looking, dear. No one in the inn saw him leave, and Captain Garlantis has thoroughly searched the Wolf's Head. It has been quite an interesting night we spent together. Is Trinames's disappearance the reason I found you lifeless, sprawled on the floor with a bloody hole in your chest? You gave me quite a start, Merina, I must say."

Casting the blanket off her, Merina sat up. In the light of the lamp she examined the circle of blood staining her blouse. Helinu was seated in a chair near the bed, watching her. Merina moved each arm carefully, feeling no pain, then swung her legs slowly off the bed.

She told the Healer what had led up to her conversation with Trinames. "He said he had to return to you in an hour and he wanted me to return with him so we could talk. That was not what I had planned to do with our time! I told him I didn't want to talk to anyone--I just wanted food and time alone with him. It started an argument." The sadness on Helinu's face told Merina the sorceress knew the cause of the fight. Merina glared at her. "He said he wanted me to meet you about testing. Did you put him up to that?"

Helinu shook her head. "No, dear, it was his idea. When he said you were coming in for Settling Day, I told him it was not a good time for me to administer the Test. If the person being tested doesn't want it to happen, the results cannot be trusted. I just wanted the three of us to talk about it in the hope of persuading you to want to be tested."

"I refused to go with him. He said it was important to him that I be tested, and I told him it was not what I wanted. We said a lot of angry things to each other."

"I know. When I came to the inn to find out why Trinames had not shown up at my home as he promised, I asked the landlord for the room number you were staying in. He gave me quite an earful about the ruckus the two of you had been making. Not hearing anything at the time, I asked if you or Trinames had left. He said neither of you had, so he was also curious as to why all the noise stopped. He suggested--"

"That we had killed each other? The landlord knows me better than that. I stay here all the time when I accompany my uncle on Settling Day. Yes, I have a temper, but I don't get into brawls."

Helinu smoothed her robe over her knees and said coyly, "No, he thought you might be making up."

Picking her way to the other chair in the room, Merina sat gingerly. She discovered changing positions made her dizzy. "He was not far wrong, Healer. We were just starting to kiss when he was jerked out of my embrace by two Tieri men and a woman."

"Tieri? The only one of the wandering tribes I've seen in town today is Delnos."

"Believe me, these were Tieri. They were trained warriors and well-armed. Before I could do anything, the woman stopped me with a sword at my heart. She blew that powder in my face, and I passed out."

Helinu sat forward and looked intensely at Merina. "I've been sitting here trying to figure out why someone would poison you when they could have just thrust deeper with the knife that made the wound over your heart. It only makes sense if they wanted you unconscious. Which means the powder was a sleeping drug--a very powerful one, and quick acting. The way you were sprawled on the floor, you must have collapsed while standing up. That means the drug works on your muscles. Oh, dear, I wish I had saved some of the powder."

Merina brushed her fingers over her face to feel for the powder Helinu said had covered it.

"I washed it off. They taught us at Byklandes to neutralize the drug before we healed the victim, that way we wouldn't be poisoned ourselves if we touched it. I should have saved some of that powder so I could send it to Byklandes. I'm sure the Mage Healers there would be very interested in finding out what it was. It could have such marvelous healing uses."

"If you want to sleep the sleep of death, it would be useful. I have no memory of anything until I heard you tell me to be still."

"No pain, nothing? My, that powder would be such a marvelous thing to have. I hope these attackers have some more on them. We must get you to the Guard and have you repeat your story. They didn't believe anything happened here!"

Confused, Merina blurted out, "Don't believe? Did they see this?" She pointed to the bloody stain on her blouse.

Helinu picked up the bag by her feet and stood. "Once I was sure you had not been killed, I went back to the landlord and told him what I had found. He was really shocked and confused. He swore no one had left your room since the yelling stopped--especially not Trinames. I told him you were alone in the room and I was treating your wounds. He sent for the Dysandesian guards, who showed up several hours ago and searched the inn, finding nothing. Yes, they noticed the stain. I had to stop them from exposing your breasts looking for the wound. We had better talk to them if what you just told me about Tieri is true."

"Sorceress, you sound like you don't believe me."

Helinu put her bag down and approached Merina. The Healer gently enfolded Merina in a hug. "I know I healed a cut. I know I found you unconscious, and my sensing your body told me you were paralyzed by something. I know you woke in a panic and I had to calm you with a spell. There was powder on your face and hair, which I removed. There may be other explanations for the existence of these things I know, so I am open to finding the truth."

Even this close to Helinu, Merina did not feel the unease the older woman often provoked in her. Merina pushed the Healer away gently to look into Helinu's eyes. She could see the sorceress was exhausted, drawn down by the time and effort spent caring for her. If the Healer really did want to find the truth in what just happened here, maybe she would be open to another truth.

"My fight with Trinames was over my lack of trust in Healers. You lied when you told me Delaphinu cared. Let's go the Guard and talk to them. Maybe they have found out what happened to Trinames."

Chapter 8

The Guard Captain was well known to Merina, and she considered him a friend. When she was growing up, about the age when little girls fall in love with heroic men, she had cajoled him into teaching her the rudiments of sword fighting. Because the weapon was too heavy for her, he switched her to the long knife she eventually mastered. Her uncle had done most of the real training, but Garlantis taught her the finer points. From his grim expression, Merina knew she was putting a strain on that old friendship.

"Mistress Merina, please be reasonable!" Captain Garlantis urged her. "We are doing everything we can to find Neophyte Trinames."

"Which, from what you have told me, Captain, is written a report and told the town sentries to be alert for his departing. I didn't see anyone searching for him as I came to your office, and the guards I saw in the street were obviously not looking interested in anyone but young females."

"You have to admit that bloodstain attracts a lot of attention, Mistress."

Merina stood from the chair she had taken while explaining what happened and stalked over to the desk Garlantis sat behind, leaning over and pointing to the cut blouse. "I was attacked, Captain. They took my fiancé by force. Why aren't you searching for him?"

Sitting up straight, Garlantis shifted his gaze from her chest and glared into her eyes. "No one in the inn saw any Tieri dragging Trinames, bound or unbound, out of the building. No one in the streets saw anything out of the ordinary, and there were many town folk out walking by the inn, enjoying the setting sun. It was not dark, Mistress."

Merina stepped back and folded her arms across her chest. She tried to speak without overemphasizing her words. "Then they are still in the Wolf's Head Inn."

Shaking his head, Captain Garlantis said wearily, "I searched the inn myself. I know every hiding place thieves have been using for years, and I checked for trap doors or newly cut entrances. Your room has no windows. They are not in the inn, Merina."

Sorceress Helinu spoke up, agreeing with the Guard Captain. "I saw him inspect the room, dear."

Merina didn't turn toward Helinu. She knew she would not get any support from the Healer, so she didn't try for any. "And the Tieri?"

Standing, Garlantis walked around his desk and halted before Merina, folding his arms in the same posture as hers. A foot taller than Merina, he looked imposing in his leather armor. "Listen, Mistress. The Tieri are not allowed to trade anywhere in Saphradea unless they report themselves, in person, to the local guard commander. We are required to report their presence to the Royal Army commander in Byklandes. The Tieri are so distrusted, here and everywhere in the Domains, that they can't move without our knowledge. The only Tieri here is Delnos Pathla m'Lothur. I have never seen him or his uncle, who really owns the trade here in Dysandes, in green armor. I have never seen a Tieri woman alone, without the presence of her clansmen, in town. The only person who has seen these people is you."

Merina returned Garlantis's stern glare with one of her own. "Are you calling me a liar, Guard Captain?"

"No, Mistress, I am not. I just don't believe your story. With all respect to Healer Helinu, I think you hit your head in the fall you took and are not thinking right."

This made Merina laugh. "You think I am crazy, Guard Captain?"

"I think you had a fight with your fiancé. You would not go with him as he asked, so when he started to leave, you threatened to take your life.

You nicked yourself with that knife I trained you with, but Trinames walked out anyway. You started after him, slipped and fell against the washstand, knocking the bath powder into the air. You continued falling to the floor, knocking yourself unconscious."

Garlantis delivered this theory with such calm seriousness that Merina could only stare at him, her mouth moving without uttering a word. He continued, "The guard did not see any powder, but he did report you had taken a recent wash. I think Healer Helinu was trying to be helpful by believing your story rather than what really happened. Even then, I told you I would continue to look for Tieri that don't exist, and we will be on the lookout for Trinames when he returns later today. Now, I am a busy man, Mistress. Good day."

Fuming, Merina left Sorceress Helinu at the Guard Captain's office, cutting off Helinu's attempt to speak with her by telling the Healer her magic had apparently failed if Garlantis was correct. Merina stormed through the hall where the off-duty guards rested, glaring at anyone who tried to greet her. She pushed her way past one guard who made the mistake of entering the door Merina was marching through, muttering "Idiot" at him as she exited the building.

Where are you going? she asked herself. Wolf's Head.

Why? her mind queried calmly. Last known place Trinames was seen.

Having convinced herself, Merina headed in the direction of the inn with such determination on her face that the few villagers she met along the route stepped clear of the angry young woman striding toward them with blood in her eyes and on her chest. By the time she entered the Wolf's Head, she was breathing heavy, but the exercise had drained some of her anger.

The landlord stepped out from behind the bar he was tending and greeted her, "Mistress Merina, I'm so sorry about Trinames. I'm sure he'll turn up soon."

"You told the guards you did not see him leave. So you believe he is missing now, sir?" Merina said calmly.

"I searched the inn with Captain Garlantis, Mistress. Trinames must have gotten out when my back was turned--how else could he not be here?" the man asked reasonably.

Merina almost suggested to the landlord that Tieri took him, but she was tired of people telling her there were no Tieri in Dysandes but Delnos. "I will be staying the night, landlord. I'll leave in the morning."

She hurried to her room and pushed the heavy door open, examining the latch as she passed. It was intact, with no signs of being forced. Closing the door, she inspected the privacy bar. It moved easily into place, and when the latch was turned down, she could not shift the bar. There was no way someone could have inched it back out of the holding bracket without scratching the metal shaft.

Merina turned away from the door and scanned the room, trying to see it not as she had as a guest, but as a hunter seeking the presence of game spoor hidden in the forest floor.

The floor was bare wood except for a square of carpet between the bed and the fireplace. At the foot of the bed was the nightstand with its washbasin and towel rack. The floor where she had been standing with Trinames was bare wood. There was no powder of any kind on it that she could see where she stood now.

Merina stooped down and studied the floor. It had been cleaned recently. Whether it was Helinu's doing, or the landlord had sent in the cleaning maid, the results were the same. No blood or powder--or tracks in the dust that might once have been there. Kneeling, she crept across the floor looking for some kind of latch that would manifest itself into an entrance of a trap door. Nothing appeared abnormal.

Could it be hidden by magic? she wondered. I don't believe in that. Don't be foolish, she chided herself.

Pulling the rug away to look underneath it only created more dust that hindered her search. She would certainly tell the landlord that his cleaning servants were shirking their duties, but more importantly it meant the good Captain Garlantis had not searched as thoroughly as he said he had. Using the table lamp, she stared under the bed, which was too heavy for her to move. There were no signs of its having been moved, although the bare floor underneath had been dusted in the past. If the trap door was under the bed, it was doubtful that even two grown men could have come from there, made their attack, and returned, moving the bed back into place. Neither could Garlantis alone do so.

Standing, Merina brushed the dust from the rug off her skirt and walked over to the basin, which she found filled with clean water. She washed her hands and wiped them off with the towel, which she saw had also been replaced. Staring at the washstand, she knew that Garlantis's explanation was plausible, but not likely. The basin was made of fired clay. It would surely have broken if dropped to the floor. She remembered clearly that she had put away her powder after using it, just before Trinames had knocked at the door.

Turning away from the washstand, she walked to the stone wall to the left of the door and started her search. Pushing and shoving at random stones frustrated her to the point that she gave up quickly, relying on holding the lamp close to the stone and searching by eye to spot any door hidden in the surface. An hour passed fruitlessly.

Merina completed her search and sat dejectedly in the chair that Sorceress Helinu had spent the night in. *He's not here! The Tieri must have gotten him out of the room. But how? No one saw any Tieri. Haven't you heard everyone say there are no Tieri in Dysandes except Delnos?*

"Delnos!" she spoke the name aloud. "I am going to pay a visit to the only Tieri in Dysandes." Standing, she headed for the door, unbolted it, and stalked out of the room, pulling the door shut with a loud thump. The landlord answered her curt question, pointing to the south of town, and watched her march from the inn.

Merina followed the landlord's direction and found the warehouse well off the main road at the southern end of town, tucked behind a long line of shops. She thought it odd that the entrance was so inconvenient to anyone interested in buying goods from the trader. Perhaps Delnos and his uncle did their trading only on the road from their wagon.

The door was small, with a thick iron bar grill latched back against the wall. The lock on the grill gate looked as if it could withstand the assault of many sledgehammers for a long time--as would the heavy wooden door it protected. No windows, just a peephole to let the owner inside look out.

She knocked on the door, hurting her knuckles with the effort to evoke a sound from the solid panel. She was reaching for her knife to use its hilt end when the door swung open on well-oiled hinges. Delnos stood facing her, a smile flirting around the corners of his mouth. Whether it signaled welcome or amusement, she could not tell. When his deep-set eyes flitted down to her breasts, as all men's did, he frowned slightly.

"You're wounded, Mistress?"

"Was--Healer Helinu fixed that. I haven't taken the time to wash the stain out. I'll save you the trouble of asking how it got there. It was done by one of your people," Merina said brashly.

Stepping out of the way, he motioned for her to enter. Merina swept past and glanced quickly around her, wondering if the two abductors might have left some evidence of their presence. The room was small, with only a desk along the front wall and a small fireplace opposite it about ten feet away. With two chairs on a bare wooden floor and the ceiling close overhead constructed from very solid-looking boards, the chamber seemed more of a wooden cell than a shop front. One single door to the right of the fireplace was both barred and locked with the twin of the lock on the gate.

"If that were true, Mistress, then it would have had to be me. I know of no Tieri in town."

"I could have taken you in a fight, Tieri, but not the two who just wrested away my betrothed from me. They were hardened warriors. There wasn't an ounce of fat on either the man or the woman. And fast."

Delnos offered her a chair, which she accepted. He sat on the corner of the desk and crossed his arms over his chest--perhaps to cover his slight paunch. "What makes you think they were my people?"

"Oh, the deep-set eyes, the long thin nose, and the same funny accent you have. Their faces were weathered like yours--spent a lot of time outside, as you have. Do you think I can't recognize Tieri, sir?"

Delnos rubbed the top of his nose, as if convincing himself it was as long as she said. "No, but I can assure you that despite what your people say about mine, we are not kidnappers. We have rarely gained any profit from ransom, and for that reason, we have an unwillingness to trade in humanity."

"They were Tieri, Delnos," Merina said firmly.

"I don't doubt you, Mistress. Can you describe them further?"

"They had on dark green leather armor, not the thick stuff like Saphradean Guard wear. No helmets. Swords were narrow-bladed and sharp on one side--at least the one that cut me was. The female did that, and she also blew a powder in my face, which knocked me out. They got away with no one seeing them," Merina added bitterly.

"Not quite true, Mistress. You saw them. Where did this happen?"

"At the Wolf's Head Inn. Trinames and I were alone in my room." A blush heated her cheeks. "We were sharing a kiss when he was pulled from my arms and a sword stuck in my chest."

"And you heard nothing? Don't you bar your door when you want privacy?" Delnos asked.

"Of course I did," Merina shot back.

Delnos spread his hands out in a gesture of peace. "Then how did they get in? A window, a trap door?"

"Neither. I checked afterward." Merina realized the Tieri was trying to be helpful and not asking questions to annoy her.

"Did you look in the ceiling?" Delnos asked.

"No," Merina said with a frustrated groan. What else did I forget to do or say? Then she remembered. "One other thing, Tieri. Both of them had tattoos on the backs of their hands. Some kind of animal, maybe a tiger."

"Ah, then they are indeed Tieri. We have a clan of assassins called the Kanchala. They receive the tattoo of a dragon when they complete their training. Which makes this all very curious. Why would a Kanchala pay you a visit?"

When Merina heard the word assassins, her heart jumped, and she barely heard Delnos's question. "Assassins? They are going to kill Trinames?"

Shaking his head, Delnos spoke calmly. "You would have found him dead when you awoke, Mistress. Why take someone off and kill them later? The Kanchala are highly trained and very shrewd. They do not make stupid mistakes, and they always complete what they are paid to do. Because of this, their services are very expensive. Someone with a lot of gold wants your young man out of your life."

Merina stared at the Tieri, stunned. "He has no money. He has no enemies--he's a healer in training--he does only good things for people."

"And you? Do you not have money?"

Shaking her head, Merina said angrily, "Not yet. What I have saved would not bribe a poorly paid thief, much less one of your Kanpalas."

"Kanchala. Is there no one who could help you pay a ransom? Your aunt?"

"Only if she sold the land I gave her. No, there is no one." Merina gazed beyond the Tieri for a moment. The thought of one who might lend her the money jumped into her mind. Dame Brischelu might be willing to do so. I love you, Trinames, but if she hired someone to get you back, that means I would have to mate with Markinis. That is too high a price to pay.

Delnos seemed to be waiting for her to finish her thought. When she looked back at him, he asked, "Do you have enemies, Mistress?"

"None. I have never cheated anyone in my business affairs. Made a few mad, but to do this to me in revenge?" Merina shook her head in doubt.

Delnos asked gently, "A jilted lover perhaps?"

Merina's eye narrowed, and she spat out, "Markinis--that snake. He has the money, and he wants me. It has to be him."

The Tieri shook his head. "No, I think not. My uncle knows the man all too well. From what Jalanos has told me, Markinis is not one to think in terms of conspiracy and intrigue--which is the way of the Assassins Guild. Markinis is a man of action--if he wanted Trinames out of your life, he would try to first buy him off. If that didn't work, he would threaten your betrothed to scare him off. Paying someone to do what he could do himself is not his way."

Merina thought about Delnos's words, remembering that she herself had said Markinis was not a bully, at least not with men. "Then maybe his father, Calandis, tried to do this without Markinis's knowledge."

"Ah, Mistress, that is a possibility. When Markinis hears of Trinames's disappearance, he will most likely appear at your doorstep and volunteer in the search. He will be entirely sincere in his wanting to help. People will see this and not suspect him. Yes, Calandis has shown himself in the past to use devious means to get what he wants."

Intrigued, Merina asked, "When was that?"

Delnos stood and turned to open one of the two drawers in the desk he had been sitting on. He pulled out a silver flask and two glass goblets, filling them with water. He handed one to Merina, who felt the chill on the glass. She took a sip and found that it was wine, not water.

"Let's just say that his taking a noblewoman as his life-mate was not done purely out of love or desire," Delnos said before taking a quick drink from his goblet.

"Then he is more than a rich farmer from the wilds of Saphradea as he likes to portray himself?" Merina asked.

"He is. His influence comes from more than money or the size of his holding. Which is why I suspect he could be the one who would know of the Kanchala and their uses," the Tieri said, finishing his wine.

"Who else would know?" Merina asked, draining her glass. The wine was slightly sweet and cool, and she found her body reacting quickly to its essence.

"Other than Jalanos or myself, no one. I am a man of trade, and as I have said before, knowing the people I trade with is useful in my business. What bothers me, Mistress," Delnos said, refilling her glass, "is that Calandis would have come to us to arrange for the Kanchala. He didn't. When did you last see Markinis? I assume that is when you told him you were not interested in his proposal."

Merina took a much smaller sip than her first one. The wine was definitely going to her head. "A month at most. Why?"

"That is barely enough time for Calandis to go to his own contacts in Byklandes to arrange for the Kanchala. Now, it is possible he has been planning this for a long time. He could have decided you were the match for his son long ago, and when young Trinames showed up, it created a problem for Calandis."

A chill shot down Merina's spine. He might have, but I know of one who made that decision long ago. The Dame! She noticed Delnos had not filled his glass. Seeing her eyes on him, the Tieri put the stopper in the flask and returned it to the desk. He looked up at her and smiled. "I am not trying to get you drunk, Mistress. The wine relaxes you, which in turn allows your mind to be open to new thoughts. The events of the day have put you on edge."

Merina took a deeper sip of the wine. "If you mean upset, then that is true."

"Captain Garlantis told me you would be visiting me. He wanted to know if any of my people had come into town without his knowledge. I truthfully told him no. He does not believe in your story, as you are well aware. I suspect if Calandis is involved, he would want Captain Garlantis and all of Dysandes to continue to not believe in Tieri kidnappers. I may be able to find out the truth by questioning Calandis. Is my approach reasonable to you, Mistress?"

Finishing the wine, Merina nodded. She was not sure if it was reasonable, or if the wine was drugged and she no longer felt like fighting. Delnos smiled and offered his hand to pull her out of her chair. "Then let's go find out how the Kanchala made off with your young man."

Merina woke coughing, her throat irritated by a dryness that she thought at first was due to thirst. As she coughed again, she sat upright, looking about in confusion. Why am I in bed? What is going on? She swung her legs off the bed and saw she was fully clothed, the bloodstained blouse obvious as she looked down to place her feet on the floor.

A memory of being in this position earlier flashed in her mind, and she remembered that she had sat on the edge of her bed to watch Tieri Delnos search her room. Merina glanced up and scanned the room for him. He was gone. She stood and ran to the door. The latch was pulled out of place. She heard a board creak behind her and, as she turned to look, started coughing hard.

The air around her was filled with dust. She grabbed her skirt and covered her nose and mouth, blinking as the dust swirled around her. It flowed past her head, and she looked up to see where it came from. A pair of legs flashed by her. She would have screamed but for another coughing fit that cut the sound off.

Delnos stood beside her, a big smile spread across his face. "As I thought, Mistress. They came from above," he said, pointing to the ceiling.

Merina walked to the washstand and picked up the pitcher sitting there. She hefted it to her lips and swallowed several large mouthfuls of water, splashing an equal amount past her lips and soaking her front. Gasping, she set the pitcher down and turned to face the Tieri.

"Damn it, man! Give a warning next time you appear out of midair."

Delnos watched the dust settling to the floor. "That explains the dust on the rug that you and I both found. They must have entered the room before you arrived from the market, then removed the dust." He looked up. "I can barely see the hole, but I suspect they hid it with a spell."

"Magic...they are sorcerers?" Merina asked.

"No, and yes, Mistress. Tieri are not like the rest of the Domain's people. We do not Test our young and send the promising to training lodges to turn them into magic-users. We have a few Tieri who learn the ways of magic from our ancients, who learned it from their ancients. Most clans have a woman who can heal and do tricks to amuse the unwary. The Kanchala do as well, except they use their magic more for illusion than healing and parlor tricks."

"So you think they were waiting in here for me the whole time I was here?" Merina said softly. The presence of the assassins watching her bathe did not bother her as much as did their seeing Trinames and her kissing. Not that they let us do much of that.

"Very likely," Delnos said, then added cautiously, "I have further news."

Taking the nearest chair, Merina sighed. "I hope it is not bad. I have had nothing but bad news today."

The Tieri took the other chair and leaned forward, resting his elbows across his knees. In a softer tone, he said, "You fell asleep shortly after I started searching. When I had finished my search, I decided to check the roof above us. This wing of the building is only one story, where the main entrance room has another floor. Rather than wake you, I decided to let you sleep and go outside alone. The streets would be getting dark..."

Startled, Merina asked, "What time is it now?"

"The first hour past midnight," he answered.

"We have lost the entire day!" Merina cried.

"Please calm yourself, Mistress, and lower your voice. They believe you alone in here."

"But we have not found Trinames..." Merina started to moan.

"We might have, if you will let me finish."

Merina shut her mouth and choked back the rest of her complaint. Her heart leaped at the hope of her love being found, and she waved to Delnos to speed up his story.

"It was better for me to search at night than with people watching me the whole time. I didn't want to be caught on the roof under any conditions. People already think Tieri are thieves, and Captain Garlantis would need no further excuse to throw me out of Dysandes."

"That he would, so..."

"I ran into Calandis talking to the Wolf's Head's landlord, who was tending the bar as usual this time of night. Calandis called me over and asked me if I had seen any of my people in town lately. He and the landlord had been discussing Trinames's disappearance. It was the perfect opportunity for me to talk with Calandis. He ordered us drinks, and we retired to a booth."

"And?" Merina cut in anxiously.

Sighing, Delnos continued, "I don't believe he knows anything about the Kanchala, let alone anyone who could actually arrange for their services."

Merina twisted her hands around each other in nervous anticipation of what Delnos would finally end up telling her. "Maybe he lied to you?"

"No," Delnos said in a soothing tone. "My uncle told me Calandis has a nervous tic at the corner of the left side of his mouth when he lies, and his eyes would betray him as well. He did not lie to me, and what's more telling, the man was more than half drunk before we talked. He is worried, all right--he thinks Markinis will be blamed if Trinames does not show up soon."

"Damn it, Delnos, how does this tell us where Trinames is?"

"Part of being successful in a search is to know where the person you are seeking isn't. I believe that Kanchala took your betrothed. I just proved how they got in and out. The Kanchala are masters of disguise and could just as easily use illusion spells to make it even harder to recognize them or their victim."

"So..." Merina stretched her hands toward Delnos as if she meant to shake Trinames's whereabouts out of him.

The Tieri shifted back out of her reach. "Captain Garlantis walked over to the landlord and told him to tell you that the village guards had not seen anyone enter or leave town except for a party of hunters that left Dysandes at noon today, and that he was not giving up on the search."

"You think--" Merina started to say much too loudly.

Delnos stopped her by reaching out and touching her lips with his pointing finger. "Shh." He nodded. "It is likely the hunters are the ones we should search for. I will leave as I arrived just now. In the morning I will meet you outside with supplies and horses to search after your young man. Be ready early, Mistress."

Delnos took the rooftop route back to his uncle's warehouse. As he crept along the roof tiles, knowing which were loose or missing and avoiding a wrong step that would send them crashing to the ground, he wondered just what the Kanchala were doing. He had not been told of any other Tieri being sent to interact with the woman he had been assigned to evaluate.

Ducking behind a row of chimneys, he watched the village guard patrol the road beneath him, their attention more on the conversation they were having than on their job. Was that the reason the Kanchala were here--to do his job? He had reported that Merina had reached the point of her maturity when she was ready to assume the role the Unnamed had for her.

The patrol passed, and Delnos continued on his own way. Had his message been intercepted, he wondered. Using a source to send the one-word signal was always risky. Had it fallen onto the wrong mind? Were the Tieri assassins he would seek tomorrow actually Kanchala-zo, the enemy of his people? Was he leading both Merina and himself into danger?

Stopping on the roof of his warehouse, Delnos wiped the sweat off his brow. He was not as young as he had once been--able to skulk through the night without ever raising a sweat. Or was it fear that soaked him?

Chapter 9

True to his word, Delnos arrived at the Wolf's Head the next morning with a horse for Merina in trail, with heavily laden saddlebags on both horses. By all appearances they were equipped to go on a hunt, which in reality was exactly what Delnos and Merina were doing--except not for game. Merina strapped her baggage from the Wolf's Head on top of the camping gear and forwent the urge to inspect the saddlebags themselves to ensure Delnos had everything she would need. The Tieri was an expeditor, trader, and seasoned traveler, after all.

Merina had selected a long-sleeved shirt of sturdy material that she wore when riding around the farm, which, along with leather pants, provided protection from the brush she rode through crossing between pastures. Her boots replaced the more flimsy sandals she had worn in the market. The long knife at her waist completed her usual work outfit.

When she mounted her horse and looked over at Delnos, he handed her a farmhand's field hat. She took it from him with a smile and placed it on her head--it fit perfectly. Delnos nodded his approval, and she wondered how he had known what size to get for her. He must have a good eye for sizing women's clothes, a skill a Tieri trader would cultivate.

"Thank you for the hat, sir. Now if there is nothing more we need to do, let's begin our search."

Delnos turned his horse around and headed south to the not-too-distant edge of town. Merina followed, noticing the landlord of the Wolf's Head standing in the entrance of the inn, with her note to her foster parents in his hand. He waved it to assure her he was on the task of delivering it to them. Merina waved back and spurred her horse to catch up with the Tieri.

Finding the tracks into the woods was not difficult. The guards who had been on duty the day before had the same watch today and readily pointed out where the hunters had entered the forest. The tracks left on the forest floor were simple to follow. Merina muttered that this search was going to be too easy.

"They are deliberately leaving us a trail, Mistress."

Merina looked over at Delnos and did not try to hide the disbelief in her voice. "Why would these phantom assassins of your people, the Kanchala, do that? They can sneak into a crowded tavern and snatch my beloved, removing him from a town full of revelers in broad daylight--a feat I am still having trouble believing--but then they deliberately leave a clue for any pursuit to follow?"

"They let you see them, did they not?"

"How could they have not? They took him from my arms!"

Delnos nodded. "And you are still alive? Did you not say they were armed and threatened you with swords? I assure you that they could have abducted Neophyte Trinames without your knowledge. They chose the time and place deliberately."

"They blew a poison at my face--how is that not trying to kill me?" Merina stopped her horse and turned it so she could face Delnos directly.

"It was not intended to kill you, but to render you unconscious."

"So I can wake up minutes later to raise an alarm and possibly foil their escape?"

Delnos rested his hands on his saddle horn and slightly relaxed his stiffened posture. She could see he did not like her angry questioning. He said calmly, "You said you were out for hours until Sorceress Helinu revived you. They escaped, didn't they?"

"No search discovered them in Dysandes--I'll give you that, sir."

"They were not afraid of pursuit, Mistress. The Kanchala made their way through Dysandes with Trinames without being seen by anyone. If they were worried about being caught, they should have left the town that night. No one saw them leave, which doesn't mean anything because the assassins would not have allowed that to happen."

"Yes, but a guard saw them entering the forest just beyond the village walls," Merina countered.

"Why else would they wait until yesterday to leave unless they were sure the Guard Captain was not mounting a real search for them. Remember, the guard did not see four Tieri leaving town--which would have been highly suspicious in itself since none were known to enter. They reported a group of hunters. You and I are making the assumption that it was the Kanchala in disguise."

Groaning in frustration, Merina forced herself to relax, wanting very much to scream at the Tieri. Instead she mirrored his calmness with her own. "Then why did they let themselves be seen by the guard?"

"The guard had no reason to chase them, so the Kanchala had no fear of pursuit by the guard. What they did need was a starting point for the pursuit they knew you would make."

"And how did they know I would be doing that?"

Removing a water skin from his belt, Delnos offered it to Merina first, who waved it away. He took a long drink, offered once again. Merina reached for it and drank. She was mildly surprised at the coolness of the water. How did he do that? When she handed it back to him, he draped it over the saddle horn.

"That is why they left you alive. They knew you would have trouble convincing Garlantis that your betrothed was taken by Tieri for two reasons. First, your argument before his disappearance was heard by many, so it was easy for anyone to surmise a lovers' quarrel led to his leaving. Secondly, accusing the Tieri of the abduction made no sense since no one had seen any Tieri in town but myself."

"All of that may be true, but it does not answer the question of why would they know I would come after them myself."

"You saw them without their disguises and would recognize them as Tieri. You would then come to me, and I would realize who they were. If there was to be any hope of ransom, you would need me to negotiate it. They reasoned we would follow them--as we have done."

"Then we should catch up with them soon enough, Tieri. With a trail like they are leaving, we don't have to waste much time tracking them."

The trail continued through the forest, staying out of densely packed trees as much as possible and cutting through glades whenever they appeared. The tracks had started east but were slowly turning to the north. The ground was becoming more hilly than flat, and riding to the top of one hill showed nothing but a sea of treetops and, to the northeast, a mountain ridge. After a day of following the Kanchala with no conversation, Merina broke her silence to ask Delnos why the assassins were leading them so far into the wilderness. The Tieri did not have an answer for her. He told her the Kanchala's trail was not going toward any town or village Delnos knew of. He told her Dysandes was the largest village this far north in Saphradea, with only a few hamlets and small holdings that his uncle had ventured into when desiring to expand his trade route.

Merina said with a nervous glance at the horizon, "We can't be very far from the beginnings of the Non-Lands."

"You are very right there, Mistress. That mountain range marks the Non-Lands."

Looking toward the west, Merina tried to judge how much daylight remained. "We should make camp soon," she suggested.

Delnos nodded. "Have you seen any sign of deer, boar, or anything bigger than squirrels all day?"

"No, and I would expect to. Plenty of birds, though," she said. "I wonder why we're not seeing game."

The answer to her question drifted from behind in an eerie howl that spooked the horses and sent a chill up Merina's spine. Wolves!

Delnos stared in the direction of the call and listened to the sound for a few minutes. He turned to Merina and said, "I don't think it has found our trail. They make a different call when they're on the hunt. Let's pick up the pace and see if we can reach that hill over there before dark. Wolves don't hunt at night."

Merina needed no further encouragement, nor did her horse.

"What is the chance that the Kanchala will see our fire and come to us?" Merina asked Delnos, tossing another branch into the flames. She had a blanket wrapped around her to block the cool night air.

Delnos laughed. "Is that why you keep feeding the flames? If so, you might succeed better than you hope. But if they wanted to talk to us now, why drag us all the way out here?"

"I asked you that earlier. It does not make sense." Merina poked at the burning log to make a bed of coals. An iron pot filled with water stood ready by her side to boil for tea. Their cold dinner of dried meat and bread needed something to wash it down.

"For all your skill with that knife, I doubt if you could defeat a single Kanchala, let alone three. So they are not worried about us recapturing your fiancé. If they really were trying to get us away from Dysandes so they could negotiate with us without fear of the guard, they would not have to go too far to accomplish that. That leads me to believe that negotiating ransom for Trinames is not what they have in mind."

Setting the pot over the red-hot coals, Merina pushed a few more coals around the bottom. She looked up and stared fearfully at Delnos.

"As you have already pointed out, if they wanted me dead, they could have done that in the inn. Why drag us all the way out here to do what assassins do?"

Delnos's deep-set eyes focused on her face, and he asked, "Is there a reason anyone would wish you dead?"

She nodded. "There is what some people might see as a reason for getting rid of me. Someone would gain my mother's holdings. I assume without me as her heir, the land I would be getting would be divided among her other siblings."

Delnos thoughtfully replied, "If the assassins had killed Trinames and you in your room on Settling Day, that would have left bodies. Your murder would have excited the guard into an investigation. Motives for the killings would be examined, and the most obvious one would be what you just stated. One of your relatives would be blamed."

Staring at the pot, Merina mused, "My uncles are all good-hearted men. I have never heard a single word dissenting from Grandfather's will. I have loved them all my life, and I'm sure of their love in return. No one in the valley would believe they would kill me themselves. And to hire a killer--it is also unbelievable."

"Someone did. What would happen if you just disappeared?"

"I haven't thought that out," Merina said quietly. "If I disappeared--that is a whole other thing. People might say I was just doing what my good-for-nothing mother had done--run off with one of the roving traders."

Delnos smiled gently. "Ah, the age-old excuses for runaway women. How many times have the Tieri been accused of that?"

Casting him a shamefaced glance, Merina muttered, "There are a lot of stories told..."

"Such stories are more legend than fact, Mistress. Many of my people have paid a price for acts of so-called justice done on the basis of lies and rumor."

"Why are your people so distrusted, Delnos?"

He glanced away from the firelight and toward the stars as if seeking her answer in them. "It has always been so, as far back as our memories go. We have never fought a war between us. We do not value the land as your people. We do not seek to control its resources. We do not owe allegiance to a king or prince, nor do we interfere in how anyone lives their life."

"You value trade--acquiring gold." Merina spoke from experience.

"Which is an understanding all the Domains have of us--something we have in common with them. And as I told you when we first met, all the Domains want to know what their friends and enemies are doing. Information is a very valued commodity for trade." Grinning, Delnos added, "As are our beautiful women and handsome men. This mixture always leads to volatile relationships."

Grinning back, Merina said playfully, "So we are back to my running off with a Tieri. Numerous people clearly saw you and me leaving town together. Your presence throws suspicion onto the Tieri, so it would not take much for Captain Garlantis to shift the blame of my disappearance onto you and your people."

"That has occurred to me, Mistress, but the Kanchala left an easily followed trail, as did we. I assume you told your foster parents in the note you sent them what your plan was, and I'm sure you did not say you were running off with me. If your disappearance would cause an alarm, your aunt and uncle would persuade Garlantis to track us down. If we had been killed out here, he would find our remains. The wolves could be blamed, as they are even now with the killing of cattle."

The pot was starting to boil, so Merina tossed some tea leaves into their cups and ladled hot water into them. Handing one to Delnos, she asked, "And if they don't find our bodies?"

The Tieri shrugged. "Then I get blamed, but that would mean the Kanchala would have to collude with bringing dishonor on their clan. They would not do that."

Merina sipped her tea, once more thinking through the line of reasoning they had followed. "It is rather hard to think someone would want me dead just for the land I will inherit. As I said, I don't believe my relatives are the kind of people who would go through all this trouble. From what you say about the cost of hiring Kanchala, I doubt it would profit any one of my uncles and aunts to try that."

The Tieri blew across his cup and took a slow drink. "This is good tea. Did you grow it yourself?"

Merina nodded, then said, "What other reason do you suggest, Delnos?"

He finished his tea and held it out for a refill of hot water. "The only thing that really makes sense about dragging us out into the wilderness is that they are leading us to a rendezvous."

Riding at a trot into the clearing gave Merina no time to react to the horrible scene that leaped into view. She reined her horse with a hard tug at the halter with both hands, yelling a warning to Delnos, who rode in trail behind her. He managed to stop beside her and, with a quick glance at what lay ahead, ordered her to remain quiet, as before. Merina stared at him as if he was out of his mind.

Pointing, she gasped out, "We have to get out of here, Delnos. There must be a dozen wolves over there."

The Tieri nodded, cautioning her to be quieter. "They have been feeding. See, the pack leader was asleep--now he is watching us. They will have no desire to attack us if we leave the area and no longer threaten their kill. It is the wolves pursuing us that pose the most danger to them."

Hearing the distant call to their rear, Merina scanned behind her to check if she could see them approaching. "How do you figure that?" she asked, struggling to keep her voice steady.

"They are hungry, these are not. And I would not want to be caught between them if the two packs got into a fight over the carcass. It looks like a horse from here, and I see a saddle on it."

Merina stood in her stirrups to look at the remains. "I don't see a body. Whoever was riding the horse might have gotten away."

"We can't do anything to find out, Mistress. If there were more of us, we might be able to drive the wolves off their kill, but even if we could succeed in doing so, we have no time. Let's ride up that slope to the left and go around them." Hearing the change in timbre of the calls behind them, Delnos added needlessly, "And hurry!"

The pack leader, a large, gray and white male, watched them ride up the hill and away from the clearing. The call of another pack downhill from him caught his attention. When he stood, a long growl poured from his throat. Merina kept glancing down into the clearing, hoping not to see a body, and, if she did, that it would not be Trinames.

"Just our luck, Mistress! The pack following is smaller than the one at the kill. They are stopping. I hope for our sake their leader thinks long and hard about trying to take the kill away."

They spurred the horses as fast as they could along the ridge, following the valley to their right as the Kanchala's trail would most likely have taken that way. Merina gestured downward. "The assassins will be slowed down now--someone will have to be riding double."

Delnos nodded toward the ridge they were riding on. "We will have to find a path downward soon. It gets too steep ahead for us to keep riding. If we lose a horse now, we will be in no better shape than they. Worse, I'm sure, because I know the Kanchala. One of them will run ahead to find a path that the other three riders can navigate better. I don't think I could do that, although you might."

Merina shook her head. "Not I." Imagining the strength of will of the assassins made her wonder if she had enough of her own to continue this chase. Delnos turned his horse downhill on a game trail that some animals used to cross the valley. They cut across the Kanchala trail by a stream that flowed down from the mountain. Boot prints, partially covered by those of horse hooves, proved Delnos was correct. Hearing the call of wolves on their trail again, he stood up from examining the prints and looked at Merina. "Seems the hungry pack would rather continue after us than wait out their brother wolves."

An hour later, they found the second horse carcass. They had been following the trail dismounted, as the way up the hill was proving to be too much for their mounts. The body lay beneath a small cliff that had prevented the Kanchala from going upward, and they had veered to the right to follow a cutback across the face of the hill. Kneeling beside the corpse, Merina could see the animal had broken several legs in a fall and its throat was slashed. Merina glanced uphill. "I'm not sure I can go any farther."

"We can't go back, they are closing on us. If the Kanchala can get up that cliff, we can. We may lose a horse also, that is a chance we have to take. In any case, this horse will serve to stop the pack to feed. We don't want to wait here to offer a choice of food."

Wearily, Merina stood and started up the gravel trail, placing one foot carefully in front of the other and hoping the horse she led would do so also. It placed a lot of strain on her thighs to move up the cliff, and she frequently stopped to rest. At every stop she scanned the tree line below them, looking for the dark gray shadows to emerge. The calls from the wolves had fallen silent. The beasts were stalking them now.

As they edged past the cliff face directly above the dead horse, a huge female wolf came out of the brush and stared up at them for a moment. She decided the scent that she had followed so long was not as interesting as the one fifty feet closer. Merina watched her approach the carcass warily until she got close enough to bite the flank of the horse. Ripping a piece of flesh lose, she chomped it down quickly. Merina saw the wolf hesitate to bite again and watched her turn and call to her pack mates about what she had found. The answering cries sounded close, and Merina's horse brushed past her to get away from the scene below.

In another twenty feet, they got clear of the cliff face, and a level clearing opened up before them. It swung around the mountain side, continuing to the right, and ended in a stand of pine trees hugging another cliff. Merina mounted her horse, which was very determined to get away from the snarling, frenzied pack behind them, and let the horse take the lead. Delnos was close behind her when they reached the end of the clearing and found a narrow path leading up through a split in the rock cliff. They had to dismount and lead the horses over the stony ground. The split was not formed by water, but it was clear that runoff from the mountain had taken its downward path that way often, although the cleft was dry now. The small stand of trees had been thinned recently. Someone had chopped down a dozen of them near the entrance to the cleft. Only the stumps, most of them under six inches in diameter and cut very close to the ground, remained of the missing trees.

As they entered the split, a gusting wind tried to shove them back, and Merina barely managed to save her hat from flying away. Holding onto it with one hand, she bent forward and half-dragged her horse through the cut, which was about fifty paces long. As she cleared the exit, she found herself confronted with another open area about twenty feet across at the point where she stood. It narrowed along the face of a cliff to her right like a teardrop, ending in a large, shallow cave in the face of the mountain. The left side of the clearing where she stood fell off into a sheer drop, which Merina did not venture to look down. When a flicker of movement at the end point of the clearing caught her eyes, she squinted against the buffeting wind. She saw a crude barricade but no sign of life.

The area in front of the fence of sharpened tree trunks was strewn with boulders, most knee high or smaller. What few trees had managed to gain a foothold in the rocky ground were stunted and twisted by the winds that whipped around this face of the mountain. She pointed at the barricade and called Delnos's attention to it, her words blown away. Her horse could not move forward, and would not, even if she had tried to force it. It shied away and backed into the cut.

Delnos took its reins and, turning both of their horses around, led them back to the clearing behind them. He returned alone and joined her. Merina put her mouth close to his left ear and yelled, "I don't see anyone!"

He yelled back, "If the Kanchala are there, I wouldn't expect us to. They will show themselves when they want us to see them." He pushed ahead of her and worked his way awkwardly though the boulders. He followed the scrape marks made by whoever had hauled the trees to the end of the traces. From the whiteness of the spear points, the barrier was very recently erected. About halfway there, he called to her that he could see a man's arm waving above the points. Stepping up on a boulder, he shouted, "I see Trinames! He's down on the ground covered by a tarp." He jumped down and started forward as fast as he could.

Merina wanted to shove past the Tieri to reach her lover, but she could barely keep up with the trader. He was not as weak as his slight paunch made him appear. When they reached the sharpened tree spears blocking the entrance to the ledge Trinames lay on, a rope hanging from the cliff face offered the only way to pass up and over the barricade. Delnos climbed over quickly, then had to help Merina up by grabbing her arms and hauling her past the points.

Catching sight of her beloved, Merina screamed his name and pushed past Delnos, and, stumbling over the rock strewn floor, she fell on Trinames. His loud cry of pain told them both he was hurt, and badly.

Chapter 10

The cave provided some shelter from the wind and had enough of an overhang to shield them from the sun, except when it was setting, as it was now. Merina checked Trinames again, saw he lay in a deep sleep, and returned to the small fire Delnos had built in the fire ring near the barricade. The Tieri had gone to collect their supplies from the horses. She was happy the potion Delnos made her lover drink to kill the pain had worked immediately, but annoyed because it put Trinames to sleep before she could find out what had happened to him after he was pulled from her arms.

The rope beside her went taut, and Delnos's head appeared beside the spear points. The expression on his face was not hard to read--he looked very concerned. He pulled himself up, stood on the barricade, and hauled their saddlebags over it. He turned toward her, his voice grim. "The horses are gone."

"What? You said you tied them..."

"I did, Mistress. As I came out of the cleft, I saw nothing, alive or dead, in the clearing. When I ran to where I had left the horses, I found our saddlebags dumped on the ground. If the horses had pulled themselves loose, the bags would have gone with them. Someone released the horses." Delnos sat, pulling the bags over to inspect them.

"The Kanchala?" Merina asked softly.

Handing her bags over, Delnos shrugged, intently rummaging through his supplies.

"Damn it, Tieri. Answer me!"

Delnos pulled out a small, square box, about three inches on a side, and opened the lid. Merina was immediately overwhelmed by a strange uneasiness when he did so, which disappeared as soon as he snapped the lid shut. He looked up at her, and, noticing the queasiness in her face, flipped the lid open again. Merina felt her body respond once more and shot an angry glance at the trader. A tiny smile chased across his lips as he closed the box and stowed it away in his belt pouch.

Merina pointed at his belt pouch. "That box you just opened--what's in it?"

He said, "I'll explain later. I searched the area where I had left the horses. I didn't find any boot prints in the area different from the ones we have been following--which we assume were made by the Kanchala. That is what worries me, Mistress. I should have found fresh tracks in the area, and I didn't! I should have found fresh horse prints or boot prints leaving the area. I didn't. If they drove the horses off the cliff and jumped after them, then I should have found something. Nothing."

"They couldn't have just disappeared," Merina spat out. "The horses have to be somewhere."

"I agree, Mistress, but wherever they are, it is not anywhere near us. Right now we need to make a plan, because our situation is getting worse by the hour."

Before she could ask why, the distant howl of the wolves below echoed in the cave. Merina listened for a minute, then said, "That is not good, not good at all. It sounds like they are calling for help. Why would they do that with all the meat available from the dead horse? Surely it would last more than a day."

"It should have. Maybe the wolves are inviting other packs to dinner," Delnos replied with a trace of humor that she had not heard from him in a while. The Tieri glanced over at Trinames, and, seeing the man was resting deeply, he turned back to Merina and said, "I am not a Healer, but I've had some training. Your young man has broken his left leg below the knee, at least three ribs on his left side are broken, and also his left forearm broke--the bone pierced the skin, creating that wound. These injuries could have come from falling off his horse, or maybe from the cliff we scaled, or both. He could not have traveled too far after suffering those injuries, so I don't think his was the first horse we found."

Merina nodded. She had seen similar wounds on field hands, not uncommon for people who work around large animals. "Someone set the breaks and bandaged his ribs," she said to Delnos.

"The Kanchala have even more healing skills than I. What puzzles me is they could have done more to ease his pain and heal the wound from the arm bone. They can use Power to heal such things," he said with a frown.

Merina jerked back in disgust. "Magic-users that kill. Talk about an abuse of Power. Maybe they wanted him to suffer."

"No," Delnos said quietly, "they probably used all the potions they brought with them, as well as the Power they stored from a source."

"Stored from a source? What does that mean, Tieri?"

Pulling the box from his pouch, Delnos held it out toward Merina. She recoiled in fear, refusing to touch it. He said, "This is a source. It sends out Power from the special rock it holds. Sorcerers can absorb the Power into their bodies in something they call a grid. It remains there until they draw out the Power to use in a spell. The amount they can store is strongly dependent on their training. Novice sorcerers, and some people like the Kanchala, store the least and can do minor spells. As they progress in their training to the levels of Sorcerer, Adept, and finally Mage, their grids hold more and more Power. They can use more complex spells for longer periods of time. At whatever level they are, they all will deplete their grids of Power, and they have to go back to a source to replenish it."

"Why do have you a source? You said you are not a Healer."

Delnos put the box on the rocky ground beside him. He must have known Merina did not like discussing magic, but she needed to understand more to grasp their predicament. "All sorcerers use Power, whether they are Healers, Provisioners, Illusionists, or Aggressors. Kanchala use Illusionist spells to hide and evade. They can also heal, as well as create food and water like Provisioners. I have similar skills, but I use mine for my own purposes. Most Tieri are like the rest of the Domain's people, they can't use Power."

"What do you mean by my own purposes?" Merina cut in, distrust sharpening her tone.

Delnos met her eyes. The smile she had seen earlier flitted across his lips again. "A little wine, a cool drink, remove an illusion--or make one. Small things that serve me well at times."

"You looked worried when you returned with the saddlebags until you found that thing," Merina said, pointing at the box. "Why?"

Delnos patted his bags. "I used the only potion I had on me to ease the pain of your lover. If I was to help further, I would have to use a spell. To do that, I needed the source. I have no Power stored in my grid. I was afraid the Kanchala might have taken the source. They are very expensive and rare."

Looking at Trinames, Merina saw the bloodied bandage on his arm and remembered his cry of pain when she had touched him. He needed healing, even if she hated the use of magic so much. "How long does it take to restore this Power you speak of? Do we have the time before the wolves get hungry again and decide to come after us?"

"For Novice level magic-users, it takes four or five hours of exposure to the source, but that will only allow me to heal the wound. I will need to repeat the exposure several times to heal him enough that we could move him."

Merina stared at the sun dipping below the horizon and grimaced at the thought that because of the time to heal Trinames they would lose the protection of the night. For this time of year, the sun would be up in eight hours. Even if they took the risk of moving him with minimum healing time, they would not make it far on foot with the two of them carrying him. They were trapped. She looked back at Delnos and said, "Do you think this barricade will keep the wolves out?"

He glanced behind him at the thin wall of points sticking out and nodded. "If the Kanchala built it, it should do the job. I doubt if the wolves have siege engineers in their pack. A hungry enough wolf might leap over the spears, but we could kill it with our weapons. I had a crossbow in my gear, but when the Kanchala took the horses, it went with them. Not that I had sufficient bolts to thin out the pack enough to discourage them from attacking us in mass."

"I doubt if we have the food or water to wait the wolves out," Merina said while searching through her bags, pulling out the rations she had left and counting them. The Tieri agreed with a grunt. She took out the small pot, closed the flap on the bag, and set the pot near the fire. "Tea?" she asked.

"So our plan is to do what, Mistress?"

Merina busied herself with the fire as she had done the previous night. Putting the pot on the raked-out coals, she sat back and said, "I don't understand why the Kanchala built this little fort for us. The best reason I can come up with is that by taking our horses and vanishing with them, they forced us to remain in place while they went for help. If we are to accept that thought, then we wait for their return. Between us, we have four days of food left each. The assassins left nothing with Trinames, so we might have six or more days among the three of us if we go half-rations." She eyed the Tieri's paunch. "You, maybe another week."

Delnos gave her a smile for her attempt at humor. He patted his stomach and held up ten fingers.

Sprinkling a half-handful of tea into the two cups, Merina set them on the ground and said, "I don't believe the Kanchala went for help, so one of us has to do it. You are needed here to tend to Trinames. It will take me three, maybe four days to walk out. Two days to get back with help. I'll take a day's worth of food. You should be able to survive on what is left. That's my plan."

Delnos took the ladle from Merina's hand and filled the two cups with simmering water. He said, "Better take three days' worth of food. You seemed to have forgotten that the shortest path back to Dysandes has at least two wolf packs in the way. You will have to go around the one at the bottom of the cliff and hope they do not find your scent and give chase. Your three, maybe four day estimate should be six days. I don't think we will starve to death since I can produce some food with spells--if the wolves leave us alone long enough for me to meditate with the source. Oh, and please do not reveal the fact that I can use Power--it would be bad for my business if people knew."

Sipping the still-too-hot tea, Merina wondered why he would prefer no one knew. *Maybe he uses magic to cheat his customers.* "Good, we have a plan. The only thing left to decide is when to leave. I think now is a good time--"

"No, love, don't leave me!" Trinames groaned, trying to sit up by rolling onto his good arm.

Merina dropped her cup and reached to stop him, afraid he might roll back onto his injuries. Delnos was by Trinames's side in an instant, helping her. He scolded the young Neophyte, "Do not move, sir. You will unset the breaks."

Moaning in pain, Trinames lay down again. Opening his tear-filled eyes, he fixed his gaze on Merina and said, "I thought I'd never see you again, love." Glancing quickly at Delnos, he turned back to her. "Those people, the Tieri, never said anything to me except to tell me to be quiet. They knocked me out as soon as the woman blew that powder in your face and I saw you fall. When I woke up, I was in a stable, sitting with my hands tied to a post behind me. Before I could cry out, that woman appeared from behind me, forced open my mouth, and poured a drink down my throat. I couldn't spit it all out, and I swallowed some--then I couldn't talk. She told me to do exactly as they said or they would let you die. Oh, love, they tried to make me believe you were badly wounded and their prisoner."

Merina held tightly onto his right hand and gave him a long kiss, afraid to press his lips too hard or hug him in any way. His breathing slowed a little, which meant the panic of his awakening was fading. She sat back and gave him a reassuring smile. "See, I'm not dead, and a free woman."

He squeezed her hand and smiled. "Yes, you are, and I am so glad." Merina brushed the tears from his face. He continued, "Two men untied me from the post and pushed me toward a horse. When I refused to mount, I heard you cry my name from the back of the stable, and I froze. I didn't want to believe it, but it sounded so much like you. The woman was standing in front of me, so it could not have been her. I had no choice but to get up on the horse."

"You couldn't have known, Trinames," Delnos said quietly, "but the woman used an Illusionist spell. You will learn during your studies at Byklandes to recognize when a sorcerer casts a spell--you can sense the release of energy. What happened next?"

Merina picked up her cup and dumped the dregs out, filling it with water from the pot. She added tea leaves and waited for them to steep while Trinames answered the Tieri.

"I did feel a wave of dizziness when she rode up beside me while the two men opened the stable doors so we could ride out. It must have been another spell she cast, because when the men mounted their horses they were both bearded, where before they weren't. They looked just like normal people..." Trinames stopped, glancing at Delnos. "I'm sorry. I meant to say they did not have the nose and eyes like you, sir."

The Tieri acknowledged Trinames's apology and reached for the cup Merina was holding out. "My people like to think we are indeed special, young man, but I can tell you we are all normal. Drink this slowly. It is quite warm." Delnos raised Trinames's head with one hand and helped him take a sip.

Merina spoke as her lover drank the tea. "The village guard reported four men left town and went into the forest. One of them spoke to a guardsman, saying, 'Wish us luck, we're off on a hunt.' The guardsman told them to be careful, wolves were about."

Trinames finished his sip and pushed the cup away, nodding his thanks. "That is exactly what happened. I couldn't talk, and when I turned to look at the guard, hoping he would recognize me, I found myself looking at a bearded man where the woman had been riding. From the glare in his eyes and a gesture with his hand I knew I was being ordered to stop looking at the guard. We rode on and entered the woods."

Trinames's voice rasped with dryness. Delnos offered another drink. "The guard would not have recognized you. When Captain Garlantis asked the guard to describe the hunters, the guard said they all had beards, were dressed in field hands' sturdy clothes, and had the usual bows and equipment hunters carried into the woods. Is that what you saw?"

Trinames finished the tea and pushed it away with his right hand. "Yes, at least the men in front of us looked like that. Once we were in the trees, the woman took the lead and told me to follow. He--she--warned me not to try to ride off. With two men at my back, I was not about to do that. After about two hours, we stopped to relieve ourselves. I felt that wave of dizziness and, looking around, saw everyone as I had seen them in the stable."

Merina felt the urge to go herself, but she didn't want to stop Trinames's story. "Did they tell you why they were doing this to you--to us?"

"No. The woman gave me a cup of something, and I drank it. It tasted really foul and I almost threw it up. Whatever it was, it let me talk again. As soon as she realized I could speak, she told me in that heavily accented voice of hers that she was not going to answer any questions. I could make simple requests and, if in danger, call for help. If I tried to do anything else, she would take my voice away again. By now I knew she meant what she said and arguing would get me nowhere with her."

Merina cocked her head to one side, remembering something about her encounter with the Tieri woman. "You said the woman spoke Saphradean with a heavy accent. She did not say much to me, but I noticed her words were strange. Yet the guard made no mention of an accent."

"You're right, love. I heard one of them speak very clear Saphradean to the guard, but I never heard that clarity again. The very few times the men addressed me, it was in that same strange dialect of Saphradean. Most of the rest of their conversation was in Tierian."

Delnos had a strange look on his face after Trinames finished talking. Merina noticed and was about to ask why when he said, "There is a very old form of Saphradean that I have heard used in isolated farms near the Non-Lands much farther to the east of us. It is in another clan's trading territory." Shrugging, he handed the cup Trinames had used to drink from to Merina, who filled it for her own use.

Delnos turned to Trinames. "We did not follow you out of town until the next day, yet your trail was fresh when we encountered it. What did the Tieri do in that time?"

Merina wondered why Delnos was not referring to the Kanchala by their name. Maybe he didn't want to waste time telling her lover what he already knew, that he was traveling with hired killers. Trinames answered the question.

"One of the men rode back the way we came, and I did not see him return until the next morning. After he left, we rode on for maybe three hours more, and then the woman stopped us for the day. We just sat around and waited. No fire, a meal of bread and dried meat, water when I wanted it, and sleep. I thought once of escaping, but whenever I looked at the Tieri, one of them was looking back. When I got up to relieve myself, whoever's turn it was to stare at me followed me into the bush. I gave up thinking I could sneak off and slept as much as I could."

"When did the missing man return?" Delnos asked.

"We had broken camp, if that is what they think we were doing, and had been riding along at a walk for several hours. I was not paying much attention when the man seemed to appear out of nowhere riding next to the woman. I don't think they said a word to each other--at least I didn't hear anything. She just picked up the pace and trotted off to wherever she was taking us. I trailed along behind."

Merina finished her tea and held the cup out to Trinames. He shook his head. She asked, "When did the wolves show up?"

"We heard them behind us toward the end of the second day. By then we were climbing up into the hills. The man who had stayed with us the night before disappeared in the direction of the howls, and the woman led us up a steep ridge and had us dismount. That was our camp for the night. When the scout showed up out of the dark, I happened to be returning from the brush with the woman watching me, and I heard him speak to the other man. I can only guess what he said--maybe he wanted to know where the leader was. She walked past me to talk to him, and I saw him pointing to the south. That's when I saw the flicker of light of a campfire on the hill about a mile away."

"That must have been Mistress Merina's fire, I suspect," Delnos mused, kneeling beside Trinames's wounded arm to examine the bandage. He gave Merina a worried glance.

"I wish I had known. It would have made me feel a lot better knowing there was a friend out there looking for me. Not that I could have done anything, because the woman ordered us all to walk away from the direction of the light, guiding the horses off the hill. We spent most of the night walking with the horses to put distance between us and you. The loss of rest didn't seem to affect the Tieri, but it just about did me in. I know we stopped at some point, but all I remember is tying the reins of my horse to a limb and sitting down against the tree. I woke up being shaken by one of the men and ordered back in the saddle. The sun was well up, about two hours after daybreak. I was really tired and groggy from getting so little sleep."

Delnos sat back off his knees and put his arms around them. "We broke our camp before dawn. With a pack of wolves behind us, we wanted to get away from them before they picked up our trail."

Trinames turned his head toward Delnos. "That must have been what caused the woman to push our pace, because we did not proceed the leisurely way we had been going. When we rode into a clearing, she took off even faster, and I had to gallop the horse to keep up. I'm not sure what happened next, but I think I tried to jump over a log, and I found myself flying through the air over the horse's head. I remember hitting the rocky ground, but that is all. When I awoke, I was on a pallet being carried by the two men, and when I looked around me, I saw a cliff wall on my left. I twisted to look to the right, and the worst pain I have ever felt shot through my body. I screamed. It was answered by a scream from a horse as I blacked out again."

Trinames's voice was rising in pitch. Merina realized how the memory of that pain must have awakened his fears of that moment. She touched his lips with a finger and told him, "Rest a moment, take a deep breath. You are safe with us now. Calm yourself, love."

Delnos nodded his approval. He spoke to keep Trinames from continuing. "Which explains what probably happened at the cliff a short way from here. Your movement on the pallet with all your broken bones caused the pain that made you scream, which spooked the horse behind you. It lost its footing and fell off the cliff. The Tieri killed the injured horse. The one that threw you must have injured itself as well, because we found it being eaten by wolves shortly before we reached the cliff. Do you remember any more?"

Having calmed down, Trinames nodded. "When I woke, I was lying here. The woman told me I was injured in the fall, and she would now heal as much as she could using the potions she had. I told her I couldn't remember anything, and she smiled for the first time since we met. She held up a pouch in her left hand and pointed to it, then put her right hand to her head and made a flying away motion. She opened the pouch and took a pinch of powder from it, then let it fall into my nose. That is the last I remember until I heard rocks falling below me and saw you," he turned to look at Merina, "and my love approaching."

Merina gave him a smile. "I know the effect of that powder. It's the same one she used on me."

Cutting in, Delnos said worriedly, "Unfortunately, it does not heal anything. She set your breaks and splinted those she could. The arm wound from the bone tearing through could be infected and needs treatment. I can do some, but it will take time to meditate with a source to get the Power I need to do the healing."

Trinames looked startled by what the Tieri had just told him. He glanced at Merina to see how she had received that piece of information. She gave him a slight nod and tried to keep her discomfort about use of magic from her face.

Delnos continued, "Someone has to go for help. The Tieri took our horses while we were tending to you. I don't know why--maybe to save themselves since they lost two horses. They could have left us one, but don't waste your time trying to figure it out. It leaves us on foot. We could use a pallet to move you like they did, but there are wolves in the valley below. I don't think we can carry you out and fight them off at the same time. They did make this barricade, which should hold off the wolves, so staying here is safer. If I stay with you, I can do some healing and fight off any wolves that get past the barricade. Merina agrees and is willing to go. Now is the best time, young sir, don't you agree?"

The anguish in Trinames's face tore at Merina's heart, but she knew it was wise of Delnos to make her love approve her decision. She packed two days of rations into a saddlebag and took one water bottle, leaving the rest. Trinames closed his eyes and began to slowly shake his head from side to side. Merina started to protest, but Delnos silenced her with a stare. Trinames stopped moving his head and opened his eyes, which now had tears trickling from the corners, and croaked out softly, "Go quickly! I love you, Merina. Please don't risk your life by taking chances. Run rather than fight and--"

Merina kissed him to shut off his worries and to say goodbye. When she raised her mouth from his, she pressed a finger across his lips and said, "Rest and heal, my love. I will return as soon as I can." She stood and walked to the rope. Grabbing it, she gave her lover, who lay watching her with such sorrow-filled eyes, the warmest smile she had and lowered herself past the spear points. Her last glance she gave to the Tieri, silently begging him to keep her lover alive. Delnos nodded and took out his source, opening it. A wave of uneasiness washed over Merina, and she quickly lowered herself to get away. The uneasiness persisted even as she passed through the cleft and made her way toward the lone entrance to the ledge and the wolves below.

Delnos watched the young woman picking her way through the boulders toward the glade entrance. He had seen the flash of uneasiness in her face when he opened his source and realized she had sensed the Power radiating from it. This confirmed what he had suspected. She was indeed ready to become a magic-user. The fact that she fought against it was probably a concern of those who had sent him.

As the Power slowly filled him, he tried to figure out what the Kanchala were doing. The barricade protecting them had been built recently, but not just a day ago. It was at least a week old. It did not make sense that the assassins would have prepared a number of sites in case they needed them. This one was placed here for a purpose.

That purpose was to protect a small party of men from wolves. How did the Kanchala know they would need such a construct? Did they really know the wolves would come after them, or both them and a party in pursuit? Were the wolves being driven in their way? The beasts were not behaving normally--they should not be gathering in the numbers they had been. Hunting in large groups would make all the less food available from a kill. No, he convinced himself, someone was controlling them.

Did the Kanchala intend to harm the lad? Not likely because of what had really happened to them--the injury hindered their plan. The Kanchala always had a plan with another plan in case the first faltered, and another added onto that. They were probably going to leave Trinames tied up behind the barricade.

If the purpose was to strand us, stealing our horses made sense. But why? What were we being driven to do, and had we done what was expected of us?

And why me? Delnos wondered. Why involve our people when we face so much hostility in this world?

Chapter 11

As Merina inched along the cliff face, she looked down into the moonlit valley below. She did not really expect to see wolves and was not disappointed when she saw none. She could not see the carcass of the horse either. To do that she would have to venture down the cliff face trail, which she was not willing to do. Knowing the body was still mostly intact would have eased her worry that if it had been devoured, the wolves would be on the hunt again soon. The trail continued eastward and up from where it split to go south and down. A quick glance at the moon let her know she had only a few hours of darkness left. It would be too risky to attempt passing through the wolves below with so little darkness left. She proceeded east, glancing back frequently to check that she was not followed.

Just how far she would have to climb eastward up the trail worried her. The cliff face was turning more vertical rather than sloping as it had where they climbed up it yesterday. At some point she might have to climb down in the dark, which was riskier than going too far along it and wasting time. From her vantage point above the little valley, she could see a ridge curving away from the cliff she was crossing, to form the eastern wall of the valley. With luck, she could get there from here.

Thankfully, the path was not steep. Whatever animal made the trail was not one of the few mountain goats she knew lived in these mountains. She shook her head in disbelief that hunters would waste the time and energy to come up here to bring home a set of horns as a reward for their prowess. She wondered if the goats still survived, considering the determination of the wolves below. She stopped and sat on the rocky ground to rest her aching thighs. As she looked around, she glanced back the way she had come and surprised herself that she still felt the sense of unease from the source. She had hiked at least two hours along the trail, putting at least two miles between her and that damn box. The sun was rising on the other side of the ridge she perched on, and she could see the southern part of the valley reflecting the sunlight back to her. The wolves would be stirring by now. The ridge she wanted to take south was close. She would make faster time going downhill than she was now.

Reaching the junction with the southern ridge, she spotted another trail angling in from her right, which joined the sparsely overgrown path she was laboring to climb. As she reached it, she noticed claw traces in the rocky dirt. Wolves! As if in answer to that thought, a howl rose from below her, soon joined by numerous others. Another pack, or the same one? It doesn't matter, Merina, move!

She could only go uphill if she didn't want to run into the pack. Her muscles protested as she doubled her pace up the path. She could hear the excited howling of wolves close behind her. She kept losing traction on the grit and loose rock, which threatened to ruin her footing and send her sliding backward. More than once her feet slipped out from underneath her and she pitched forward, slamming her knees on the rocky ground. After the second time that happened, her right knee really began to hurt, and she had trouble walking on it. The pains made her wonder if she should turn and face the threat or continue fruitlessly trying to run up the trail. A glance behind gave her the answer.

From what she could see of the trail, three wolves had followed her, at their lead a huge, white male. Not more than twenty feet away the pack leader sat watching her as she stared at him. There was no doubt in her mind that he could climb the steep slope as readily as she could not. The snarl on his lips said he was not happy at stopping, but halting he was. They're not following! Merina faced backward and sat gingerly on the mountain trail.

A low-throated growl reached her ears above the whistling of the wind down the path, and it sent a chill down her spine. This was one angry wolf. The two wolves behind him whined at their leader, but he would not climb farther. She could not see around the bend in the trail but knew the rest of the pack had to be lined up along the path behind their leader.

Why did he stop? Merina felt a flow of wetness running down her right leg and groped along her pants to her ankle, where she touched the warm liquid. She raised her hand to her face and saw her fingers coated with blood. Not knowing why, she turned her hand to show the alpha, which responded with a more intense growl.

You smell that, dog? Come and get it!

The wolf did not move. Its tongue licked out, as if tasting the scent, but it stayed immobile, staring at her. Merina pulled up her pants leg and found the source of blood. A rock had badly gashed her knee even through her tough riding pants, which surprised her. She pulled a wiping cloth from her pocket and tied it around the wound to stop the oozing of blood.

Merina gingerly stood and began walking up the path again. She placed each foot carefully on the rock trail before putting her weight on it. Foot by foot she moved away from the wolves below. Her knee screamed in pain with each step, but it was nothing compared to what she would have felt under the tearing jaws of the pack below. She inched upward, following the narrow trail until the lead male was long out of sight.

They are not following. That doesn't make sense. Struggling ever higher, Merina let the surge of fear that had been driving her go and tried to think beyond it to what she was doing on this upward sloping path. She pushed herself upward for another fifty feet before the path began to flatten out and widen.

Now able to limp on the wounded leg, she paused to survey what was happening ahead. The path led up to a cave entrance, a large hole in the mountain ahead, taller than any man. It was strangely round, as if drilled into the stone. From the cavity emanated the same uneasiness that Delnos's source gave her. Is this one of those source mines Uncle Tomanis mentioned? But it is not guarded. Surely it can't be, there are no roads leading to it!

She approached it warily, stopping when she reached the entrance. The sun was high above her, and the shadows in the cave started almost directly below the beginning of the cave's ceiling. Reflected light from the rocky ground let her see perhaps a dozen feet into the interior. From what was exposed, the hole seemed to extend into the dark at the same dimensions as it started.

Loose gravel and dirt swirled around her feet as the wind, which had blown constantly on her since she entered the barren mountain range, flowed past her into the cave. Merina found a fist-size rock on the ground near the wall to her right and threw it into the cave. The sound of its hitting the floor was followed by a clicking as the rock rolled farther in. It seemed to be picking up speed, and the sound quickly got lost in the dark. It's sloping downward?

Merina put her back against the wall and begin edging sideways into the cave. With her right hand groping forward on the wall, she found to her surprise that it was almost without roughness, like the walls of her home--except no mortise joints. The farther she went in, the footing became more difficult as her boot soles began sliding on the dust. She looked to her left at the cave entrance and saw she had advanced about thirty feet. The circle of light that defined the opening appeared only slightly smaller than it had before.

The air was still wafting past her, but not in gusts. It was definitely flowing into the cave. The stone beneath her fingers was not as cold as she would expect of rock not directly heated by the sun. She looked to the right again and waited for her eyes to adjust to the blackness. It did not really help much, so she closed them to force her mind to rely on her hearing and sense of touch to make her way forward.

Merina slid her right foot forward to what she thought would be a foot's length, then brought her left up against her right. The only sounds of her progress were the gritty scrape of her boot on the floor and her intake of breath. The air was cool and dusty-smelling. She counted her steps, and at a hundred she looked to her left. The circle of light was definitely smaller. Step and recover, step and recover. At two hundred her hand touched an outcropping of stone. When she groped along it away from the wall, she found it was another wall. As high as she could reach, the wall extended.

Putting her back against this wall made her face the entrance with its white circle of light, which hurt her eyes, so she closed them again. At ten feet her boot kicked a rock away from the wall, and a surge of disappointment flashed through her mind. Not the end? Fifteen feet later her fingers touched stone again coming off the wall, and her boot toe hit the rock. Damn it!

She used the tips of her fingers on the seam of the wall joining but could not feel a hole anywhere. The air flowed upward now, but she could not find where it was exiting the end of the cave. It was above her, but beyond her reach. She thought of tossing the rock up in the hope it might go through a hole above her, but after several tries it broke in smaller pieces. She gave up and sank down with her back against the wall.

"Well, wolf, I guess we are going to get a dance together after all." Her voice echoed off the wall, and she sighed in defeat. She let her despair send her off to sleep.

"The subject is ready."

"Yes, she is physically where we planned her to be. Mentally--not yet."

"You are going to fix that now. Isn't that why she is here?"

"My changes to her are physical. I cannot change her will. That would be the same mistake the Others made."

"I don't understand, Mother."

"It is because you think like the Others--you do not take into consideration the difference in our perception of time and hers. You think I am acting too slowly."

"You are being very cautious, Mother. That is important if we must avoid detection, but..."

"There is still time. The margins for error are very narrow, but to rush now would risk failure of our plan."

"Theirs has been in motion for centuries."

"So has mine, my son."

"But yours needs more time to come to fruition, and theirs--"

"Is past due. It has failed."

"Then my father is--"

"Unknown. There is still a probability the Others could succeed."

"But you believe not before our enemies return?"

"There are many other ways this can end, my son."

"You mean your plan?"

"That too."

"There are too many variables when dealing with these people. It is irritating."

"True, but, oddly, their randomness is not. What bothers you is that you can't control the variables, knowing you should be able to--or think you should. The Others tried and, well, did not succeed."

"But, Mother, it forced them to execute their original plan."

"Because they saw their experiment fail and thought to erase it. That was a mistake--one I will not make."

"From it came Lenora."

"Fortunately they did not see."

"Why worry now? So little has really changed."

"This one will, so we must be careful. All must proceed as it would if left untouched by any of our hands. I will make my changes now."

Merina sat on her stool under the sitting tree. She looked around and wondered why her house was not nearby, nor were any of the farm's many outbuildings where they should have been. She could not see the neighboring homesteads for the forest that should not have been there. But this was her tree on her hill. She wondered aloud, "Where am I? Is this a dream?"

"Yes, it is, my daughter." A woman's voice spoke from behind Merina. She turned on her stool and saw an elderly woman dressed in a black robe standing out of reach of the knife Merina clutched in her right hand. Merina gave the weapon a puzzled frown and dropped it. The knife passed through the ground and disappeared as mysteriously as it had appeared.

The woman had a gentle smile on her wrinkled face, and her eyes were a piercing blue that sparkled in the sunlight filtering through the leafy branches above. Her hair was short, once red but now streaked heavily with gray. Although taller than Merina, even in the flowing robe she looked thinner. Her hands were smooth and fine-boned--the hands of an artisan, not a farm maid.

Merina stood and offered her seat to the woman, who declined with a shake of her head. "You sit," she said. Merina obeyed as if compelled.

"My name is Lenora. Your name is Merina. We are family."

Merina gave an explosive laugh. "Of course your name is Lenora. This is a dream, you said. Delnos said you were a powerful Mage sorcerer hundreds of years ago. He spoke of you with awe because you were the first leader of some council. Do you have a spell for immortality? If so, you are getting older and had better use it again."

The older woman laughed with merriment that Merina's laughter had not had. "No, no spell. I did die of old age, but long after I had a daughter, who had a daughter--how many before you were born? I am not sure. It has been a long time, granddaughter."

"If you are dead, and talking to me, then there must be life after death. No one believes that, Magess. Is that what I should call you?"

Lenora smiled. "The people of the Domains hold many beliefs, but all four factions have suffered much through their short lives. It is not surprising they believe only in life, then death. I am not the proof of anything, Merina. This image you see is from a memory of what she was. I have borrowed her memory. If I appeared in my true form you would be horrified, and we would not get very far in our meeting. I choose this age because it is grandmotherly and I want you to feel comfortable. Are you?"

"I'm not sure." Merina glanced at her hand and saw the knife back in her grip. "This seems to say I am not, but I don't feel threatened by you. Wait! There is that feeling of unease that I get from Helinu and Delnos. What is that?"

"You sense the Power I hold in myself--the place you were told about, my grid. No magic-user alive can sense Power being held within a human. But you do, my child. That makes you special. It is as I thought it would be."

Merina looked away from the old woman, saying softly, "I never asked to be special, Grandmother. I just want my life to begin as I have dreamed."

"And it will, Daughter. But you are very defensive, dear. Are you more afraid of magic, which I represent, or of death?"

Merina reached for her face with both hands, the knife gone before she touched her skin. Rubbing her eyes, she moaned, "I don't know."

"It is what you are meant to do, Daughter."

"Die? I am to climb down off this mountain and be killed by that wolf pack?" Merina asked defiantly.

"It will be your choice," Lorena said, folding her arms across her chest and frowning at Merina's tone.

Merina took a breath and tried to cleanse the anger from her voice. "If you mean being torn apart by fangs or dying of hunger, I can see the choice you offer."

"That is not the choice I speak of. You were made for Power use, Merina. You can deny it all you want, rage at anyone who suggests otherwise, and defy all who have tried to help you."

Merina shot up from the stool but found herself slammed back down, pushed by some force that seemed to emanate from a command softly spoken by Lenora, "Sit and be silent."

The old woman's eyes narrowed, matching the anger that Merina sensed written all over her own face. "You think you can stop the forces of nature that created you, daughter of Delaphinu? You descend from a long line of women who have wielded the Power, some willingly as I did, some forced by circumstances beyond their control. Each and every one was shaped by changes the Power wrought."

Merina choked, trying to talk. Whether it was the anger and tears, or the spell Lenora had used to silence her, Merina barely managed to croak out, "Like my mother was--the Power destroyed her life."

"Not true, Merina. She lives still." Lenora waved her right hand, and Merina found she could speak again.

"It turned her from a loving daughter to a drunken whore who sold her body for wine. She lost sight of her goal, failed at Inhestia, and ran away from her family and from me."

Lenora turned away, the rigidity of her back speaking silently of the anger that she was trying to hide from her many-times granddaughter. Merina sat quietly, wondering if saying the same thing over and over about her mother was ever going to hurt less than it did.

Lenora shook her head. "No, and repeating your complaint gets you nowhere. You should know that your mother did not fail at her training. She excelled in all the tests and could have been made Sorcerer, a step beyond the Novice training she had received. Her drive to succeed forced her to take risks beyond her level of control, and she suffered a backlash of Power. It damaged her mind. The Healers tried to help her, and as was their wont, they locked her away to hide her illness from the rest of the magic-users. She escaped and came home. With child, she could remain only long enough to bear you and foster you to her sister. She drank because it numbed the pain and the depression she suffered. When she was able, she fled, knowing the Saphradean Lodge would search for her once the Delmathians told them of her illness and confine her again."

Merina wept quiet tears, glad in one way because this was a story she wanted to hear, but sad because she had no cause to believe it. "This is just a dream, Magess Lenora, my dream. Everything you say either comes from my memories or it is what I want to hear. How am I to believe anything said in a dream?"

The old woman sighed and turned back to Merina. Tears shone in her eyes as well. "So it has been with humans from the beginning. You question everything not confirmed by smell, touch, sound, or any of your senses. Would you believe if your aunt had told you what I just said, or Florinu, your friend? Let me answer that. No, you would not because you might expect them to tell you a happy ending to your sad tale. Would you believe if Sorceress Helinu had told you? No, because you will not listen to anyone you distrust. Helinu knew most of what I said, but she could not tell anyone the secrets of the sorcerers. Who would you believe then, Merina?"

"My mother. Where is she, Grandmother?"

"She is cared for in a place no one has ever found. Her madness has grown since your birth. If you could even talk to her, you would not believe her. Do not even make that attempt."

"Then my father. I have no memory of him, nor does anyone else know what happened to him at Inhestia. All I was ever told was that my mother seduced him to keep him from informing the authorities about her drunkenness. He never acknowledged me or helped my mother that I can discover. I have asked, Grandmother."

Lenora's sadness deepened. "The records are there, but magic-users fear greatly any open mention of grid burnout. It was a primary cause of the Sorcerer Wars. Sorcerers learned they could change their abilities, not knowing of the dangers if control was lost. They pushed the limits of their skill and became overconfident in what they thought they could control. The changing of Power into a spell can result in Power flowing back into the mind. The mind can sense what is happening and counter the flow with increased speed and control. The mind grows, and the sorcerer becomes more powerful. It is the same process used by all the training lodges. It takes years of study to go from Novice to Adept. In a burnout situation it is near instantaneous."

"That is what happened to my mother!" Merina gasped.

"And your father, but he did not have the help your mother found, and it killed him. His name was Trilistes. He was Delaphinu's mentor. A highly skilled and respected Provisioner Adept, he was also a Mage candidate. The work he was sharing with Delaphinu would advance both of their candidacies."

Merina thought, He had everything to gain, and everything to lose by my mother's failure.

"Your father had no fault in what happened to them. Delaphinu and Trilistes were lovers long before they experienced the burnout. He was aware she was pregnant, and they were making plans to become life-mates when Delaphinu graduated to Sorceress and was no longer his student."

"So she was not a whore as we were told?" Merina asked quietly.

"No, but they were in violation of the Inhestia's rules about students and instructors mating. It was an easy twist of thinking to come up with that tale. And as for her drinking, it was no more than any students of that age indulge in and was never a problem until afterward."

"Afterward?" Impatience sharpened Merina's tone.

"As I told you, she drank because of the pain. Your parents were discovered together in their laboratory near death after their experiment failed. Delaphinu was less experienced in her control of Power, but she had the stronger mind. The Healers wondered if her being with child made her more cautious about their experimentation, but for whatever reason, she recovered her sanity. Trilistes never did. He stayed in a coma for over a month, and the two lovers were kept apart the entire time Delaphinu remained at Inhestia. He never knew of her recovery. He died thinking she was dead."

Oh, Father! I have been so wrong about you. I am so sorry. Merina broke down into tears and moaned aloud so painfully that Lenora almost went to her side to comfort her. When Merina saw dimly through her tears the old woman turning away, she realized again that she was not really living this. She wiped the tears from her face with her blouse sleeve and stared at the ground.

"Do you now believe what I say, Merina? Or is it just something you have wanted to hear all your life?" Lenora asked.

"I don't know, Magess. How can one have proof with magic?"

"Ahh, child, you have asked the question of the ages. Womankind has the miracle of birth given her and accepts that it happens because she has a child. In wondering why she becomes pregnant, she eventually discovers it is because of the union of man and woman. She then feels she has the power to control whether she bears a child or not. She believes she has the answer and therefore the truth. But does she, Daughter?"

Merina looked puzzled. "Everyone knows it takes mating with a man to have a baby. Simply said, if you don't mate, you can't get pregnant."

"Does that make you in control of the birth process? Let me suggest the answer is no. Assuming no rape, the woman is in control of the non-birth process," Lenora said firmly. "There are spells, drugs, herbs, and other ways of stopping a pregnancy before it starts, or even afterward. But what if a baby is desired, and all the mating a woman could stand does not create a child? There are no spells, drugs, or herbs known that can make a woman pregnant. Is she in control of the birthing process then, Daughter?"

Shaking her head, Merina wondered what this all had to do with the question of the age. "No, but--"

"Then the woman is not even in control of the non-birth process either. My point, Daughter, is we think we know so much about some things that we use that knowledge to define what truth is and then make future decisions based on what we believe is true. It is the same in magic use. The non-Power user sees the results of magic--I see the baby. Since they don't understand the use of Power, it is a miracle--or is magic."

Merina thought through Lenora's last words. "The results are the proof that magic exists. But does it follow that magic can provide the proof to one's belief?"

"The question of the ages, Daughter. If I use magic to prove to you everything I have said in this dream, you would still have cause to disbelieve because you lack the knowledge of what Power can or cannot do. You fear magic use for the same reason. You have no knowledge of it. Therefore, you fear it, because you have no control over it. That is why we sorcerers study the use of Power. We hope to figure out how magic works so we can control it better, so that maybe one day we can use it to prove everything--by showing we have control. That is why we created the Council of Magi--to get Power use under control.

"But you have a dilemma, Daughter--one you do not fully know but sense within yourself. You were born to Power use, as was your mother before you, and hers before her. You come from my line, and I was chosen for the purpose of giving you that gift. But long ago, your ancestors left the sorcerer's fold and found a new path for their abilities. They became farmers, and their minds lost the wonder of magic and took up the reality of the land."

Merina shook her head. "My mother--"

"Was forced by circumstances beyond her control--as you have already admitted earlier. Helinu told you that magic is dependent on the kind of person you are, which determines what kind of magic you do. Facing the harshness of living off the land tempers the way one thinks and leads you to solidify what you believe, or don't. My Saphradean line became stuck in the changeless life of tending the land. After Romanus brought in a young housekeeper, Delaphinu believed she had no recourse but to leave farming--which was not true, but she believed she had no other way. Thinking that, she opened herself up to the possibility of another way of life. For one to use Power, one must have an open and inquiring mind."

Merina bristled. "You are saying I am closed-minded! You're wrong. I try to think of every side of argument before I make any decision."

Smiling, Lenora asked, "As you have with magic use, Daughter?"

Caught in Lenora's trap, Merina tried to dodge answering the question. "You said I had a dilemma I was not aware of. And you said I had to decide if I was more afraid of magic or of death. Is that the dilemma?"

"With your present beliefs, you would be correct. With what your future holds, no. Remember I told you why we created the Council of Magi. Another reason, not revealed to the people of the Domains, was to watch for deviations in the use of Power. If any were found, the Council was to eliminate it before it could get out of hand, as magic use did during the wars."

"Deviations?" Merina asked. "Like grid burnout?"

"That is a result of a process. Bleeding results from being cut. Sensing stored Power is a deviation."

So that is why I am special, Merina thought, a tremor of uneasiness running through her mind. "As leader of the First Council of Magi, you have been sent to warn me, Grandmother?"

"Yes, and no, Daughter. Your gift of sensing stored Power, if discovered, could lead to your destruction. Whether or not that happens depends on what you do next in your life."

This is all so unclear. Why am I bothering to talk to a dream image?

::Would you prefer to communicate this way?::

Startled, Merina looked up and found herself back in the cave. She was chilled to her very core and stiff from sitting against the stone wall. The light from the tunnel entrance had disappeared. She reached out and found a shard of the rock she had been throwing. Its presence affirmed that she was awake.

::Yes, you are no longer dreaming.::

"Lenora?" Merina whispered, the sound swallowed up by the pitch blackness of the cave.

::I no longer need her memories to reach you. We are bound now.::

The voice spoke in her head, for no sound came through her ears--she was sure of that. "Who are you?"

::Who I am is not important. You have been awakened. Find Trinames where you left him. He and Delnos are in grave danger.::

Merina cried out desperately, "I know--I was trying to get help when the wolves drove me up here. I can't do anything against the wolves alone!"

::Time is against you. Find a way to save them yourself.:: A wave of calmness coursed through her, and for a moment her mind reacted as it had when the Kanchala powder felled her in the inn. Just as suddenly, she became aware of her surroundings. The unease she had felt before the dream was gone. So was the voice, and Merina knew it would talk no more. She struggled to stand up and found her knee no longer hurt. The aching weariness from climbing the path was also gone. She felt no chill, hunger, or thirst.

"How long have I been here?" she asked the dark, not expecting an answer, nor did she get one.

Stretching out her left arm from her side, she walked sideways until she touched the wall, then retraced her earlier steps toward the cave's mouth.

Chapter 12

When Merina stepped out of the cave, there were no wolves in sight. The bright moon's light covered the harsh rock mountainside, casting its shadow into gullies where the pack could be hiding silently, awaiting her approach. She searched more with her hearing than her eyes, closing them to enhance her ability to pick up panting or a threatening growl. If the wolves had found a less combative prey, they might be busy eating and ignore her as she escaped past them. The wind whistling by carried no scent of blood. Uneasy but determined, she pulled her knife from her belt and tiptoed across the clearing toward the mouth of the trail. The skittering of gravel there told her she was not alone.

The huge male stood in the path, the rest of his pack out of sight. His eyes reflected the moon above, and their eerie brightness made him appear more monster than animal. The grin across his face, with fangs showing starkly against the blackness of his mouth, should have made him look even fiercer--but it had the opposite effect on her. Dogs grinned that way in friendship. Was it not the same for wolves?

The absence of a wagging tail cautioned her to keep her guard up. "Come to say goodbye, fanged one?"

The wolf cocked his head to one side, as if taking a moment to think before replying. He sat and, turning his head, nipped at his left haunch.

"I guess not. A flea is of more interest than me. I'll just take my leave of you." When she started to edge past him, he snapped his head around. Merina stopped.

Down below, around the bend in the path, Merina heard the chorus of howls the pack made when picking up a prey's scent. She thrust her knife forward. "That's the game, Killer? Waiting for reinforcements?"

The wolf glanced away in the direction of the pack, and Merina tensed to lunge. He looked back at her and the shining glint of her blade, then turned and trotted away down the trail. The leader never looked back again. Rounding the corner, he rent the air with his response to the pack. The howling stopped as quickly as it had begun. In moments she was alone.

What is going on? She was too stunned to follow for several minutes. "Were you holding me back, wolf?" she wondered aloud.

Replacing her knife in its sheath, Merina started down the steep path. She glanced upward at the moon and, from its position in the night's sky, wondered if she had been in the cave since before its rising tonight. That short a rest could not explain her condition. Lenora must have healed me, but what else did she do? What did she mean, I "have been awakened"?

Merina found going downhill faster, but only marginally so. The loose gravel and rocks still threatened to make her lose her footing, and she took to making small leaps to any patch of clear ground she could see. It was that or chance sliding the way one would on ice and risk falling down the steep slope. The path ahead was clear of wolves, although their tracks showed in the first beams of daylight flooding over the mountain at her back. She reached the split in the path where she had intended to go south along the ridge and stopped. Decision time! she chided herself.

Glancing west, Merina could not sense the Power from Delnos's source. Now that she was "awakened", and knew what to look for, not sensing the source made her worry. It must mean he was not using it. Either he didn't need to or he couldn't. The Tieri had said he would need several meditation periods to draw the Power he needed to heal

Trinames. Perhaps this was between those times. The other alternative was that she was too late.

They were only a few hours away. Merina sat and reasoned aloud, "If Lenora truly meant for me to hurry to them, then I could be there in a short time and know if they really are in trouble. And if they are, the most I could do would be to get the wolves to chase me. If I can draw them far enough away before they catch me, it might allow Delnos time to complete Trinames's healing, and they could escape on foot. On the other hand, if I go for help now to the south as planned, I may come back to find them dead because I took too long."

A gust of wind from the east blew up the trail and whipped her hair back from her ears. She turned her head away to keep grit from getting into her eyes and found herself staring into the eyes of the pack leader. In shock, she couldn't move. She had been thinking so hard she had not heard his approach. The wolf licked the sides of his mouth with a long, pink tongue, as if tasting the fear that immobilized her.

He glanced behind him at the rest of his strangely silent pack, most of which lowered their heads submissively to his glare. He then trotted past Merina, the other wolves giving her a wide berth as they followed him eastward.

Merina finally released the pent-up air from her lungs and took several rapid, deep breaths. The dominant wolf, at the edge of the trail before it disappeared downward, stopped to look back at her. She said to him, "Lead on, wolf. I trust you will be able to control the other pack because if you can't, you will lose your kill to them."

The wolf seemed to nod, then led his pack downward. Merina mused to herself, "Did you just agree with me? Why do I feel so uneasy? I know I just received the shock of my life when you appeared out of nowhere, but since you didn't kill me just now, I should be feeling relief. Wait! Is that the source I feel?"

She was following the pack only as close as necessary to keep them in sight. There was that same unease coming from the east, but she noticed it seemed to move with the wolves, not fixed in place the way it had been when she climbed up the trail yesterday--or was it days ago? How could it be moving, unless Delnos was moving? Why would he be moving with an open source if he was meditating with it?

The lack of answers to her questions frustrated her and added to her anxiety. She stared at the leading wolf and yelled at him, "Something is very wrong here, fanged one! Things are not as they should be--nothing is making sense, least of all you." With her refusal to believe in what was happening, the pack leader ahead disappeared and Merina thought she saw a dark-cloaked figure in its place.

"What?" Merina choked out, then the huge white wolf looked back at her for a brief moment and gave her a wide, open-mouthed grimace before turning back to lead the pack down the trail. Merina stopped for a minute to rub her eyes. "Am I still in a dream?"

Opening her eyes, she glanced at the sun, whose brightness made her squint. She could hear the wind whistling past the scrub trees along the path and smell dust in the air. Her senses said she was awake. But am I?

Merina hurried after the pack, which was no longer in sight. She knew she was approaching the cliff where the horse had fallen, and she knew the danger that lurked there if the wolf pack that had been feeding on the carcass still lingered. She slipped once and fell, skinning the palms of her hands when she tried to break her fall. The burning pain assured her she was not asleep. As she passed the path downward to the corpse, she heard from the west, the direction of the barricade, the howl of a distressed wolf. It shot a bolt of fear through her body. She ran past the cliff and into the clearing where the trees had been cut down.

No animals waited between her and the cleft. Neither her wolf pack nor any other. "My wolf? Since when is it mine?" She swore as she wiped the blood from her knife hand on her pants leg. She paused, listening to the faint snarling and barking coming from the cleft. "Make a plan, Merina. First, bandage the hand so you don't lose your knife when you need it. Second, approach with caution and don't run headlong into a fight until you know whose side you are on. Third, make sure you have a place to retreat to."

Nodding to herself, she pulled a shirt from her saddlebag and tore the back out, wrapping it around her hand. As she did so, she hurriedly scanned the trees ahead for one she could climb. They were all too small. No retreat there. The cleft was too wide for her to defend it by herself, and climbing its rock sides was out of the question with her injured hand. She stood a better chance of retreating to the cliff face and defending that path. That damn wolf better help. Where is it? she thought furiously.

Merina sprinted to the cover of the tree line in front of her, then edged along it southward toward the cleft. She passed the stumps of the trees cut down for the barricade and scanned the area where they had left the horses. She hoped Delnos had missed finding some of the gear they had left on the horses that might have been discarded by the Kanchala. A rope would be very handy right now, but she saw none. She started into the cleft.

The noise of the angry pack swelled as she crept down the trail. A sharp yelp cut through the air, and the barking response doubled. Merina neared the entrance to the rock-strewn clearing, which faced more southerly than east, and glanced around the corner. The scene before her made her heart jump, and for a moment she could not comprehend the mayhem ahead. Wolves were everywhere. One hung from the palisade, pierced in its chest, the back legs kicking spastically in the air. Another lay beneath the wall. A sea of gray wolves milled back and forth in front of the barricade, snarling, their heads lowered in kill lust.

Delnos stood to the left side of her love, a bloodied knife in his right hand and a club in his left. Trinames sat against the wall of the cave, his broken arm tied across his chest, with his right arm waving back and forth in front of him, the knife he held covering any wolf that moved toward the barricade. One broke from the pack and sprinted forward, jumping high into the air, clearing the points. It crashed into Delnos, who managed to push it slightly to his left with the club and stabbed into its side with his knife. Another sharp yelp of pain, and the maddened animals below raged in response.

Merina looked wildly around for her white wolf and its pack. She saw two massive wolves at the rear of the pack before the wall. It looked as if they were driving the pack forward. That can't be. They should be leading the attack. And since they are both pack leaders, they should be fighting each other, not joining forces.

When she looked to the edge of the cliff next to her, she saw her wolf. There were no wolves around him. He was just sitting on his haunches, watching the battle. He was panting, his tongue lolling outside his fanged maw, occasionally wetting his nose. He looked in her direction and saw her watching him. The huge white wolf tilted his head to one side, then the other--as if he was wondering when she was going to act.

"Where is your pack?" Merina yelled at him above the noise of the crazed beasts.

The wolf looked at the sea of snarling animals and then back at her. Confused, Merina glanced at the wolves but saw no white ones fighting the grays. She yelled, "You are supposed to be helping me, damn you--do something!"

He did. Her wolf reared back his head and howled the most chilling sound she had heard in her life. It seemed to last forever, and when he stopped, the only noise in the rocky glen was the cold, gusting wind whipping past her. He stood on all four feet, gave her a look that seemed to say he had done what she asked, and trotted back through the cleft. All the eyes in the glen followed him out, and when Merina looked back at the battle scene, the eyes rested on her.

The nearest pack leader lowered his head and charged straight for her. Few boulders blocked his path, and he would be on her in seconds. Merina dumped the saddlebags from her shoulder and shifted into her defensive stance. She swung her knife low from her hip and twisted to one side as the wolf lunged for her throat. His momentum carried him past her, ripping her knife out of her hand as he crashed into the cleft wall behind her. The blade had stuck in his chest. Merina tried to yank it out, but the thrashing, dying animal made it impossible to do so. She looked behind her at the remaining wolves, which took only moments to swarm away from the barricade and begin a rush in her direction.

Merina jumped past the dying leader and ran through the cleft. Her only hope was to outrun the pack, who had to weave through the rocky ground where she had a clear path. Maybe she could get to the cliff wall and climb down far enough to escape their jaws. Reaching the edge, she realized there were few handholds or ledges she could step to, and she looked back to see how much time she had even to try. The second dominant wolf was halfway through the gap and would be on her before she had covered another foot. She got ready to dodge his attack.

Sensing she was trapped, the wolf ran around her to approach from her rear. A dozen more wolves charged through the cleft, rushing to support their leader. Her heart was racing, her chest sucking in great draughts of air. Her body was preparing to expend every bit of energy it had to fight, and she was helpless before the pack. Merina looked around for the white male and saw him sitting by the tree line, doing nothing. That sight filled her with rage.

::Good. Take the Power I offer. Now release your anger.:: The voice was back in her head.

Merina turned on the wolves bounding toward her and thrust her hands out, as if to push them away. She screamed, "Go away." And felt a release of built-up tension in her mind. A ball of flame rushed away from beyond her clawed fingertips and exploded in front of the charging wolves. The blast knocked her backward, and she almost fell. Her eyes were blinded for a moment, and she blinked, trying to refocus where the wolves had been. When her vision cleared enough, she saw dozens of blackened bodies on the ground, twitching in death. A snarling growl at her back warned her of the other pack leader, and she spun to point her right hand at him, in mid-jump. As she felt the release, a dazzling flash leaped from her fingertip and a thunderclap stunned her ears. A bolt of lightning blasted the wolf backward and threw him over the cliff edge.

Merina whirled around, but she could not hear for the ringing in her ears or see past the sparkling flashes that dazzled her eyes. Fear surged in her body, and she fought a rising panic because she could not tell if she was still under attack. What just happened? What have I just done? The knowledge that she had used magic filled her with horror.

::Calm yourself, Daughter! You and the others are safe.::

A wave of healing calm washed through Merina, and she found her senses flooding back. She was alone in the clearing, the only thing alive-- except for the huge, white pack leader. As Merina stared at him, his image blurred and in his place stood Lenora. She was dressed in the black robes of a Mage; around her neck hung a chain bearing some sort of badge of office. She beckoned Merina to approach her.

As Merina warily picked her way forward, Lenora looked to the cleft for a moment, then turned and said, "Your lover is worried, and the Tieri is...confused. As are you. You must decide what to tell them."

"What can I tell them but the truth?" Merina asked as she got within a few feet of Lenora. An aura surrounded the Magess, but Merina did not now feel the unease she associated with sorcerers. She stared at the wavering background behind the Magess and for a moment saw only the trees.

"Ahh, another growth in your skills, Daughter. Yes, I am an illusion. Now, what can you tell them? If you tell your lover about your use of Power, you will lose him to envy and jealousy. Tell Delnos Pathla m'Lothur a lie and you will lose the trust of his people, which you sorely need. Tell them each what you know, and let them decide what they will tell others."

Merina looked at her hands, then at the smoldering corpses. "I don't know what I know. I know I loathe magic, but I think I just did it. I was told that magic-users get their Power from meditating from a source--which I don't know how to do and don't have a source to do it with. Delnos said it takes a lot of time, which I didn't have. Therefore, everything I know about the use of Power could not have happened. But the explosion--"

The image of Lenora stayed Merina's rushed babbling with a finger that approached her lips but didn't touch her. "If I tell you what has happened, then you will have knowledge. Knowing, you will have to decide what you will lose."

Merina moaned fretfully, "I know I saw you earlier as the pack leader when I could not believe what was happening, then lost the truth moments later, until now. I can see past your illusion. That means--"

"Nothing of consequence," Lenora said softly to settle Merina. "Disbelieving illusions could be seen as a result of your hatred of the use of Power. Use that. Your hatred of magic will serve to protect you for a while, but you must not be seen using Power. Even if you have reconciled yourself to its use, there are those who will kill you if you do."

Merina reeled back in shock. "Helinu is begging me to be tested. Couldn't I conceal this Power-sensing? If I can use magic, I could go for training with my life-mate. It will bring me the happiness I have been denying myself all this summer."

"You know Byklandes will not allow life-mates to train together. It is not their way. And it is not anyone you know who wants you dead, Daughter. There is a reason you have been awakened to Power, but it is not time for you to know why. What I can tell you is that in time you will come to know what you need to know. It is then you will have to make even harder decisions than the ones you face now. Now go. Your friends are beginning to believe you were killed by the wolves."

Merina retreated from Lenora's dismissing hand. She turned and staggered toward the cleft. It was as if all the energy she had demanded from her body in the last hour was taken at once, so that she felt drained of life. She looked down at herself and saw that the blood of the first wolf she had killed had saturated her shirt and pants. Her own blood soaked her bandaged hand, and she smelled the singed hair around her face. *I must look dreadful.* Then, passing the exit of the cleft, she picked up her saddlebag and pulled her knife from the corpse of the leader, wiping it off on the wolf's fur. Hearing a shout from the barricade, she saw her lover struggling to stand. She yelled in alarm, "Stay there. I am coming!"

She hurried as fast as she could up the rocky path to the barricade. The look on Trinames's face was one of joy, where the one on Delnos's face showed puzzled relief. She found strength from somewhere to pull herself up the rope and was met by the Tieri, who gave her a long hug both because she was alive and to keep her from throwing herself into her lover's arms. Merina realized his caution and lowered herself to kneel beside Trinames and give him a lingering kiss.

Merina heard Delnos clear his throat and ask her, "Are you injured? The wolves?"

She sat back, reaching for Trinames's uninjured hand and squeezing it tightly. She reluctantly looked away from his adoring eyes and glanced toward the cleft. "Dead," she said, then found herself sobbing in relief, realizing they were indeed safe at last.

Delnos lowered himself to sit on the ground and reached over to steady her shoulder with a hand that itself was not too steady. Merina rubbed the tears from her eyes with her free hand and started to wipe it on her shirt when she remembered the blood on her clothes. "I'm fine, really I am. It's not my blood."

The Tieri tore off a piece of his now useless spare shirt that he had ripped into bandages and handed it to Merina, who wiped her face and took a deep breath to settle herself.

"We saw you kill the pack leader at the cleft entrance, and then you ran away, pursued by all the other wolves in the glen. What happened next?" Delnos removed his hand from her shoulder and pulled his water flask from his belt, offering it to Merina.

::What do I say now, Great Mother Lenora?::

The wind gusted around the edge of the shallow cave and swept through her hair, blowing it into her eyes. She took a sip of water, waiting for an answer, but none came. She took another, then handed the flask back to Delnos. She cleared the hair from her face and, feeling the burned ends, groped for her eyebrows. She sensed the two men's eyes on her as she rubbed where her eyebrows used to be.

Merina spoke in a dazed voice, which was how she felt at the moment. She was not acting, but a part of her mind seemed to tell her she was. "There...there was an explosion of fire in the pack. It spun me around, and another large wolf jumped at me. I heard a clap of thunder, and the wolf disappeared."

"How?" Trinames cried out, gripping her uninjured hand even more tightly.

"I don't know, love. I was blinded and couldn't hear, and the next thing I know I see a huge, white wolf staring at me."

"Is that the one, Mistress?" Delnos asked, pointing at the cleft entrance.

Merina looked in that direction and saw Lenora in wolf form sitting there. "It's him," Merina gasped out.

The wolf image shimmered away, and a black-robed figure stood where the alpha had been. Even at that distance, Merina could tell it was not Lenora, but a man, a Tieri. He pointed at Delnos with his right hand and made a series of gestures, ending with a warning sign that everyone in Saphradea knew the meaning of: "Beware the danger." He turned and disappeared into the cleft. Merina looked at Delnos, finding the set expression of someone who had been admonished on his face. She asked cautiously, "What did he signal you? That was Tierian sign language."

Delnos glanced at her, then at Trinames. "He thanked me for my services and told me I would be compensated. He warned me not to interfere in this business deal, or he would make it his business to interfere with mine."

"What business? Who was he?" Merina asked, wondering what Lenora was trying to do. *Was this my answer?*

"I don't know, Mistress. Most of our magic-users are women--your people call them bush witches. They do not learn their spell use in the training lodges. They would not be invited to train, nor would they want to leave their clan. There are very few male Tieri sorcerers, myself being one. I can only do minor Novice-level spells. In all the Domains, there is only one Tieri who has risen to the level of Mage, and her name is Tierii Chalinee Rhuhani v'Nomeles. She is in the Hermanian Coven and lives a month's journey from here. That Mage could not have been Tieri--why he disguised himself as such is worrisome."

Merina stroked the back of Trinames's grasping hand to pull his attention off Delnos and to get her lover to free her aching limb. She removed the saddlebag from her back and used it to help prop him up against the cave wall. When she had him settled, she glanced at Delnos. Though he was staring in their direction, his eyes did not focus on them.

She stepped over to him, touching his left arm, which brought him back to their presence. "And his business--was he angry because you used Power? Is that his business?"

He closed his deep-set eyes briefly, then focused on her face. "I do not know what he means by 'his business'--perhaps I misinterpreted his sign. My uncle holds the claim for all trade in this part of Saphradea. No one else is allowed to conduct business here unless they are doing so against our Clan laws. And we do not settle claims by threatening one another. That is a matter for the Ruling Clan to decide. If he was Tieri, he would know that."

"So you don't know what service you provided or why you're getting paid?" Merina asked.

"Apparently, but that is not how we Tieri conduct business," Delnos said with a grim look on his face.

Is Lenora trying to shut Delnos up? That isn't going to work on him. The wind whipped around them, its chill reminding Merina that she was still wet from blood. She reached down, grabbed the slain wolf's back legs, and began to drag it toward the barricade's spear points. Delnos helped her to push the corpse over the edge. She turned to do the same with the dead wolf hung by a spear, but it was too deeply impaled for her to push it off. She gave up after a half-hearted try and trudged to the meager pile of wood that remained near the extinguished fire, gathering small twigs to rebuild it.

While she made her preparations, Delnos checked Trinames's wounds, removed Merina's saddlebags from behind him, and lowered Trinames so that he was lying on his back. The Tieri gave her love a drink from a flask that lay by Trinames's side. Some of the tension in her love's face eased, and he half-closed his eyes while watching her.

"He is almost well enough to be moved, Mistress. Will you be able to do so in the morning?" Delnos asked in a low voice.

"Can you do no more for him?" she asked.

Shaking his head, the Tieri knelt away from the flames that began to lick up around the logs. "There is more healing that could be done, but it is beyond my skills. I made a potion to ease the pain. It is the best I can do to make him able to move."

Looking around for her cooking pot, she spotted it near the edge of the fire pit where she had left it. She pulled travel rations from her bag and decided they needed all they could eat now rather than go to half-rationing. She muttered loud enough for Delnos to hear, "Could that Mage have healed Trinames?"

"If he was the one who killed the wolf pack, probably not. The spells I heard used were Aggressor spells. Domain sorcerers do not train in other disciplines' area of expertise. Healers would not have the kind of mind that would release Power to destroy or kill, nor would a Provisioner. That is what they are taught in the training lodges, especially as they advance their skills beyond Novice. If he was a real Mage, then he must have studied at either Delmathia's Inhestia lodge, Saphradea's Byklandes lodge, or Hermania's Wendelia lodge. If he was Tierian... We have been able to use simple spells from other disciplines, which the training lodges don't allow. I'm curious why you asked. Do you now believe it is all right to work magic?"

Careful! Merina warned herself. She busied herself putting the dried rations in the pot and covering them with water to soak. She sat back and gave Delnos her attention. "I know so little of magic. I have always seen it as a weakness that people too easily fall back on. Yet, when Trinames"-- she looked at her now sleeping lover--"was so badly hurt, I wanted him to be healed so we could escape the wolves. It was selfish, I know that now, but our lives were in danger. Having accepted its use for healing, I saw how you and Trinames could survive starvation by stretching the rations with food and water provided by Power--and thought that was good. Only..."

"Magic was used against us from the start," Delnos cut in, seeing where Merina was going. "Yes, Mistress, it has, and will always have, a bad side. The Kanchala hid their attack using magic. Something drove those wolves to pursue and attack us far beyond what they would do naturally."

Merina caught her breath. "That's so true. The wolves had fed before they followed us here. We would have been a very small meal for them if they were starving."

Delnos chuckled. "Now you say I am a mere mouthful."

His laughter distracted Merina, and when she realized he had made a joke to break her tension, she relaxed a bit. "The thought had occurred to me to throw you to them to save us."

"No--now I know you enough not to say that."

The seriousness of his response made Merina quickly say, "I meant it as a jibe, Delnos."

"But it has truth behind it. We talked about the Kanchala luring us up here for a reason. Could we have been bait for a trap, Mistress?"

Merina caught his train of thought. "Let's say for the moment the Mage was Tierian. I know--you don't agree to that, but let's propose he is. He would have known about Kanchala. He could have hired them."

"That would be true if he was of my people. Why hire them to kidnap your young man asleep over there? Why not just have them kill the wolves?"

"Could they have? They seemed very skilled," Merina mused.

"There were a lot of wolves. Kanchala never do anything that would involve such an unknown risk. How would they know how many wolves would show up? It would have been a major hunt for even your valley folk to make."

Merina nodded, then said, "So they needed to ride a party of humans through a forest infested with hungry wolves to a spot where the wolves could be concentrated and an easy target for the Mage to kill them. The Kanchala grab a town resident..."

"Who better than a Healer?" Delnos mused.

"But Trinames isn't one," Merina protested.

"He was wearing the robes. That was their big mistake. And an even bigger one was that his disappearance did not cause any special alarm for the people of Dysandes."

"Except for us!" Merina added quickly. "By exposing their true selves to me, they hoped I would raise the alarm--which I did. But no one believed my story. They eventually got their pursuit, as small as it was, but it would have to suffice. Since I identified them as Tierian, the Kanchala, or the Mage, knew you would become the focus of an investigation of some sort, so that would mean he knew you would get involved. Maybe because you got dragged into this that he felt he needed to offer compensation."

Delnos used his knife point to lift the pot next to the fire and scooped coals around its base. "So far this is making sense, but a question jumps into my mind. Why keep us alive?"

"That is easy enough to answer," Merina said, laying her bare knife blade on the glowing coals to cleanse it. "He would need witnesses who could tell Captain Garlantis of the Mage saving them by killing the wolves."

Merina used the cleaned knife blade to stir the simmering water in the cooling pot. The truth is I was lured to a cave in the Non-Lands to have my Power awakened by whoever cast the illusion of Lenora. Did that person actually make a business deal with the Captain? If not, we are going to be in big trouble explaining what happened up here.

"When we return to Dysandes we should very careful what we tell the good Captain," Delnos said, as if reading her mind. "But I am very curious to know what happened to you after you left three nights ago."

Three nights? Merina wished she knew herself. "I went past the cliff face where the horse fell and decided to keep going east up the hill, following a game trail. I saw I could connect to a ridge coming up from the south and hoped to avoid the wolves in the valley below. When I got to the ridge, a new pack of wolves picked up my scent and drove me back up the mountainside I was on. The pack was led by that white wolf."

"Ahh, I see," Delnos said, "the Mage was luring more wolves to his trap and found one of the bait, you, had escaped. What happened next?"

"I fell several times and injured my right knee. I found a cave in the side of the mountain and went inside. The wolves did not follow me in. Perhaps there was something in there they didn't want to meet. I was so exhausted I feel asleep. When I awoke, my knee was no longer hurt. Maybe the Mage came in after me and healed it. I walked out of the cave just before morning--I thought the morning of the next day. It would seem I was asleep for several days." Merina looked at her sleeping lover, then glanced at Delnos. "What happened to you in that time?"

"The wolves started arriving late in the afternoon of the first day. I continued to heal Trinames as best I could, and we took turns watching the gathering wolves while the other slept. I was surprised when I woke the next morning that the wolves were still in the area. I could see another pack leader had arrived, and the two packs seemed to be getting along with each other, which is very odd. I noticed that white wolf late in the afternoon sitting near the cleft entrance watching the other wolves. They were all made very nervous by his presence."

Merina stirred the pot again. "Do you think the Mage was driving the wolves to this place?"

"Someone was, as well as keeping the wolves gathered and making them more and more tense. Hunger may have been doing that. The next morning, I saw the white wolf come through the gap and excite the packs into attacking us. He watched the whole thing from where you found him when you entered. The rest of the story we both know. What did you do when you left the cave? Why did you return?"

Lifting the pot off the coals, Merina set it on a nearby rock to cool. She took out her cup and pointed to Trinames's, sitting by Delnos, who retrieved it and handed his own cup over to her as well. "I started back down the trail. I wasn't sure why the wolf pack had not attacked me when they could have, but I had a nagging feeling that I had been driven to the cave for a reason I came to where I had first seen the huge white wolf. I sat to consider what I should do next--go for help, which meant encountering that wolf pack again, or return to Trinames and you. I'm not sure why, but I had the strongest urge to get back to the barricade because you were in danger."

"Was the Mage around?" Delnos asked, looking at Merina with his eyes slitted, as if trying to visualize her story in his mind.

"I don't know, but really, yes." She explained how she had followed the white wolf.

Merina used her cup to dip out some trail stew and filled Delnos's cup. He accepted it from her and took out a spoon from his belt pouch, blowing on the stew to cool it further before eating. Merina refilled her cup and sniffed the steam rising from it. "Needs salt," she said, rummaging in her own pouch for the small bag of seasonings she kept there.

"And a nice red wine would go well with it, if you have that in there as well." Delnos chuckled.

"Sorry, Tieri, that was my mother's area of expertise," Merina said, but with less bitterness than she would have used a week ago. "Water will have to do."

Delnos glanced at her, apparently sorry he might have irritated an old wound. He must have hoped she would be more open to the use of Power after this past harrowing experience of theirs. Merina caught the look and said lightly, "Unless you..."

"No, Mistress, I have no Power available and would rather eat this excellent meal while it is warm." Delnos dipped his spoon in to replenish his cup from the pot and looked to see if Merina wanted more. She peeked into the pot, saw there was plenty for her lover to have seconds, and held out her cup.

Delnos filled it and, looking at Trinames, said, "I will volunteer to feed the young man over there his share when we are done so you can have an empty pot to brew us all some tea."

"Gladly, sir. And before you wake him, let me thank you for all you have done for Trinames--and myself!"

"I thank you in return for trusting me to do the task you hired me for. I know your people view Tieri as only doing what we must to get the most gold out of every business trade we make. And in many cases that is accurate, but this has been an adventure I would have undertaken at cost because it has been so mysterious and intriguing. Not that I would say it was enjoyable almost being eaten by wolves, but we weren't. It is a tale worthy of being told around my clan's campfires. Plus, I find that I am being paid to do a job I have done nothing for. So I say 'thank you' once more."

Merina remembered what Lenora had warned her about having the ability to sense Power in another magic-user and said nothing to the Tieri about her dreams in the cave. When Delnos had said he was not able to do a Provisioner spell to change water into wine because he was drained of Power, she had already known that because she felt no emanations from him. When he suggested after dinner that he meditate to regain Power so that he could heal her wounds and make further potions, she did not protest the idea as she would have earlier. He waited until Trinames was asleep and suggested she follow her lover's example. She was very tired and glad to move to Trinames's side to share his blanket and give him her warmth.

When Delnos opened his source to begin, she felt awash in the unease that the presence of Power gave her. She did her best to ignore it, and the stress of all she had experienced that day quickly overcame the feeling. She fell into a deep sleep.

How long she slept before she awoke enough to recognize the uneasiness again, she did not know. Perhaps what broke into her unconsciousness was that the uneasiness was blinking on and off. Not really flickering like a candle flame, but full on, then off. Not wishing to let it awaken her, she pushed the irritation the blinking created as far away as she could, as if it were the whine of a mosquito in the summer night's air.

Chapter 13

Merina had watched her uncle and his men lift a pallet of hay bales into the loft of the barn on numerous occasions, but she had never rigged the ropes to get this simple task accomplished. Not having a pulley system was going to make it all the harder to lift Trinames's stretcher over the spear point barricade. Only the fact that it would take her forever to chop through the spears with her knife kept her from abandoning her plan. Delnos had gone to search the corpse of the dead horse to see if any useful equipment was left, leaving her to devise a plan to move her love from the shallow cave.

"We could do with more rope," Merina said to Trinames.

"Not much chance of that, love. Have you thought of making a ramp of small trees to slide me down?"

"Yes, but that amounts to as much work as cutting the barricade down."

Trinames nodded, seeing her point. He had already tried to suggest he could get up out of the stretcher with the Tieri's help, but Merina and Delnos did not want him putting any pressure on his healing breaks. He had just started to repeat the proposal when they heard Delnos call from the clearing entrance. Looking up, they were surprised to see him standing there with two horses. He tied the horses to a scrub tree and hurried toward them.

"Those look like ours!" Merina yelled to the Tieri as he approached the barricade.

"They are, and not a scratch on them. I found them tied up on the trail you followed away from the cliff. There is little chance they were there yesterday. You would have had to pass them on your return. All our gear is on them, including this extra rope." He raised the coil up to hand it to her. "Someone is looking after us, but the question is who?"

"Or why?" Merina added. "Could it have been the Tieri Mage?"

"Doubtful," Delnos said as he pulled himself up. "The horses were hobbled military style. My guess would be the Kanchala did it."

"Kanchala?" Trinames asked, sitting up in the stretcher to hear better.

Delnos looked at Trinames, then Merina. She knew he had avoided using the Tierian name for the assassins before because he did not want to have to explain they were hired killers. He apparently figured the young man was well enough now to be told the truth of what had happened to him. Merina nodded to the Tieri, letting him explain what a Kanchala was. Merina watched Trinames's face twist in fear when Delnos told him of the assassins.

Trinames shook his head in disbelief. "So we were bait for a trap. And this Mage Merina spoke of?"

"The wolves were killed by a very powerful fireball. I took a good look at the corpses of the pack as I passed them, and there was little left of them but charred remains. I was surprised to find anything because a fireball does more damage from the blast than from the heat. The Mage expertly aimed the fireball above the pack, smashing them into the ground. He certainly knew his business," Delnos said with a certain amount of respect in his voice.

Gazing at his love, Trinames said, "A magic-user saved us, Mer. See, Power can be used for good!"

Merina nodded slowly. Not that she was agreeing with him, but wondering how she managed to produce an expert fireball with no training. "Yes, love, but it was almost pure chance that he didn't kill me in the process. The wolves were really close."

"We owe him a debt, Merina."

Delnos shook his head. "Actually, young sir, he owes us one. At least he said he did. You see, I think he was the one who set this plan in motion. We were the bait for his trap. He must have hired the assassins to capture you. He is Tieri, and very few people of the Domains know of the Kanchala except my people."

Trinames said with mounting anger, "You mean this whole sorry adventure was just a business deal? That is what Tieri are known for. We could have all been killed."

"But we weren't, love." Merina soothed him, squeezing his hand. "At first we thought that's what the Kanchala intended. I thought Markinis might have arranged with them to make you disappear. I was so worried for you!"

"But you came after me knowing they were assassins! Why, after I tried to trick you into taking the Test?" The anger vanished from his voice, replaced by regret and wonder.

"I love you, Tri. And I know you love me because you thought you had to do what you did to keep yourself in the competition with Markinis. There is no other suitor, love. I want you as my life-mate--only you." Merina kissed him with tears streaming down her face, hugging him as close as she could considering his injuries.

Delnos's cheeks reddened, and he turned away to give the young people a moment of privacy. He busied himself slinging the new rope over the same tree limb the Kanchala used for the first rope.

Drying her tears and Trinames's, Merina stared at the Tierian's back. The sight of him working re-awoke her to where they were and the danger they still faced. She left her lover's side to help.

Although Delnos had healed the torn skin on Merina's hands that morning, the remaining injuries made tying knots difficult. She succeeded in tying one end of the rope Delnos had put over the branch to the bottom of her love's stretcher, making a loop around the two poles. Seeing her difficulty, the Tierian took over the job. With surprising expertise he rigged the rope so that the two ends of the stretcher were suspended by a single line going up and over the tree limb supporting the original rope used to climb into the cave. When Merina stood to help him pull on the line to lift the stretcher off the ground, he told her to use her strength to guide the unwieldy burden as close to the barricade as she could. She found as she started to pull it toward the spear points with her back to the points that the stretcher swung up like a pendulum, making it hard for her to pull it horizontally. This arrangement was not going to work, as she told Delnos after minutes of trying.

"I see your point," he said, lowering the stretcher back down. "We can't use the climbing rope to pull upward because it is tied to the limb."

"I could climb up it and untie it," she suggested.

Shaking his head, Delnos said, "It is too short to loop over."

Studying the rig, Merina saw the answer. "Let's tie the climbing rope to the point where your rope holds the two ends suspended. We'll do this after you have lifted him a few feet off the ground. If I make the climbing line as tight as possible, it will help hold him up. Then, when you lower him a little, the stretcher will swing toward the climbing line."

"Ah, an excellent suggestion. We will have to do this many times, because we will have to reposition the pulley rope closer and closer to the climbing line. Eventually it will replace the climbing line so we can lower Trinames down. I am very impressed, Mistress. You have the quick mind for moving cargo."

Busy tying the climbing rope in place, Merina smiled in thanks. "Watching the boatmen at the docks helped. Too bad we couldn't rig a boom like they have to move heavy loads so easily."

In return, the Tierian said, "I'll bet given more time, you could do just that. Let me lift him now. I suppose you learned knots by watching the dockworkers."

"Them, and my uncle. That should hold him, lower away."

Keeping the stretcher level, Merina watched as it swung toward the edge a foot or so before settled on the rocky ground. "This is going to take a while," she muttered to no one in particular. And it did.

It took them all morning to get Trinames past the barricade to the spot where the horses stood waiting. Merina knew by the time she reached the clearing entrance she was not going to be able to carry the stretcher much farther. Her hands ached continuously, and blisters were beginning to appear. Seeing her tiring and in pain, Trinames again insisted he could make it to the horses. Merina seriously thought through the idea. Delnos shook his head. He told Merina the movement of the stretcher itself was bad enough as they threaded their way through the boulders in the clearing. They could not risk the patient's falling. He stopped the young man from badgering them by given Trinames several sips of a potion that made him sleepy. Thus they were able to get him into the clearing beyond the cleft with no further arguments.

Studying the path that led by the cliff face, Merina felt the strength drain from her body, realizing they still had to carry Trinames down the steep incline. Their plan to get him home was to rig a travois behind her horse and drag him slowly through the forest they had ridden through to get here. There was no possible way the horse travois could get down the hill safely. That meant they would have to carry him down.

Merina slumped to the ground and stared at her feet, not wanting to look toward the problem that felt overwhelming at the moment.

Delnos spoke above her, "Rest a moment. Drink some water and think of the day we met. Remember the bath you were so eager to take, to relax by the flowing water on the warm grass of the island you swam to. It was--"

Looking up at the Tieri, Merina said flatly, "I am too tired to think of that day, Delnos." Before he could counter with more soothing words, another realization flashed into her mind and she said with much more spirit, "Wait a minute. I saw you row away before I ever went into the water. How did you know I swam to the island?"

Sitting down wearily beside her, he shrugged. "Where else could you have gone?"

He asked the question innocently enough, and his face betrayed nothing else, but Merina felt a surge of energy course through her body. With mounting anger she pointed a bandaged-wrapped hand at him and poked him sharply in the chest. "You were spying on me! Did the sight of my naked body make you excited, old man?"

"I'm not an old man, Mistress, and yes, you are a woman of great beauty and very alluring. But I am still a man. Isn't that what you expect of men?"

"Yes," she said with anger, "and when I finish cutting off your manhood--"

"Before you do so," Delnos said, backing away from the knife that appeared almost magically in her hand, "I could use some of that energy to help lower your fiancé down the cliff yonder."

Merina looked in the direction he was pointing and then back at him. "Nice trick, sir. You best hope that energy is used up by the time we reach the bottom, or I might just follow through with my threat."

She stood and untethered the horses, walking them to the cliff edge and retying them where the Kanchala, or the Mage, had left them before. As she worked her way back to where Delnos stood by the stretcher, she had to acknowledge he had probably found the one thing that would have awakened her anger faster than anything else he could have said.

And waking that anger evoked the strength to go on. *He knows me well, this Tieri.*

Delnos took the lead down the slope, since he was slightly taller and had to lift his end higher to keep Trinames from sliding off the stretcher. The shuffling passage down took forever, with several stops that got increasingly longer as they neared the bottom. It was all Merina could do to drive herself an additional several hundred feet beyond the rotting corpse of the horse to get away from the smell and horde of insects feeding off the viscera. As she stumbled past, the thought crossed through her mind that the wolves should have eaten more of it than was missing. Why hadn't they? What would drive them off a kill uneaten? How had Lenora done that?

Merina collapsed beside the stretcher while Delnos trudged slowly back up the way they had come to retrieve the horses. She wanted to help, knowing the horses would not want to pass the rotting corpse, but she could not will any more energy into her trembling leg muscles. Trinames woke and called her name, giving her the excuse she needed to turn her attention from the Tieri's retreating back and lean over to reassure her love.

"Where are we?" he asked, struggling to sit up and look around.

"Near the cliff where the horse fell and died. Do you remember that?"

"No, no, I don't. I heard you talking with Delnos about searching a body. We couldn't have gone very far. Look at the sun! The day is almost gone. We'll never get home at this pace."

Merina shushed him, touching his lips with a shaking forefinger. He took her hand in his and examined the blisters, murmuring that he wished he could heal them. Because she was afraid her own despair would only deepen his, she forced her voice to sound light and spirited. "Look, here Delnos comes with the horses. Once we rig the travois, we will make much faster progress."

Catching some enthusiasm from her, Trinames patted her hand gently and smiled at her, saying, "First, rest awhile. You need to wash the sores and re-bandage them. I could do that much for you."

Merina turned to gaze into his eyes. "I would like it if you could wash my whole body. I really do smell terrible."

Sniffing the air, Trinames shook his head. "I'm afraid what you smell is me--or the dead horse. I can't figure out which is worse. I've gone over a week without bathing."

"My point exactly, love. First we must find a stream we refill our water bottles from, then we can indulge in a nice wash..."

Trinames lay there grinning.

"What are you smiling at, Tri?"

"That is what I love about you. Taking charge--planning every detail. And the image of you sitting in a stream washing--"

Delnos cut in, stopping next to the stretcher. "Careful, young sir. Your betrothed has threatened to cut off my manhood for doing just what you are suggesting. At least this time, she will know I, too, am truly watching, not just because she thought I was."

Blushing, Merina had forgotten her threat in her weariness. "What point would I make cutting off my love's manhood? Yours, though, is still not safe."

"Then to be sure, we men will watch each other to ensure neither looks. Is that fair, Trinames?"

The young Neophyte looked unhappy but nodded.

"Good! And by the way, Mistress. I'll wash your young man. Wouldn't want you to see anything you shouldn't."

Merina's jaw dropped open. She started to protest, then realized Delnos was pointing out her hypocrisy. She closed her mouth and said tightly, but with no anger, "Fine. That is how it should be. Now let's get moving before I stiffen up so badly I wouldn't be able to ride."

The bath in the stream had brought a cold shock to her body that made her heart race and gave her another boost of energy, which she used to do a hurried wash of her shirt and undershift. She didn't bother with her leather pants--she had no replacement, and they would never dry in the cool night air. The men did give her the moments of privacy they said they would, but she knew both had glanced in her direction when she gasped after splashing water onto her chest and arms.

The remains of the shirt she had torn for bandages did a poor job of removing the chilly water from her skin. She was glad to put on her last wool shirt. It clung to her breasts, and the memory of the last time that had happened flashed into her mind. It made her all the more eager to seek the comfort of Trinames's side, even if he would be asleep long before she could do so.

Delnos had less skill as a cook than one would expect from a man who traveled alone. At best the stew was warm and filling, with a strange taste that Merina could not identify. He had made it while she bathed, so she didn't see what he put into the pot. It could not have been the dried meat or crackers from their rations. The presence of torn stalks of reeds from the stream hinted at roots of some kind.

The Tieri gave Trinames a draught of the potion in his flask, and her love dropped off to sleep. Delnos returned to his seat by the fire, putting the potion away. He turned to Merina and said in a low voice, "If we retrace our path here from Dysandes, it will take nearly a week dragging the travois. We barely have the food to do so, even supplementing it from what we can forage along the way. We might take a bird or two with my crossbow, but I am as good a shot as I am a cook."

Merina smiled at the wryness of his comment. "What was that you put in the stew?"

"I don't know the Saphradean word--it may not have one. My people call it ponilta. It will thicken a soup or stew and helps prevent bloating."

"I hope it is digestible," Merina said, rubbing her stomach.

"It is not poisonous, Mistress. But do not worry, we will not starve to death with my wood lore. I am more anxious that we get Trinames to a Healer faster. There is a road to the east, about two days from here."

"The road to the Barrens?" Merina asked, puzzled that he would suggest that route. The Barrens was only a collection of small homesteads scattered along a rutted path traveled at most twice a year by the poor farmers living there to bring their produce to town. "They are farther away from us than Dysandes, and they have no Healer there. How is that a help?"

Delnos looked toward the east, hesitating. "My uncle travels that route regularly. He has found himself stranded on occasion and needed to make use of supplies he has hidden along the way. In one cache there is a small cart--"

Merina cut in, excitedly clapping her hands. "Now that is exactly what we need."

"--and proper food and wine. My uncle believes in traveling well. There are even trade goods there, dresses and such," glancing at Merina's bloodstained pants, "which we can use to make ourselves a bit more presentable before reaching town."

Glancing down at her disheveled clothes, Merina asked meekly, "Do I look so bad, Delnos?"

Trinames answered sleepily, woken by his love's clapping, "No, you are beautiful."

The buzzing at the back of her mind from the source was less irritating that night than it had been the previous. As she snuggled contently against her love's warm body, letting her mind skip through the tiring but fulfilling day, she felt the stirring of a strange attraction to the emanations of the source. This was totally at odds with the unease it had caused her before. Or maybe it did not bother her as much because she was even more exhausted at the end of this day than before. She tried to think through what really made her uncomfortable, but sleep whisked her away before she could find a reason.

Since the travois was hitched to Delnos's horse, the stallion being larger and stronger than Merina's filly, this arrangement left Merina in a position to ride forward to scout out the best path through the trees. She was glad to do this because when Trinames was awake, he would pester Delnos about healing spells and the use of Power. Their conversation was difficult to hear with the scraping of the travois logs on the ground, and Merina was not very interested in the subject. From what little she heard, she could not reconcile what had happened to her at the cleft with what they talked about. As she rode off to search for a clearer path, she wondered if she had even done what Lenora said she did. Grids and speed of spell transmission, visualizing the joining of skin and blood vessels--none of that made sense to her.

Borrowing the Tieri's crossbow, she rode into a meadow she found on her scouting expedition and tried her luck at hunting pheasant. With her bow at home, and the services of the dogs, she could do as well as her uncle. He used a crossbow, having been trained in its use in the Prince of Prince's army. It was heavy and awkward for her to handle. Delnos's was a lighter version, made for game and not armored men. This difference was fortunate for her because without a dog to put the birds to flight, she had to carry the bow at the shoulder ready to shoot. The birds would explode out of the brush and be gone before she could shoulder the weapon and fire.

The thought jumped into her mind after the first few misses that if she really knew how to do it, she could simply point at the bird and shoot a lightning bolt into it. She aimed the index finger on her right hand at a tree and yelled "kill" at it. Nothing happened, and she had to laugh at how stupid she must have looked. She lost half of her available bolts to misses before she managed to down a bird. She hoped the Tieri would not be angry over the loss of his bolts. When she rode up to the men, she held the bird aloft and got a cheer from her love.

"How many bolts did it take you, Mistress?" Delnos asked, accepted the crossbow back.

"Ten. I'm sorry, Delnos."

Grumbling, the Tieri congratulated her on her success. "I would never have tried, Mistress. This will be the most expensive meal I have had this month."

"Just don't spoil it with ponilta, sir. And it does not ease bloat much, at least not in Saphradeans," Merina quipped back. "How much farther, do you think?"

The Tieri took his source out of his belt pouch and opened it, a move that took Merina by surprise. She flinched. Delnos gave her a strange look, closing the box with a snap. He stared at Merina, as if she was supposed to do something. Confused, she glanced around to see if he was looking at someone else. Off to the east she felt the uneasiness she knew came from a source.

"Not far, Mistress. Care to lead us?"

Merina shook her head.

The constant bumping and swaying of the travois took its toll on Trinames. He did not complain about the pain much, but Merina could see it in his face. As the day progressed, he became less talkative and took to staring at the scenery slowly drawing away behind him. Delnos saw the change in his patient and slowed their pace considerably. He made the decision to camp much earlier than they had been doing, which raised a protest from the younger man, who didn't want his injuries to prevent their getting home sooner.

Merina tended to Trinames's comfort as well as she could under the circumstances. She washed the sweat from his face, giving him little kisses every time he started to say something about the delay. Trinames finally gave up and watched the preparation of the pheasant. Merina baked it in a pit of coals, covered by wet leaves, with herbs she found along the stream they camped beside. The bird was not very large but would supplement nicely the bread and dried meat stew that simmered near the fire.

Trinames made an effort to praise her attempt at cooking the meal, but he did not want to eat much. She managed to coax him to eat his portion of the bird and got a fair amount of hers into him before he realized what she was doing and refused to take anything from her. She made a show of eating the pasty stew, commenting on how she was beginning to like the roots Delnos kept putting into it. After the pot was emptied, she washed it out and made tea. With the promise of finding the cache on the morrow, she made the tea extra strong. Delnos gave Trinames a large drink of the potion, which acted quickly to put the injured man to sleep.

Merina sipped her tea and stared at the fire, finding the flames more interesting than the Tieri who sat across from her.

"Tieri rarely take the Test. Once or twice in a decade, a Tieri shows great promise and is given permission by our clan leader to be tested. Since most of the Domain's magic-users despise my people, taking the Test usually costs the clan a great deal of gold and puts obligations on us that we do not wish to be beholden to. Tierii Chalinee is the last one I know of. She is sister to the ruler of all the clans. We call that clan the Rhuhani. She is Sorcerii Hitalna-ar, which translates as 'Magess'. A very powerful Aggressor, probably the most powerful in all the Domains. The Hermanians were the only people who would accept her into their Coven, their word for Council of Magi."

Merina glanced at Delnos, wondering why he was telling her this again. She found him staring back at her with those deep-set eyes, a slight frown on his face.

"I asked her once what the Test consisted of. She gave me her sternest glare and told me it was a secret not to be revealed to the uninitiated. I asked why the Tieri had no need to test their people, since so few of us learned to use Power. Tieri find that you either sense the source or you don't. She just smiled but said nothing more on the subject. I suppose she wanted to maintain the mystique of the uniqueness of sorcerers."

Sighing, Merina busied herself refilling her cup. Delnos held his out, which she filled. "Why, sir, are you telling me this? I refused Trinames's request to have me tested and made it clear to Helinu I would not be."

The Tieri set his cup down to cool. He chose a small branch from the wood pile beside the fire and broke it, tossing the pieces onto the glowing coals. Flames shot up from them, and Merina blinked at their brightness. He said, "When I was tending your lover's wounds after you left to go for help, I would meditate to get my Power back up. He would ask me what I was doing, and I explained it to him. He nodded, saying that it would take months of training, according to Sorceress Helinu, before he could learn to fill his grid."

"I know, he told me that himself. What--"

Delnos cut her off. "Part of the Test is whether the person being tested reacts to a source. He never did. That is not to say what Helinu said was a lie or that she passed him after he failed to react. I believe a person can be taught to seek Power, then be taught to use it, but many sorcerers I know scoff at the idea. So Trinames may be a perfectly normal candidate, but I don't think so."

Merina avoided Delnos's intense gaze. She stared into her cup, swirling the hot liquid to cool it. "I have my doubts, Tieri, whether Trinames will learn to be a Healer. His heart is set on it, but..."

"He didn't react. You did. And you sensed a source being exposed at a distance. That is something all sorcerers can do. Whether you like it or not, you would pass the Test. What you do with that knowledge is up to you."

Merina looked into the Tieri's eyes. "I will never be tested, and I will never be trained. I am a farmer, I will remain so. I do not need Power to do what I do best."

Delnos smiled and nodded his acknowledgement of her message.

Merina noticed the thinning of the trees ahead and hoped she had found a sizable clearing. The last few miles of forest had slowed them considerably. She found in her scouting foray that she was being forced to head north, away from Dysandes, to find a path that supported the passage of the travois. Breaking out of the tree line, she found herself on an overgrown and deeply-rutted road.

"Saved at last!" Merina said aloud, as if the horse could understand. The road ran slightly downhill from the northwest to the southeast. The choice of which way to continue was easy. She was about to turn her horse and ride back into the trees when a flash of light from the crest of the road to the northeast caught her eye. She stared at the spot for several minutes, wondering if she had really seen anything, when the top of a wagon cover slowly rose out of the road. Pulled by a team of horses, the wagon crested the hill. The shape of the wagon was distinctive, Merina having ever seen only one like it in the valley. It was a Tieri caravan, belonging to Delnos's uncle.

Merina rode up to meet the ancient Tieri, who waved at her when his old eyes could focus on her. She greeted him with a shout. "Jalanos! What a surprise to find you here. How are you?"

She didn't expect him to answer, as she had never heard him speak much louder than a whisper. It was a wonder that he still breathed. When the wagon drew abreast of her, she turned and rode alongside the driver's side. The old Tieri gave her a warm smile, which made his wrinkled face even more lined. He expertly reined in the team of horses, braking the wagon to keep it from rolling down the hill.

Once the wagon was secure, he turned to her and said in his oddly-accented Saphradean, "My nephew? He is well?"

"He's fine. He is pulling a travois with my betrothed behind him. I scouted ahead to find a better path for him. He is about an hour away."

Nodding, the Tieri looked in the direction where Merina knew Delnos was--how he identified it, she did not know. He said, "That about right. I wait here, you go get."

Merina said hesitantly, "Of...of course. My betrothed needs to get to a healer as soon as possible, he--"

Shooing her off, Jalanos barked hoarsely, "I know, I know. You waste time--ride!"

Merina turned in the direction of Delnos, focusing on that sense of uneasiness she knew was his Power grid, and urged her horse into the trees. Before looking away, she glimpsed a knowing smile on the ancient Tieri's lips.

Chapter 14

Merina was surprised at the strength of Delnos's uncle. When she gripped her end of Trinames's stretcher to lift him into the wagon, the old man made a disapproving sound in his throat and said something rapidly in Tierian. Delnos waved her away, and Jalanos stepped in to take her place. The two men maneuvered the stretcher up the back steps of the caravan, and in a few moments her love was loaded aboard. One side of wagon was stacked high with securely stowed trade goods; the other had a bed running the length of the wagon. Into it Trinames was secured and covered with a blanket against the cool air of the mountains. Delnos gave him a dose from the flask.

Jalanos motioned them out the back of the wagon, saying something to Delnos in their language. Delnos told Merina his uncle wanted their horses tied in trail behind the wagon, with the two of them riding up front. There was wine and food up there for them.

And there was. Jalanos had the wagon rolling down the road at a pace Merina thought faster than she would drive it, but the Tieri caravan was made for such roads and the driver obviously skilled in its use. She tried to thank Jalanos as she climbed up onto the bench seat in front next to him, but he waved at the basket under their feet and made eating motions. The next hour passed in relative silence as Merina and Delnos pulled bread, cheese, and fish from their wrappings, relishing the freshness of the food and flavors their tongues had forgotten existed.

When Merina opened the wine, she looked for cups to pour out a portion for herself and Delnos. Jalanos, seeing her search the basket, grunted and reached for the bottle. Holding the reins in one hand, he drank a swig from the bottle and, using the index finger of the hand clasping the bottle neck, he pointed at the other bottles lying in the basket.

Delnos understood Jalanos's gesture and said to Merina, "You'll just spill the wine if you try to drink from a cup. There is a bottle for each of us."

Merina nodded, having seen numerous bottles. "More than one each, I suspect. Is he trying to get us drunk?"

Laughing, Delnos shook his head. "The bottles have corks, Mistress. He is trying to keep us from making a mess in his wagon. These are our homes, you know."

Merina pulled the cork on a bottle that appeared to hold white wine and followed Jalanos's example. She nearly spilled wine down her front in the process but managed to swallow it before it escaped. Holding the bottle upright against the sway of the wagon, she tried to read the emblem embossed on the front. "This is Dame Brischelu's wine."

"My uncle's favorite and our best seller." Delnos held up his bottle. "She makes an excellent red as well. Try it, if you don't mind sharing mine, or open another bottle."

Merina thought of all they had just gone through, shrugged, and traded bottles with Delnos. The red was delicious and went better with cheese. The two continued to eat and trade bottles back and forth until the wine was gone. There was more food in the basket than they could finish, including cookies that Merina had passed over going after the cheese. She sat back filled and slightly drunk. The swaying motion of the wagon made her think of the rocking chairs on her porch at home, and her mind wandered off. She felt drowsy and saw Delnos was already asleep on her right. Her final conscious thought was that they were safe at last.

Merina's dream was broken when the wagon hit a large hole in the road and bounced its occupants off their seats. She had been drifting in and out, dimly aware of the wagon's movement, and wanted to return to the scene in her mind where she and Trinames were sailing on the river. She heard him say something, but he was speaking in Tierian. She queried aloud, "What? What?" and was awake.

The two men looked at her. "Did we wake you?" Delnos asked.

"I heard my name, then the words 'Sorcerii Hitalna-ar'. That means Magess. I am not..."

"You misheard, Mistress," Delnos soothed. "I was telling my uncle about the Tierian mage. In Tierian, we use a double 'i' to speak of women, and a single 'i' for men. That is why you call me 'Tieri', and I would call you 'Tierii'."

"Oh, I see," Merina said, but she was sure she had heard them talking about her. "Does your uncle know," she struggled to say the name correctly, "Tierii Chalinee Rhuhani v'Nomeles?"

Jalanos nodded.

"This Magess, Tierii Chalinee--you said she was a ruler of your clan."

Delnos shook his head. "No, I said she was of the ruling clan. My people are divided into many clans. Each of us has a clan leader, usually a position inherited from his or her father, and theirs before them. Each clan holds a territory that they, and they alone, have trading rights in. Our territories don't coincide with any of your boundaries. We found, over the centuries, that to prevent the kinds of border wars prevalent in your peoples, we should allow one clan to act as adjudicator of any disputes. They are what you could call our ruling clan. They are the Rhuhani."

"And your clan?" Merina asked, curious that the Tieri were so different from the rest of the Domains.

Jalanos glanced quickly at Delnos, as if warning him about something. Delnos said, "Pathla."

Merina wondered if she was treading where she shouldn't. The Tieri were so secretive about their people. "And the last part of your name--m'Lothur?"

"Son of Lothur. Isn't it curious that your people, the Saphradeans, as well as the Hermanians and the Delmathians, usually only have one name. If they have any other word to tell of their family, it is a title. Do you know why?"

Merina had never thought about her name. One name was all you needed. She shook her head. "No, but why does anyone need any more than one name?"

"To remember your heritage, your past," Delnos said quietly.

"Why is that necessary? You inherit what your parents leave you, but you don't need their name. You make your own. That's why we honor titles. Dame Brischelu says Saphradean titles are bought and sold--or earned. Any respect that is due you is because of what you have done."

"I see," Delnos said, a sadness in his voice that Merina did not understand.

"And Jalanos, he is Pathla?"

The expression on Jalnanos's face approximated a smile but came closer to a grimace. He said nothing, and Delnos gently laughed. "Best leave this subject alone, Mistress. My uncle's past is very interesting, but only to those who care about the past. Let us say he is trading on the land he is allowed to trade on. We are near to Dysandes, but traveling this road at night is risky. We should stop soon. We will reach town by midday at the latest."

After all had enjoyed a wash in warm water and a change of clothes, Jalanos served the meal. He was a wonderful cook, and, from his tiny kitchen in the back of the caravan, he produced a dinner that Aunt Alanu would have been jealous of. Trinames ate heartily and seemed to enjoy it immensely, now that he was rested from the day's travel on the road. The Tierian's bed was supported by coils of metal that diminished the shock of the road far better than the springs under the driver's seat. Trinames had awakened with almost a song in his voice when they had stopped for the day.

Trinames's mood showed further improvement with the wine Delnos allowed him to have, albeit far less than Trinames asked for after his first taste. Trinames actually did sing for his supper, insisting he had no other way to pay for the kindness shown him. The tune was a bawdy tavern song popular among men his age, for which Merina smiled at the right places, but she did not really see the humor in much of the song. Trinames had a strong, deep voice, and she loved to hear it.

Merina's own mood improved after she had changed her clothes and combed her hair. She found a dress among Jalanos's trade goods that was slightly smaller than what she normally wore, but the other dresses were made for women whose figures had rounded out in their middle age. Her dress was tight across her breasts, and she did not button it to the neck. She knew that would please Trinames.

She spent the early part of the evening holding his hand and comforting him with hugs and kisses. The Tieri, with knowing smiles on their faces, watched the two lovers. When Delnos helped Trinames into the bushes to relieve himself, he told the young man that Jalanos had offered his wagon for the night. Upon their return, Trinames informed Merina of Jalanos's offer. "But I assured him you would not approve of that." After that remark she made a point of sitting away from him. The shawl she had draped over her shoulders was wrapped around her neck, and she gave the Tieri men a frown of disapproval--although she should have expected nothing less from any man.

The filling meal and wine had its effect on her love, and Trinames started drooping. She encouraged him to retire to the bed in the caravan, but he murmured that he wanted to sleep by the fire. After she spread out his blanket, he eased himself on the ground with his head in her lap. Within minutes he was asleep. Delnos came over and checked Trinames's injuries, then covered up the younger man.

He said, "He's healing well, but he needs to be monitored by Sorceress Helinu. I don't know how good the Kanchala were at setting his breaks, and he has been tossed around quite a bit. He may also have scars from the cuts and the bone piercing his skin. She could reconstruct those, provided there are no infections beneath."

"Thank you for all you have done, Tieri Delnos. You have saved him from serious injury, or even death," Merina choked out.

He moved to sit on a log by the fire, opposite her and next to his uncle. "It was you who saved us, Mistress."

Dashing the tears from her eyes, Merina denied his words. "I was just the lure for the pack. I did nothing but run."

Jalanos looked at her with squinted eyes, as if he had trouble seeing her, even though she was only a few feet away. "You came back to help. Knew the danger, but became bait willingly. Shows much courage."

Merina did not want to respond to their praise. For one reason, she knew she had not really had any choice but to do what she did. And if she acknowledged that, her use of Power, however that was possible, would endanger her far worse than anything she had faced before. She had been warned, and she believed the Tierians knew what she had done. She had to shift the conversation away from herself. "If anyone deserves credit for saving us, it is you, Tieri Jalanos. It was fortunate you were on that road to meet us."

Shaking his head, Jalanos turned to Delnos and spoke rapidly in Tierian. Jalanos knew Merina was having a hard time understanding his Saphradean, as most valley residents did. Only the farmers near the mountains close to the Non-Lands did not complain of his accent. Delnos explained this to Merina as he translated what his uncle was saying.

"Where Jalanos was born, in a far distant part of Saphradea, they speak a much older form of your language. It is possible that area was where your people originated from. Few people have ever returned to that valley. The Tieri clan that has the rights to trade there are also very different from my people. Jalanos is more likely my great-uncle, considering his age. It is too confusing to explain, as I have said earlier."

Merina stopped him. "I understand all that. If I am not to know something, please don't tell me. If I repeat it wrong, I will not be repeating the truth."

Both men nodded. Merina wondered if they understood what Lenora had told her to do.

"Jalanos wants you to understand that he is more likely the one that caused you all this trouble than he is your savior."

The shock on Merina's face stopped Jalanos talking. "What did he just say?"

"Let me finish translating, Mistress."

"Please do, Tieri Delnos."

"My uncle was approached by the Tierian Mage. His name is Styreki. Because the Mage would not state his clan and lineage, which is allowed but denotes lack of trust on his part, Jalanos was wary of him. Jalanos did not know of any Tierian Mage other than Tierii Chalinee."

"So the Mage has a name. Styreki. How odd."

"Jalanos was sure the Mage wore an illusion spell, but he could not see past it. Styreki wanted Jalanos to work a deal with Captain Garlantis. The Mage would remove the wolf threat from the valley in return for a large sum of gold."

Merina frowned. "I thought magic-users did not approve of getting large payments of gold for their services."

"That is true, Mistress. But if this mage was not from one of the Training Lodges--let us say he was a rogue magic-user, then what he was asking for was not out of the question. Styreki is unknown to my people. It is questionable that he is even a Tieri. Remember, he was disguising himself."

"How very odd," Merina mused, glancing at the old Tieri sitting opposite her. Jalanos nodded in agreement.

"My great-uncle asked the Mage how was he going to do the job, but Styreki would not tell him anything except he had laid a trap for them in the mountains just before the Non-Lands. My uncle knew the troubles Dysandes was having, and it seems reasonable that he could talk Garlantis into the taking the deal, so he went to see the Guard Captain."

"When?" Merina broke in.

Delnos looked at Jalanos, who gave the answer in his strange Saphradean. "Last Settling Day."

Merina started to ask more questions when Delnos halted her with an upheld hand. "Wait, let us finish."

Frustrated, Merina blew out her breath, then quickly glanced down to see if she had awakened Trinames. He was fast asleep.

"As you well know," Delnos continued, "Captain Garlantis does not trust my people. He told Jalanos that he would not pay any sorcerer to do the job when he had able-bodied soldiers and farmhands to do it, let alone a bush witch. Jalanos showed the good Captain that he would save a lot of gold by paying the Mage vice the cost of hiring all those men. Garlantis told my uncle he would pay half what the Mage was asking and only after the job was done. He did not believe the Mage could do the job. Jalanos returned to Styreki with the new offer, and the Mage accepted."

Merina was gently stroking Trinames's hair while Delnos was translating. She paused when she heard him stop. Jalanos's eyes fixed on her, waiting for her to ask a question. "So Styreki had already put his plan in motion before he made a deal. How does that make your uncle--or is he your great-uncle--responsible for our troubles?"

Jalanos answered for himself, "If known what Mage planning, would not have put Delnos, or you and boy, in danger. Could not stop deal."

How very clever of you, Magess Lenora, Merina thought, staring at her love's peaceful face and trying to keep from swearing under her breath. She, and everyone she knew, had been manipulated and used. It was well she had not known any of this because she would surely have fought every effort that led to this end. She looked at Jalanos. "Not your fault, then. What did you do after making the deal?"

Delnos replied, having not translated that part of the story yet. "He tried to warn me, but we were too far away. Knowing he would get no help from Garlantis, my uncle loaded his wagon and proceeded out of town to the place where the road came closest to the Non-Lands."

"Warn you? Oh, I see. That source box. You signaled him the night the wolves died."

Delnos nodded.

Merina shifted herself from under Trinames's head on her lap and laid it on a pillow she made from her shawl. "I still thank you for coming to our aid, Tieri Jalanos. And I don't put any blame on you for our troubles. You were used just like we were. Now I suppose all we have to worry about is collecting the Mage's money." As she walked toward the bushes to relieve herself, Merina paused next to Jalanos. "I am looking forward to meeting Mage Styreki."

Since Jalanos's caravan was a familiar sight in Dysandes, no one showed any interest as it made its way through town. Merina had decided to remain in the interior of the wagon with Trinames. Her plan was first to take her lover to the home of Sorceress Helinu and see to his immediate care. After he was being treated, Merina planned to go with the Tieri to Guard Captain Garlantis's office to report what had happened to them over the past week. Merina was very curious to see if the Mage Styreki had made an appearance to collect his fee, or whether he was waiting for them at Jalanos's warehouse.

As the caravan entered the side street that led to the Healer's home, the uneasiness Merina now associated with the presence of a Powered magic-user told her she need not fear that Helinu was out on her rounds. Helinu emerged through the gate to her house as Jalanos drove up. The old Tierian stopped the caravan when the rear door pulled even with front gate, and Helinu, used to having patients delivered to her home, mounted the steps into the wagon and pushed through the door. Merina rose to meet her.

"Merina! Thank the Power you're alive. And Trinames!"

Helinu hurried to the bedside and extended her hands toward the young man. Merina had seen the Healer do this in the past and knew she was going to use magic to read the health of the patient. When Helinu evoked the spell, Merina felt the release of Power as if someone had slapped her in the face. Merina reeled back slightly, but Helinu did not see, being intent on Trinames. Delnos entered from the driver's bench and told Helinu what he knew of Trinames's injuries. Merina stepped away to give the Healer room to work.

"Who did this healing?" Helinu asked.

The question surprised Merina, but then she realized it should not have. She should have guessed Delnos did not tell people he knew magic. Being Tieri made people suspicious enough without also being labeled a bush-witch.

Delnos said almost apologetically, "The kidnappers had a bush-witch with them. She was the one who used the poison on Merina. In their flight from Dysandes, they were attacked by a pack of wolves. Trinames's horse threw him, and he got those breaks. The young man has been through a lot and has quite a story to tell."

Helinu, bent over the patient, turned to look up at the Tieri. "I'm sure you all do. Whoever did this has a good understanding of the Healer's trade. There is scarring I'll have to fix, but the breaks are healing nicely." Turning her attention back to Trinames, she asked, "And how do you feel?"

"My arm, ribs, and leg still hurt, but Tieri Delnos has a wonderful potion that makes the pain go away. He brews it himself. I think he is the one who really healed me."

Delnos gave Trinames a warning look and shook his head. "Your Neophyte was delirious with pain for many days after his fall. The bush-witch left a supply of that powder when she and her companions abandoned Trinames in a remote cave in the Non-Lands. I just followed her directions in making the potion." The story of the powder was actually true, as far as Trinames could know.

Helinu asked excitedly, "Do you still have some left?"

"No," Delnos said sadly, "I used the last of it days ago."

"Too bad, but at least we know it can be used as a painkiller, like I thought. Now let's get my Neophyte into the house where I can examine him more fully." Glancing around, Helinu checked the condition of Delnos and Merina.

"You have been burned?" she asked Merina, pointing at Merina's singed hair.

"I was standing too close when the fireball hit," Merina said with no emphasis on the nature of that spell.

"A fireball!" Helinu's eyes widened in astonishment.

"I am fine for now. There will be time to tell that story after you take care of Trinames."

Merina rode up front on the way to Captain Garlantis's headquarters. A few townsmen recognized her and waved--past customers and tradesmen she had done business with. No one seemed in the least surprised to see her, even in company with the Tieri. To Merina that meant the town was not aware anything unusual had happened to her, which was good, in a way. She wondered how Garlantis would receive her news.

As Merina climbed down from the caravan, the guardsmen standing by the door paid the Tieri wagon more interest than they did her. It was not usual business for Jalanos to visit the headquarters other than on foot, and from what she knew of the old man's relationship with the Guard Captain, he did not visit often.

"I'm here to see Captain Garlantis," she told the nearest guardsman.

The man barely looked at her, waving her through the door. His eyes fixed on the two Tieri following her, but he made no move to stop them.

"Thank you, I'll announce myself," Merina said with a tinge of bitterness in her voice. She now realized how the Tieri must be treated all the time. She swept into the main room of the small headquarters and marched through the open door to Garlantis's office. The Guard Captain, seated at his desk, looked up at her entrance only when she rapped her knuckles on his door.

"Ah, Mistress Merina. Have you found anything"--Garlantis glanced at the two men behind her--"besides my old friend Jalanos and his nephew?"

Merina spoke as calmly as her rising anger would allow. "I found my betrothed, Captain--barely alive."

Garlantis stood, a shocked look on his face. "Barely alive? What happened?"

"Perhaps you should ask who did it. I told you he was kidnapped. Had I not tracked down the Tieri who grabbed him from my arms, he would be dead."

Garlantis gave the Tieri men a hard stare. "I told you no one has seen any Tieri but these men."

"But you knew of others, at least after I left with Tieri Delnos. Why didn't you mount a search then?" Merina quickly retorted.

"What others?" Garlantis coldly asked, his eyes fixed on Jalanos.

Melina saw his focus. "A Tierian Mage--named Styreki. He hired the assassins who kidnapped Trinames. He used them to try to draw a search party out of Dysandes, but he only got me and Tieri Delnos. You're telling me you didn't know this?"

"No! But yes, I knew of the Mage. He offered to rid us of the wolves troubling the valley. Jalanos said the Mage wouldn't say how he was going to do it. I thought it was a typical Tieri shady deal."

"As I told you, Mistress," Delnos said quietly from behind her.

Merina stalked over to a chair in front of the desk Garlantis still stood behind, and sat. "Well, Captain, you made the deal, so pay up!"

The confused look on Garlantis's face was worth the aggravation Merina had worked herself into. She folded her arms and waited for him to speak.

"He...he killed them," Garlantis said with a stutter, sinking slowly into his chair.

"Their charred remains rest on the slope of the mountain at the entrance to the Non-Lands," Delnos said. "You have Mistress Merina's and my word--which you may not believe, I understand. Send a search party if you don't. My uncle and I can await payment, although the Mage will be most annoyed if his services are not paid for much sooner."

Garlantis glanced back and forth between the two men, then over at Merina. She gave him her best judgmental expression, the one she used when waiting for a tradesman to pay her his due.

"But...I didn't agree," the Captain said.

Jalanos looked sad, slowly shaking his head.

"Wait, I did, but there is no money to pay for this. If I use the gold I have on hand to pay you, I can't pay the guardsmen their salaries. The mayor will be--"

"Happy," Merina finished for him, "because you rid the town of a problem that was hurting its trade. Once the valley men hear the problem is taken care of, they will expect to be asked to contribute to the bounty. You'll get your gold back for the wages."

"That will take time, Merina. I--"

Merina shot him a frown. "The Tieri made you a fair deal. You offered half of what the Mage wanted, and he took it. You should not have made the offer if you did not have the money. I don't know about Tieri Jalanos, but if I were a powerful Tieri Aggressor Mage, I would make an issue of this to the Prince of Princes. The valley will get the reputation of not following through on their trade deals. I'm sure Alexus will not pay the debt himself, but it solved a problem he was unwilling to face, and he can extract payment from Dysandes by increasing the road taxes. Profits will be lost. And no one wins in that situation."

"True, all true, Mistress. But I need to know what happened here before I can go the Mayor to ask for the gold. He won't believe it unless we tell him the truth," Garlantis said, almost begging.

Merina nodded. "Well, here is the truth--from a landholder and the Tieri tradesman who helped her to save her future husband."

She told the story as she knew it. She made no mention of what had happened in the cave, for that was a dream. And she had no need to mention her use of Power, for all would assume it was the Mage Styreki who had wielded that.

The heavy door of Jalanos's warehouse thudded shut behind Merina's back, and she turned to see who had closed it. A Kanchala swordsman stood poised, his sword extended toward her chest, but his eyes tracked the guardsmen she had been following. Their hands were burdened by the chest they held between them--the heavy, wooden box containing the gold to pay the Mage's fee. Neither guard was aware of the assassin behind them, nor was Captain Garlantis, who had led the procession into the warehouse. Jalanos had opened the door to meet the party, but he had worn no expression on his lined face to warn them of any treachery.

Merina began to cry out a warning as she turned to face Jalanos, but the sight of the sword at Garlantis's throat told her she was too late. The male Kanchala holding that sword had his eyes fixed on the Captain's, and he was slowly shaking his head. "No move, all live."

"Why?" Garlantis asked with a calmness that surprised Merina, whose own heart was pounding with fear.

"Collect fee. Our money." Merina wondered at how much the assassin's accent so closely matched Jalanos's.

The guardsmen stood unmoving, their eyes darting between the face of the man threatening their captain and the shadowy figures standing at their own sides. Merina slowly looked around and saw Delnos watching her from behind his uncle's back. For all the time she had been with him, she had never seen fear in his face, until now. She felt the tension in the room growing, as if everyone was getting ready to react violently, the pent-up energy about to be released.

Then she felt the unease of stored Power and knew that was the source of tension she felt. Another shadowy figure stepped through the back door of the office and spoke rapidly in Tierian.

Delnos translated, his voice a little shaky. "The Mage thanks you for paying his fee promptly."

"At sword point, Tieri! Is this necessary?" Garlantis growled.

The Mage pointed at Jalanos's desk, motioning that he wanted the chest placed there. The guardsmen slowly edged over and lowered the box onto the table. The swords poking against their exposed necks cautioned them not to try to drop it and reach for their weapons.

Merina stared at the Mage, watched as he moved toward the box. She knew that Styreki could not exist--was probably Lenora in disguise--and did not believe what she was seeing. The Mage blurred, and Merina saw it was not a man, but a woman--the Kanchala leader, not Lenora. But her voice was male. Another illusion? And doubted. The assassin leader became the Mage once again.

Styreki spoke to Jalanos in their language, and Jalanos nodded. He told the Captain, "The Mage wants me to open the chest and ensure the contents are gold."

"Damn bush-witch," Garlantis muttered. He received a bloody nick for his utterance.

Jalanos lifted the lid and removed a handful of coin, digging below the surface layer with his other hand to confirm the coins underneath were also gold. He spoke to the Mage, who motioned the bleeding Garlantis to step back away from the desk. Once the path to the chest was clear, Styreki walked to the desk and held out his hand for the coins in Jalanos's. Receiving them, the Mage counted the coins and handed them back.

"You may take ten more, Tieri Jalanos," Styreki said in a perfectly clear Saphradean. "That is our agreement, I believe." Merina thought it odd that the Mage didn't say that in Tierian. Maybe the Mage wanted to let us all know of the deal with Jalanos.

The old man nodded, dropping the coins in his hand into a pouch at his waist and withdrawing ten more gold from the box.

Styreki said, "And you, Tieri Delnos--take out ten for yourself, as I told you I owed you for your service. And Mistress Merina--for being such excellent bait for my trap, you may take an equal share, as I should compensate you for the trouble I caused you. Are we even now?"

Merina thought for a moment to refuse, because the lives of her lover and herself were worth far more than that, but then she realized Styreki, or Lenora, was offering her a way out of having to bring charges against the Mage--which would only end up exposing Merina's use of Power. She nodded in agreement.

Garlantis disagreed, carefully choosing his words with that sword still near his throat. "Your attack on us today will not be forgiven, Mage."

Styreki walked to the open box and took out a single coin. "You insulted me, Captain, and my people, as you are wont to do. I have extracted my revenge. Do you want to continue this feud with me? If so, I will register the fact with Alexus. Then we can bloody each other for years to come without bringing in all the Clans of the Tieri."

"Here is your compensation for the wound, Captain," the Mage said, handing the gold to Garlantis. Styreki looked over at Merina, adding, "I hear Sorceress Helinu does an excellent job healing sword nicks."

Merina glanced down at her cleavage, as did all the men in the room.

Styreki walked over and picked up the chest, seemingly without effort. The guardsmen's faces showed shock, the Captain's disbelief. "Knowing your reputation with my people, Captain, I am sure that you would not allow my guards to escort myself and my money away from this office. I do not want our meeting to end with loss of life after all everyone went through to prevent it. Because of that belief, I will be locking you all into this office. If you want to waste your strength, I can assure you that these doors will hold you in place for more than enough time for us to leave town. If you can be patient, I will send the key back by a messenger to let you out."

Merina watched as the Mage slipped out the rear door, followed by the Kanchala edging slowly away from the guards. The click of the door closing and the rattle of a key in the lock were the only sounds for many moments afterward.

Chapter 15

"He departs on the morrow," Dame Brischelu said, nodding in Trinames's direction, where the young man stood next to the long bar of the Traveler's Rest.

Merina sipped from her glass of wine, a frown shadowing her face before she answered, "Not as I would want--but it is his choice."

"He is well?" the Dame asked, signaling the bartender to bring more wine. It was on her invitation that Merina, her family, and her closest friends had come to the tavern to attend a farewell for the Neophyte Healer. Farmer Calandis, Markinis, Denathis, and Tomanis were standing with Trinames and, from the expressions on their faces, were getting along despite the earlier tension of having the rival lovers in the same room.

"Enough to take a ship downriver. He will ride a coach from the port to Byklandes. He limps when he walks, but Sorceress Helinu says the Mage Healers will be able to correct that. Otherwise, he is fit enough."

"It was quite a trial for your young man and for you."

Merina forced herself to relax in the Dame's presence. The two women were seated at the far corner table from the one they had occupied the first time they had met at the tavern. That table was being used by Alanu, Florinu, and Serafinu, with Merina's three cousins running back and forth between the groups of men and women. She accepted a refill of her half-empty glass. "It was a strange interlude compared to what I had expected to happen in our last month together before he left."

Smiling, Dame Brischelu said, "You had expected to be the center of attention for two ardent men--one defending his position and another trying to replace him. I would have loved to be in your position, as would every woman in the valley. It is the way young love is supposed to work."

Shaking her head, Merina inspected the wineglass. "The kidnapping worked to prove to me that my love belongs to, and was always with, Trinames. You opened my eyes to the realization that I was allowing my hatred to force the path my life would take. I found myself pitting love against magic--actually pitting one emotion against another--hatred. Magic is the use of Power, a force of nature. I was fighting the wrong battle."

"But you saw what magic did to your life..." Brischelu started to say.

"I saw what my knife did to a wolf and how it saved my life. The same goes for magic. It helped Trinames's kidnappers escape, it drove the wolves to come together against their nature, it forces people to do things they wouldn't normally do--but it is not the reason why they do it. It is a tool, a weapon, a healing balm. My mother became who she is because she learned to use the tool. I have chosen not to use it or to train for it even if I could. Having made that decision for myself, I have learned I do not have the right to make that decision for the ones I love. It is Trinames's decision to make, not mine, or mine to influence. He knows the dangers--at least he swears he does now, seeing the full range of what magic has done to him. I will not force him to change."

Glancing at Trinames, Dame Brischelu shook her head sadly. "He is a nice young man, Merina, but he will not succeed in his dream. You know this, I am sure."

Merina put down her glass and waited for the older woman to meet her eyes. "Whether he does or doesn't--that won't change my love for him. I also know your son will not settle down with a woman who will run his life for him. If that was not true, he wouldn't be trying to escape your home. He wants a purpose for his life, but it is not a family. Maybe, like his grandfather, he should find his purpose serving the Prince of Princes. I'm sure you could make that happen if you wanted to."

The Dame's eyes slitted, and a smile played at the corners of her lips. "You have grown wiser in the past month. Perhaps having a life-threatening experience has broadened your world beyond your farm and this valley."

Merina had expected Brischelu to take offense at her son being called mother-controlled. When she did not, Merina relaxed and took a sip of her wine. "A number of people have spent my summer presenting me with challenges. Why they chose to do so I have not reasoned out. I thought I understood why you made your proposal to me, but I don't understand why you gave the gold to Captain Garlantis to pay off the Mage."

That question made the Dame laugh loudly and drew the attention of the room to her table. Brischelu drained her glass and waved for another refill. Her guests smiled at her and assumed the Dame was just enjoying herself.

"Not very subtle, my dear. Yes, I have been meddling in your life, but you knew I was doing it for my own purposes. You were so concerned about your love life that you lost track of your trade sense. When I heard from Garlantis that you'd thought my family might have been the ones who arranged your lover's disappearance, I was not surprised. I did not hold that against you."

Merina blushed. "I didn't mean to imply anything, Madam."

"That I was paying all that gold to hide the fact I had arranged Trinames's kidnapping? Both of us know I was not guilty of doing that. I paid the fee simply because I have a financial interest in doing so. Merina--think trade, instead of your obsession with me interfering in your life."

"Of course, the Tieri!" Merina said, embarrassed that the Dame had heard of her accusations.

"Now you are thinking like a tradeswoman. I told you the Tieri are the ones who bring in my wine. I must keep my deal with them viable. Having them refuse to trade with Dysandes or get banned by stupidity on the part of the Mayor or his Guard Captain--that does nothing but hurt me. My gold will be returned, and then some. Alexus will ensure that and get his share as well."

"Then it all worked out well for you," Merina said with relief.

Filling Merina's glass with the pitcher of wine the bartender had conveniently left on the table, Brischelu said with a broad smile, "Even better. Alexus owes me a favor since I solved a problem for him, because he would have been hard pressed to find a hundred in gold as quickly as he needed to. I'll suggest to him the Duke's grandson is looking for a position in court."

Merina looked at Markinis, who was downing a large tankard of ale with much encouragement from her uncle and her lover. She felt even more relieved. Perhaps her problems were all solved as well. "From the way you spoke of Alexus's ladies-in-waiting, your son may find court life very much to his liking."

Dame Brischelu nodded and pushed aside her glass of wine. "I can tell it is time for me to remove myself from your party. I would like to stay and talk more, but I know that when my son begins to accept challenges to his ale-holding ability, I need to take him home. His father taught him that skill only too well."

Merina was in the middle of thanking the Dame for her hospitality when she saw Trinames sliding backward along the bar, hopping on his good leg in an effort to distance himself from Denathis and Markinis. The two men were glaring at each other, fists raised between them, and it was apparent a fight was about to start.

"Oh, dear! I'm too late." Brischelu sighed.

Florinu stood and yelled at her life-mate to behave.

Markinis pointed at her and said something to Denathis that made Florinu's life-mate yell, "That's it!"

Merina winced at Denathis's hard blow to Markinis's jaw. The much-larger man rocked back, staggered a step, then crumpled to the floor.

The silence in the room was broken by Dame Brischelu calmly ordering the bartender and his assistant to please put her son in her wagon, then bring her the bill.

She turned to her guests and said, "Everyone, I apologize for my son's behavior. If you would be so kind, stay and enjoy yourself at my expense. I bid you all a good evening."

After Denathis and Merina's uncle helped the bartender to carry Markinis from the room, Merina walked over to where Trinames leaned against the bar. He had a sly grin on his face. "What just happened, love?" she asked.

"I just mentioned that I had not seen Markinis holding his beer so well since the night he tried to take Florinu to the barn and you stopped him."

Merina stifled a laugh, not wanting to encourage Trinames in thinking he was so clever in provoking the fight. "You should have realized that would end our party. Everyone will be too embarrassed to stay now."

Looking at her, a broad smile on his face, Trinames said, "I did know it would. That was my plan. I don't want to spend my last night with you before I leave tomorrow listening to my competition bragging about his conquests. I'll give my thanks to the Dame and meet you at your wagon."

There was a chill in the air, a reminder to all in the returning wagon that summer was nearly over. Even with the threat of the wolves gone, no one wanted to remain on the dark road for very long, least of all Merina and her lover. The rattle of the wheels made conversation hard, so very little was said on the return home. Tomanis let everyone off at the porch and drove the wagon to the barn to put it away. Alanu herded her sleepy sons into the house and softly called out a goodnight to Merina and Trinames.

"A walk to clear my head would be nice, Mer," Trinames said to Merina.

"Just a short one, love. I didn't see you drink that much," Merina said, supporting his left side.

"I didn't. I made sure everyone else was too busy drinking theirs by constantly refilling their glasses for them."

"Ah, another plan to hurry the evening along."

Trinames grinned, his teeth easily visible in the moonlight. "Another part of the plan," he whispered in her ear.

"Are there more parts left, Tri?"

"Several. Here comes your uncle. He is swaying a little, I think. Perhaps I served him too much."

Her uncle passed them, humming a tune that Merina knew was a favorite of her aunt. He waved gaily at them and gave Trinames a knowing smile, then wished him luck.

Merina, puzzled, looked at her lover. "What did he mean by that?"

"Maybe he feels like you do--that I need all the help I can get learning magic."

Merina frowned. "I doubt that. He believes whatever Sorceress Helinu tells him, or, for that matter, my aunt. They believe in you."

"I wish you did--but I will make a believer of you yet. Let's check on the horse. Your uncle may have not bedded him down for the night in his haste to get to his own bed."

"Tomanis would never neglect an animal for his own comfort, but he was rather quick about it. To the barn we go."

She guided him through the wide doors of the barn, still open. Merina lit the lantern hanging by the entrance and looked around. The wagon had been left in the entranceway instead of parked against the back wall as it usually was. The horse was standing in his stall, busily munching from his oat-filled tray. He had been wiped down hastily with hay, a few strands sticking to his hide.

Suspending the lantern on its hook above the stall, Merina took a brush from its rack and started to give the horse a more thorough brushing. The stallion looked around at her, then turned back to his meal. Trinames leaned against the stall wall and watched her.

Bending over to brush the horse's back fetlocks, Merina heard Trinames sighing and glanced up at him. His eyes were locked on her cleavage and the view she had just presented to him. She smiled at him. "See something you like?"

"Oh, yes, love, I do."

Straightening up, Merina stowed the brush back in its place and strolled over to her lover, unlacing her bodice. When she came within his reach, his hand cupped her breasts and pushed them up until his lips could kiss the exposed tops. He continued kissing up her neck and found her waiting lips. Merina hummed her pleasure as his fingers caressed her nipples, making them hard.

The image of her uncle doing the same thing to Alanu that night so long ago flashed into her mind, and Merina did the same thing that her aunt had done. She pulled Trinames's face down to the exposed nipple on her right breast and sighed as he eagerly licked it, his warm breath flowing around the damp skin.

Trinames's breathing was becoming more rapid as his excitement grew, and Merina gasped as he squeezed her breast with too much enthusiasm. He stopped suddenly and looked up at her.

"Gently, love. Come, lie here in the hay." She lowered him to the barn floor, directing his lips to the untouched left breast, and gasped again with the surge of pleasure as he kissed that nipple. Her body awakened much more intensely than on the night she had watched

Tomanis and Alanu making love. Trinames's lips and hands were now doing to her what her own hand had done that night.

He paused. "Are you sure you're ready for this?"

"Yes. I want to belong to you completely."

"But when I must leave for so long..."

"I don't like that any better than I ever have. But I know that is what you must do. I was wrong to stand in your way."

Trinames looked up at her face with a loving smile that made Merina's heart rapidly beat. It was clear to her that he loved and wanted her so very much--as she did him.

His smile broadened into a grin. "I won't be gone that long, love. We will be together at spring planting. Just the time to--"

Pushing his face back to her aching nipple, Merina finished his sentence. "I know, to do planting of our own."

Trinames pulled away from her breasts and struggled to a kneeling position. His hands found her skirt and pulled it up her thighs, while she raised her hips until he uncovered them. He examined her underpants, searching for the drawstring to release them and not finding it. She smiled, knowing men had such fastenings for their clothing although women did not. She reached inside the waistband and pushed the pants down, past her knees, tossing them to the side.

Trinames had glanced shyly away as she exposed herself and busied himself with his belt. His injured leg, still stiff and sore, made it awkward for him to pull his trousers off. Merina pushed him back onto the hay and effortlessly removed them. His underpants followed quickly. She had undressed her cousins many times in her day, so the male anatomy was familiar to her, but this sight was much different. She remembered Tomanis's erect penis and Alanu's murmurs of appreciation as her aunt had stroked it. As Merina did the same now, Trinames writhed slightly under her hand and she stared into his eyes, seeing them widen with his growing need for release.

Whether it was his first time or not, she did not know. That he was not going to be able to check his pleasure was evident by the slick drops on her fingers. From the answering wetness between her legs, she knew she was ready to receive him. She pulled the dress over her head and dropped it beside them. Her flesh tightened and tingled in places no hand but hers had ever touched.

A thrill coursed through her when his eyes locked on her bosom as she shifted her body over his, straddling his hips between her thighs. His hands caught her breasts as she leaned forward. His lips eagerly sought a nipple. A few seconds of awkward fumbling followed while she adjusted her legs to receive him. Her fingers directed the head of his organ to her mound and seated it. She slowly sat up, pulling her nipple from his lips as she did so, and gazed into his eyes that sought hers as well.

She was a virgin, and as his shaft slid into her, it tore her. The momentary but startling stab of pain made her pull upward slightly. Trinames winced at her withdrawal, but she smiled down at him.

"Did I hurt you, love?" he asked.

"Only a little, but it's a pain I've long looked forward to."

She lowered her hips, pushing him as far into her as she could, enveloping him until he filled her. A flood of pleasure drowned the lingering hurt. The joy of having him deep inside satisfied her for a moment, but she felt the need to experience it again. When she raised her hips, he started to come out, slipping easily in the moist folds of her cleft. A wave of sensation rippled through her.

He groaned, and his hands flew up to her hips, stopping their rise. He pulled her down, filling her again, and her pleasure grew even more. Now she understood why Alanu and Tomanis had rutted so forcefully that night. It was the give and take, the thrust and sliding out, with the tantalizing glide of skin against skin that created the mounting pressure.

When Trinames convinced himself that she was not going to pull off, he returned his hands to her breasts, and she leaned into his grasp. He supported her chest as she learned how much she could move up and down his shaft. Her pleasure grew and grew, more so as he kneaded her breasts and licked the nipples.

But she knew from that remembered night the pleasure would end sooner than she, or Alanu, would have wanted. Trinames's breathing became more rapid, and his hands shifted to her thighs. She sat upright, forcing her hips down on him as he bucked upward. The urgency of his thrusts matched her need. Her breasts bounced up and down with the rhythm. It distracted her, and she grabbed them to stop them from disrupting the tension she felt building.

Her excitement crested, and she released a groan like the one she had heard that other night from Alanu, quickly followed by Trinames's own. A surge of heat flushed through her. Merina collapsed on top of her lover. Trinames held her tightly to him as their breathing slowly settled to normal.

There was no turning back now. With this mating, they belonged to each other. Exhaustion overtook Merina. Faintly aware of lingering soreness between her legs, she fell asleep.

Merina sat on her stool under the sitting tree. She looked around and wondered why her house was not nearby, nor were any of the farm's many outbuildings where they should have been. Then she remembered she had been here before. This was where she had met Lenora the first time, and thinking of the ancient Mage brought her into focus, standing a few feet away.

"Why am I here?" Merina asked sleepily.

"You have questions which only I can answer, and I don't want you returning to the cave. It is too dangerous."

"If you can visit me in a dream, why didn't you do that the first time instead of dragging me up to the Non-Lands and nearly killing me and my friends?"

Lenora settled gracefully into a stuffed chair that looked exactly like one of the chairs in Brischelu's den--and had not been behind her seconds before. "Until I awakened you in my presence, I could not speak in your mind. I needed you to come to me."

A sense of annoyance was building in Merina, replacing the peaceful mood that had filled her mind when she fell asleep in her lover's arms. "You could have invited me to a meeting like Dame Brischelu did."

Arranging her black sorcerer robe across her lap, the Magess gave Merina a cold glance. "It would not have served the purpose if I summoned you to me, and do you really believe you would have ridden to the Non-Lands to meet a perfect stranger? No, you would not. You would run around and ask everyone in the valley if they knew of me, and by doing so, alert those whom I don't want to know of my interest in you."

"You have enemies? You risk my life for what purpose?"

"They are not enemies, just people who oppose what I believe in. They could stop me by eliminating you."

Merina shook her head sadly. "And I thought all my problems were solved. The valley farmers believe a Tierian Mage killed the wolves. No one suspects I used magic."

"Tieri Delnos and his uncle know, but they will keep the secret. They now share the risk of their people being killed."

"Because of the Kanchala? Why did you use them?" Merina asked, distressed by the growing endangerment of those who had touched her life.

"No," Lenora answered less sternly. "They are not from the Kanchala, they are my allies."

Merina frowned at the old woman. "Please don't lie to me. I know they are Kanchala. They are Tieri, and I saw the markings."

Lenora's voice snapped like a whip. "Suffice that you know this... They are not of the present clans of Tieri."

"You use them as servants?"

"They are willing subjects. They can move freely in the Domains, where I can't."

Merina nodded. "As I suspected. It was not you I saw impersonating the white wolf leader on the mountain trail, or talking to me after I killed the wolves, or taking the gold from Captain Garlantis. It was the woman assassin."

"Yes, she was one of several I used for my purpose."

"And that purpose is?" Merina asked softly.

Lenora folded her wrinkled hands in her lap. "For now, to protect your awakening to magic. You are not ready to fulfill the purpose for which I awakened you. You must be trained, but not by Domain sorcerers. They are a greater risk to you than my people."

"How is that, Great-Grandmother? Helinu only wants to help me. She was the first to want to develop my magic skills."

The old woman gave Merina a wry smile. "Your people want to find the magic they lost so long ago, but they have learned to fear it as much as they want it. The thing that awakens magic in you is the very thing they dread. Look at your mother, Merina. Her rapid development led to her downfall. The Delmathian Order imprisoned Delaphinu for her grid burnout. Whenever that happens to a sorcerer, they sequester them--hide them from the public eye because it exposes the Order's inability to control their people. No sorcerer can be your friend with this belief."

A flash of anger shot through Merina, and she spat out, "So my lover is to become my enemy? You would do this to me?"

Calmly, Lenora said, "See? That is why you need training. You cannot control your emotions. Until you learn control, you cannot use Power. That makes you a danger to all."

Struggling to rein the urge to lash out at the old woman, Merina throttled back from the harsh tone she wanted to use and said through clenched teeth, "Damn it, you are turning Trinames against me?"

"No, Trinames is safe if you keep your secret."

"What does that mean, Magess? Are you saying he will not become a sorcerer? Is he really not able to use Power?"

"No, he, like many of your people, can be taught to use magic. Whether he does so or not is up to him and the skill of his instructors."

Merina did not feel pleased to hear Trinames could succeed at being a Healer. She wanted him to make the effort and then fail. She selfishly wanted him to return to the valley after this winter and become her life-mate. While she was mulling over this prospect, Lenora spoke out.

"It would be better for you that he not."

"What? You want him to continue to become a user of Power?"

Lenora's eyes darted away from Merina's. "What I need is for you to be available to be trained. That is one reason why I encouraged him to be tested."

Shocked, Merina gasped out. "You did that, not Helinu? How?"

"The same way we are talking now--only less obvious. Dreams have always been a way to influence your people. You know I can read your thoughts--I did so just now when you thought about wanting him to fail."

::Then your plan for me would have failed I had chosen Markinis.:: Merina glared at the old woman.

"No, you would never have become Markinis's life-mate. Not because of what I would do to prevent it, which I could have, but because you do not want the man. Trinames is the man for you. His going into training gives me time to teach you what you need to know to survive the dangers that are facing you."

::And how are you going to do that?::

"By dreams, dear. But know this. When you think so hard as you have just done, your thoughts can be heard far away. Do not do this unless you have to--it will bring enemies."

Merina clutched her head and stifled a moan. "I don't understand this difference between talking in a dream and thinking."

"That is why you need to learn control. Especially if Trinames becomes a Healer. Healers are exceptional in reading emotions, expressions, attitudes--all the unspoken language you use every day. If your life-mate truly believes you have the ability to learn to use Power, which we both know he does, then he will try to teach you his skill. He may even continue to enlist the aid of Helinu or his teachers at Byklandes. Drawing the attention of sorcerers to you is the danger. You must continue to discourage him from trying to make you into one."

"And when," Merina asked with weariness in her voice, "will I be free to not be afraid for my life?'

Lenora gently smiled at her. "You have many years of happiness in front of you, my dear. And many exciting and fulfilling challenges to keep you moving forward, striving to succeed--but you will never be free from fear. It is fear that keeps us all alive. That is how we are made. Rest in peace, Great-Granddaughter. We will meet again soon enough."

You can find ALL our books up on our website at:
http://www.writers-exchange.com

all our fantasy novels:
http://www.writers-exchange.com/category/genres/fantasy/

All our romances:
http://www.writers-exchange.com/category/genres/romance/

All Margaret's Books:
http://www.writers-exchange.com/Margaret-Carter/

About the Authors

Margaret L. Carter

Marked for life by reading *Dracula* at the age of twelve, Margaret L. Carter specializes in the literature of fantasy and the supernatural, particularly vampires. She received degrees in English from the College of William and Mary, the University of Hawaii, and the University of California, with her dissertation published as *Specter or Delusion? The Supernatural in Gothic Fiction*. Her other works include *Dracula: The Vampire and the Critics*, *The Vampire In Literature: A Critical Bibliography*, and *Different Blood: The Vampire As Alien*. She is also the author of a werewolf novel, *Shadow Of The Beast*, and four vampire novels, *Dark Changeling* (2000 Eppie Award winner in Horror), *Child Of Twilight*, *Sealed In Blood*, and *Crimson Dreams*, along with a fantasy novel, *Wild Sorceress*, co-written by her husband Les Carter, and a horror novel, *From The Dark Places*.

Margaret and Les, a retired Navy Captain, have four sons and several grandchildren. For fans of "Vamp Tales", please do not hesitate to visit her website: The Vampire's Crypt at:

http://www.margaretlcarter.com/

You can keep track of all Margaret's books on her author page at Writers Exchange E-Publishing:

http://www.writers-exchange.com/Margaret-Carter/

Leslie Roy Carter

Born into a Navy family in Washington, D.C., Leslie Roy Carter lived all over the United States, as well as in Argentia, Newfoundland, while growing up. After receiving a B.S. in Physics from the College of William and Mary, he was commissioned as an Ensign in the U.S. Navy. While serving as a naval officer, he earned an M.S.E.E. from the Naval Postgraduate School. His career as a surface line officer took him to many ports such as Pearl Harbor, Long Beach, San Diego, and Charleston, culminating in command of the Oliver Hazard Perry Class Frigate, U.S.S. Reid. He then switched to the acquisitions specialty, eventually becoming a major program manager before his retirement in 2002 with the rank of Captain.

In retirement, he turned his attention to writing as well as his volunteer service in the Maryland Wing of the Civil Air Patrol.

You can keep track of all Leslie's books on his author page at Writers Exchange E-Publishing:

http://www.writers-exchange.com/Leslie-Roy-Carter/

If you enjoyed this author's book, then please place a review up at the site of purchase, and any social media sites you frequent!

If you want to read more about books by this author, they are listed on the following pages...

Crimson Dreams

The summer when Heather was eighteen, her dream beast's nightly visits warded off loneliness and swept her away in flights of ecstasy. Now, returning to the mountains to sell her dead parents' vacation cabin, she finds her "beast" again. But he turns out to be more than a dream. She meets Devin in the flesh, apparently not a day older. His first human lover, centuries in the past, died horribly because of her devotion to him. Does he dare expose another mortal woman to that risk?

Publisher: http://www.writers-exchange.com/Crimson-Dreams/

Heart's Desires and Dark Embraces

When Margaret L. Carter first read *Dracula* at the age of twelve, her spontaneous reaction was to wonder how the undead Count saw the events in which he was portrayed as the villain. She's always been fascinated with the "monster's" viewpoint and relationships between human and nonhuman beings. Most of the stories in this collection can be described as romances, and all involve love and passion in some form. Here you'll encounter vampires, elves, ghosts, and at least one human-monster hybrid. The vampire stories in the first half of the book are part of an ongoing series in which the creatures we know as vampires belong to a naturally evolved, nonhuman species secretly living among us. Readers can get better acquainted with them in *Crimson Dreams, Sealed in Blood,* and *Passion in the Blood.*

Publisher: http://www.writers-exchange.com/Hearts-Desires-and-Dark-Embraces/

Different Blood: The Vampire as Alien

Different blood flows in their veins--but our blood quenches their thirst. From Bram Stoker's 1897 creation of Count Dracula, portrayed as a foreign invader bent on the conquest of England, the literary vampire has symbolized the Other, whether his or her otherness arises from racial, ethnic, sexual, or species difference. Even before the bloodsucking Martians of H. G. Wells' *War of the Worlds*, however, popular fiction contained a few vampires who were members of alien species rather than supernatural undead.

Even more intriguing than interplanetary invaders are humanoid and quasi-humanoid beings who have evolved to live on Earth among us, often camouflaged as our own kind. The boom in vampire fiction that began in the 1970s engendered a variety of "alien" vampires, many of them portrayed as sympathetic characters. The science fiction vampire is especially suited to the presentation of vampirism as morally neutral rather than inherently evil.

Different Blood surveys the literary vampire as alien, whether extraterrestrial or a different species evolved on Earth, from the mid-1800s to the 1990s, and analyzes the many uses to which science fiction and fantasy authors have put this theme. Their works explore issues of species, race, ecological responsibility, gender, eroticism, xenophobia, parasitism, symbiosis, intimacy, and the bridging of differences. An extensive bibliography lists dozens of novels and short stories on the "vampire as alien" theme, many of which are still in print.

Publisher: http://www.writers-exchange.com/Different-Blood/

From the Dark Places and Against the Dark Devourer

From the Dark Places

When Father Michel Emeric and Dr. Ray Benson warn young widow Kate Jacobs of occult danger stalking her, she dismisses them as deranged fanatics. The eerie disappearance of her four-year-old daughter, Sara, changes her mind. Ray and Father Mike rescue Kate's child, but the fight has only begun. Dark powers from beyond our world want to destroy Kate and Sara and prevent the birth of a future child foretold to have extraordinary psychic powers and a destiny as a great warrior against evil. Kate must develop her latent wild talents and allow Sara to do the same, in a universe weirder--and more dangerous--than she's ever imagined.
Publisher: http://www.writers-exchange.com/From-the-Dark-Places/

Against the Dark Devourer (Sequel to From the Dark Places)

All her life, Deborah has known she and her older sister have extraordinary psi powers. When their mother dies suddenly, Deborah learns she's meant to use her gift against the forces of darkness in some special way. How, she doesn't have a clue, but she wants no part of this alleged fate. Yet with evil forces stalking her, can she avoid the battle ahead?

All his life, Victor has known he and his twin sister have a unique destiny. Bred to serve inhuman entities from another dimensional plane, he's instructed to either seduce a strange young woman who poses a grave threat to the cult he belongs to...or destroy her.

Unexpectedly, he finds Deborah not only attractive and intelligent but his equal in psychic power. Although his cult views religion with contempt--and she's an unabashed Christian--he's helplessly drawn to her. For her part, Deborah finds in Victor a kindred spirit. For the first time, someone other than her sister can empathize with her differences from "normal" people. Is prophetic destiny written in stone, even for two potential foes falling in love? A paranormal romance inspired by C. S. Lewis's *That Hideous Strength* and the cosmic horror of H. P. Lovecraft.
Publisher: http://www.writers-exchange.com/Against-the-Dark-Devourer/

Passion in the Blood

Cordelia and her twin sister don't realize the mother who left them soon after their birth bequeathed them a dark bloodline. They're half vampire. Although human in most respects, they possess certain psychic gifts. A friend of their late father's, Karl, also a vampire, has been watching over their family for generations in honor of his love for their distant ancestor. When her sister is kidnapped and Cordelia must beg for help from Karl, she learns the truth about his vampirism and her own heritage. In the process, she and Karl form a blood bond that leads to deeper intimacy than either one could have anticipated.
Publisher: http://www.writers-exchange.com/Passion-in-the-Blood/

Prince of Hollow Hills

When her sister mysteriously dies, Fern takes over the care of her baby nephew. She has no idea that his missing father wasn't an ordinary man or that baby Baird is heir to the throne of Elfland. Two rival elvish princes invade Fern's life--one hostile, the other alluring. One wants to kill the child, the other to guard him. But both intend to take him away from her. How can Fern fulfill her promise to her late sister while falling in love with Kieran, Baird's fiercely protective--and not human--cousin?
Publisher: http://www.writers-exchange.com/prince-of-the-hollow-hills/

Sealed in Blood

Science fiction conventions attract some strange people, but Sherri Hudson never expected to spend a con weekend helping a sexy man in a cape steal photos of a winged alien. When the photographer is murdered and Nigel Jamison reveals to Sherri that the "alien" is actually his sister, the situation gets intriguingly complicated. Unwillingly swept up in Nigel's quest to rescue his sister, Sherri can't help being fascinated with him. By the time she finds out he's a vampire, the fascination has become mutual--and too strong to resist.
Publisher: http://www.writers-exchange.com/sealed-in-blood/

Sealing the Dark Portal

Almost nothing Rina remembers about her life is true. Rather than the ordinary librarian she believes herself to be, she's actually a sorceress who fled from another world to ours when creatures from an alien dimension devastated her home and killed her family. Now they've pursued her to our world, summoned by a sorcerer who plans to open a portal and invite monstrous entities from the void between dimensions to overrun this planet. Rina's former bodyguard, a cat shapeshifter who was once her lover and still yearns for her, helps her true memories to awaken. She must come to terms with the truth about her past so that together they can save their new home from the fate of their old one.
Publisher: http://www.writers-exchange.com/sealing-the-dark-portal/

Shadow of the Beast

After the mysterious deaths of her brother and sister at the fangs of what looks like a feral dog, Jenny Cameron develops nightmares and blackouts. The quest for the truth about herself leads to her long-lost father, who deserted the family before her birth. He seeks redemption for the curse he carries, but has his bloody past condemned him beyond salvation? When Jenny discovers the secret of her dark heritage, she's no longer sure she can trust her dangerous nature enough to be with the man she loves, and she may ultimately be forced to destroy her own father. Fearing she has inherited the violence that rages in him, she struggles to find her true self under the shadow of the beast.

Publisher: http://www.writers-exchange.com/Shadow-of-the-Beast/

Windwalker's Mate

Windwalker's Mate

Shannon's little boy Daniel has disturbing psychic powers. He talks to the wind--and it listens. All Shannon wants is a normal life. She wants to forget the cult of the Windwalker, a dark god from another dimension, and the terrifying night when her child was conceived. But her first love, Nathan, son of the cult leader, contacts her for the first time since that horrific ceremony. He claims his father is stalking Shannon and Daniel. Whose child is Daniel, Nathan's or the Windwalker's? Nathan's father plans to use Daniel to open a gate between dimensions and unleash chaos on our world. To save her child and become reconciled with her first love, Shannon may have no choice but embrace the strange powers she previously rejected.

Publisher: http://www.writers-exchange.com/windwalkers-mate/

Wild Sorceress Series
By Margaret L. Carter and Leslie Roy Carter

In a world where hostile nations wield magic in combat, twin sorceresses separated at birth and brought up on opposing sides of the war find each other. Together, they face persecution for using wild magic, fight against traitors and assassins, explore family secrets, and discover the hidden origins of magic itself. Above all, to protect their world, they must deal with ancient, powerful dragons that most people don't even believe exist.

Prequel: Legacy of Magic

Most people in the country of Saphradea admire sorcerers and dream of having magical powers. Not Merina, a young woman who detests magic because she thinks it ruined the life of her mother, a failed sorceress candidate who abandoned her in infancy.

When Merina's fiance, Trinames, announces he's decided to go for training as a Healer sorcerer, her personal world turns upside down. Merina is heiress to a tract of rich farmland, and she wants only to manage her own property and bring up a family in peace--a dream she thought Trinames shared. Yet events conspire to force her into a realm of magic and intrigue she never wanted.

When Trinames is kidnapped and she strikes out across the wilderness to rescue him, in company with a wandering trader who turns out to be more than he appears, she runs into a crisis that awakens magical powers she shouldn't even possess.

Publisher: http://www.writers-exchange.com/Legacy-of-Magic/

Book 1: Wild Sorceress

In a world where warring nations use magic in combat, years ago young sorceress Aetria's untamed power caused a disaster on the battlefield. Temporarily banished and retrained, she's returned to the army to redeem herself as head of a company of novice mages. She uncovers a traitorous plot by her own commander, renews her bond with her "imaginary" childhood friend, and meets her long-lost twin sister. While also becoming a trusted friend of the commanding general of the army, Aetria unearths secrets of the true nature of the magic she and her comrades wield.

Publisher: http://www.writers-exchange.com/Wild-Sorceress/

Book 2: Besieged Adept

While learning to control her wild sorcery, Adept Aetria has defeated a pair of traitors trying to kill her, found a long-lost twin, and uncovered secrets of the source and nature of magic. Now she continues her research while battling the remnants of the Neo-Aggressor rebellion and integrating raw, untrained talent into the Sorcerer Corps. Meanwhile, she discovers deeper secrets of her own family background, along with a surprising new foe and a destiny she never dreamed of. Furthermore, she learns that her "imaginary" dragon friend Rajii actually exists...but so do less friendly dragons. What does their agenda mean for the future of humanity and magic in Aetria's world?

Publisher: http://www.writers-exchange.com/Besieged-Adept/

Book 3: Rogue Magess

Sorceresses Aetria and Coleni discover that both their own births and the history of their world have been manipulated in secret by an ancient, powerful race of dragons. Some, like Aetria's lifelong friend Rajii, have benevolent intentions toward humanity while others want to restore the people of the Domains to total slavery. All, however, have their own agendas with human beings and mortal magic as pawns.

Emerging from their long-lost mother's hidden home in the deserted Non-Lands, Aetria and Coleni find themselves targeted by assassins under control of the dragons. While the sisters' powers continue to grow, so do the magical gifts of Coleni's baby daughter, but will their magic provide adequate protection?

Meanwhile, still viewed with suspicion for their "wild sorcery", they can't convince most of their rivals and allies, including Aetria's old mentor and the commanding general of the army, that the dragons and the danger they pose are real.

Publisher: http://www.writers-exchange.com/Rogue-Magess/

Series Page:

https://www.writers-exchange.com/wild-sorceress-series/

You can find ALL our books on our website at:
http://www.writers-exchange.com

all our fantasy novels:
http://www.writers-exchange.com/category/genres/fantasy/

All our romances:

http://www.writers-exchange.com/category/genres/romance/

All Margaret's Books:
http://www.writers-exchange.com/Margaret-Carter/

www.ingramcontent.com/pod-product-compliance
Lightning Source LLC
Chambersburg PA
CBHW060911140726
47996CB00001B/207